FOR BREAKFAST

Girls

FOR BREAKFAST

DAVID YOO

Published by Laurel-Leaf
an imprint of Random House Children's Books
a division of Random House, Inc.
New York

Originally published in hardcover in the United States by Delacorte
Press, New York, in 2005. This edition published
by arrangement with Delacorte Press.

Laurel-Leaf and colophon are registered trademarks
of Random House, Inc.

www.randomhouse.com/teens

Educators and librarians, for a variety of teaching tools,
visit us at www.randomhouse.com/teachers

ISBN-13: 978-0-440-23883-6
ISBN-10: 0-440-23883-8
September 2006
Printed in the United States of America
10 9 8 7 6 5 4 3 2 1

for my mom and dad

Thanks for the support, education,
and inspiration to the following:
Krista Marino—my editor/soundboard/thorn;
Beverly Horowitz and everyone at Delacorte Press;
and the lovely Steven Malk of Writers House.
My teachers: Steven Millhauser, Steve Stern,
Tatyana Tolstoya, and Reg Saner.
My friends and family, including Jessica Jackson, Joe Gillis,
Paula Yoo, Dave Cullen, Ashley Simpson-Shires,
Bo Boddie, Doug Kleinman, Jesse Blockton,
the Jackson family, and Boris Yoo.

Lastly, thank you,
Lucia Berlin and Liza Nelligan,
my lights.

Although I knew
I loved her,
I didn't like
anything she
did or said.

—Dylan Thomas

SUNDAY
10:00 AM

I'm standing on top of the water tower behind my house, thinking about my death and the inevitable bronze statue the graduating class will erect in my memory. Today is supposedly the most important day of my life so far because I'll be graduating from high school this afternoon—and yet here I am, the only senior skipping commencement rehearsal right now. The rest of my class has fanned out in waves into the woods beyond the football field in a frantic search for me. Some are joking at first, grateful to have a break from sitting on metal folding chairs in the hot sun, but before long it's obvious this is serious: *Nick Park is missing.*

The rumor mill has started churning, based on lies, but nobody knows the truth, so they have to rely on a nameless student hollering that he witnessed me entering the woods to take a leak. An hour passes before I'm finally discovered; word spreads quickly that I was attacked in midpiss by a bear in heat or something. Is there still time to dedicate the graduation ceremony to me, or have the programs already been printed?

Renfield High School
Commencement, June 18, 19__

Dedicated in loving memory of Nick Park
(July 6, 19__–June 18, 19__)
Senior Nick Park, who for four years was the num-
ber one tennis player at Renfield High, was mauled to
death by a Kodiak Long Cut bear, just hours prior to this
ceremony. The cause of death is precisely how we
should always remember Nick: courageously fighting a
semistarved and therefore far more aggressive than
usual man-eater. Preliminary autopsy reports of the
bear's intestines suggest—since all the bones in both
hands and feet were broken prior to being playfully
gnawed at and eaten—that Nick refused to turn himself
into a ball and instead went down swinging and kicking.
Tragic as this morning's events have been, it is fitting
that Nick, in death, has once again personified all that is
great about this year's graduating class. The Class
of __ refused to bow to the frustration of having to use
temporary lockers for one semester, and took the initia-
tive and handled the reconstruction of the cafeteria dur-
ing the spring with aplomb by creating the Brown Bag
picnic series, which will continue at Renfield High in the
future; Nick similarly refused to cave in to unfortunate
circumstances and fought for what is just, in this case
the right to urinate in peace and with dignity.

The statue will be unveiled this fall in a private ceremony at the edge of the woods behind the football field. All
the football players will tap or head-butt it for luck before
running out onto the field at the start of home games. I'll become a local folk hero for simply peeing in the wrong place
at the wrong time. Toxicology reports released to the public
will detail the abnormal amount of adrenaline in my system;
I did everything I could to fend off the bear, even as I slipped

in and out of consciousness following the first in a series of strangely alligatorish, furry death rolls.

I'm having trouble picturing the statue. It depicts the final struggle, teenager versus bear, but it's hard to picture my face—specifically, my eyes. I have to admit I'm picturing myself wearing sunglasses, further proof that I am a banana: white on the inside, yellow on the outside, because surely only a banana or a blind guy would picture a bronzed likeness of himself wearing fucking sunglasses.

Though after last night I'd be lucky to be memorialized in balsa.

I'll admit there's something majorly wrong with me if a bronze statue depicting my graphic mauling feels like an acceptable alternative to entering the real world this fall. Tilsen College—a small liberal arts school in upstate New York—is the ultimate microcosm of today's society, where I'll get my first taste of something besides sheltered New England life based on the fact that the student body is composed of prep school *and* public school kids from thirty-six states; where I'll be surrounded by at least 9 percent blacks, Hispanics, and Pacific Islanders (i.e., Samoans and me); where I'll share community bathrooms with flaming gays who aren't necessarily members of the drama club and tall girls, truckloads of really tall girls that I'll think are beautiful, because college is when I'll finally start appreciating them. My surroundings will be different, and hopefully so will I.

So then why am I all alone on a water tower during the rehearsal for what should be the greatest celebration of the most significant day of my life up till now? That much I do have an answer to: it's because I can't stop thinking about what happened last night.

The majority of my shortcomings can legitimately be blamed on the town I live in and my clueless parents. I'm just your average guy. I like girls, therefore I like parties because that's where girls are, therefore I am forced to give two shits about popularity. That doesn't make me shallow—it makes me normal. And how can a normal guy find himself completely alone on the last real day of high school?

This, my friends, is the question.

It wasn't until my first year here that I noticed that being Asian meant being different, and it coincided with the start of a lifelong proclivity toward lying. This was also around the time when I first noticed girls, which I guess means it was when things started to fall apart.

one

We moved here—Renfield, Connecticut—during the summer before third grade because my dad, an engineer, got transferred to nearby Farmington Springs. Renfield is the fifth-richest town in Connecticut. Unlike in most towns, there is no Main Street. No sidewalks. No gas stations, even—just a series of hills topped with immense houses, shrouded by conif-

erous trees. At night the town turns pitch black, but it doesn't matter, because the community is free of crime and murder. This in addition to a strong school system convinced my parents that Renfield was the ideal paradise in which to raise their only child. As usual, they were wrong, because this was true only if the child had friends, and by the spring of my first year in Renfield I still had next to none.

I clearly remember on the first day of school in the fall, Ms. Trebold introduced me to the class and then led me to a desk in the back row. I sat down and two seconds later was poked in the ribs by Mark Steeley, who had bright blond hair and psychotic eyes. I could feel Mark gaping at me as I bent over and started working on the first lesson. "You already know cursive?" he asked loudly. On the page in front of him were a zillion jumbled curls and scratches that looked more like numbers than letters. I glanced at the other students' papers, which were similarly littered with sad attempts at human language. I barely nodded. I could feel everyone staring at me as I focused on my shoelaces.

I spent the first week watching the other kids. They squinted at the chalkboard and dug holes in their workbooks. Mark Steeley flicked rubber bands at Ellen Gurvey, Andy Cordello constantly picked his nose, and Glenda Berrenger always chewed on the back of her thumb. They knew each other already, and I scrutinized their every movement, trying to discern some secret code to help me break into the ranks. I couldn't figure out, for example, how one day all the boys wore parachute pants except me. I covertly listened in on every conversation, yet failed to capture a

single sentence on the topic of purchasing parachute pants, or going to the firemen's carnival in neighboring Avon over the weekend, or watching the TV miniseries V.

Ms. Trebold did her part to accelerate my nobody status. Every Friday she held a raffle. At the end of the day she'd pick out a numbered card from a fishbowl, and the prize for the winner was the honor of bringing the class hamster, Marvin, home for the weekend. It was the one thing the students were rabid about. Everyone wanted to win. The first two Fridays Ellen Gurvey and then Craig Kessler won the raffle. Just by winning the lottery they suddenly became the most famous students in the third grade. Kids mobbed Craig when he tried to leave the classroom, trying to steal a glance at Marvin or at least touch Craig's shoulder. Kids in other classes would whisper and point at Ellen and Craig during recess. At night I'd pretend kids were pointing at me. I figured that given half a chance, Marvin could flourish in my care, and I brainstormed tricks to teach him in order to distinguish myself from the previous winners.

On the third Friday of the school year I went to school determined to select the winning ticket, but to my chagrin Ms. Trebold announced there wasn't going to be a raffle. I sat near my classmates at lunch and noticed it was the topic of every conversation. They speculated that Ms. Trebold missed having Marvin home herself. Some blamed Craig, who must have mistreated Marvin the previous weekend. The students were in titters the entire day, until twenty minutes before the final bell rang, when Ms. Trebold coughed to get our attention.

"Ladies and gentlemen," she said, hands folded in front of her, "the reason we're not holding a lottery today is because the greatest gift you can give is to welcome someone new into the fold. Being good to others is what really matters in life. And Nicholas Park, our newest addition, is in the process of finding his place, so I've decided to allow Nick the opportunity to take Marvin home for the weekend."

Immediately the students shouted in revolt. Mark Steeley nailed my forehead with an expertly aimed rubber band. Ellen cried. Apparently she had dreamed that she was destined to be picked for a second time.

Someone kicked the back of my chair.

"Nick, please come up here," Ms. Trebold solemnly instructed.

I trudged to the front of the class and participated in the passing-of-the-cage ceremony. Usually everyone stared unblinking as Ms. Trebold handed over the cage and instructed the winner to face the audience so that everyone could watch Marvin repeatedly smash his face against the cold metal bars, but this time the students booed throughout the ceremony. Glenda Berrenger glared at me with bloodshot eyes, and Ms. Trebold snapped at the masses to quiet down. Though I had often dreamed of one day being on the receiving end of the passing-of-the-cage ceremony, I knew all this didn't bode well for me. My hands shook. The bell rang. None of my classmates tried to touch me.

As I walked down the hall with kids bumping against the sides of the cage and running past me, I noticed that

none of my classmates seemed to be in the hallway. At the end of the hall I looked behind and saw that the majority of Ms. Trebold's class was following me like a funeral procession. My forehead streamed impure sweat. My hands were so wet the handle nearly slipped out of my grip, and every ten feet I glanced at the reflection in the gray lockers and saw that my classmates were keeping pace, giving me five feet of breathing room. They were going to crucify me and then steal Marvin.

The only kid I'd talked to on a regular basis since arriving in Renfield was my next-door neighbor, Will Fahey. He'd moved in around the same time, so neither of us knew anybody, and we were always stuck watching kickball games by ourselves during recess. He had shaggy brown hair and so many freckles on his arms and face that he looked tan from a distance, but really his skin was extremely pale, since he was half Irish. I spotted him looking at me through a window near the back of the bus and I prayed thanks for having someone on my side. I stepped on the bus, and as I made my way toward the back where Will was sitting, I felt the undercarriage of the bus heave and lower a few inches as the kids of Room 18 followed me on. "We can't fit all of you," the bus driver complained. I silently cheered her on, but they moved as one past the driver and she quickly gave up. "Okay, then, triple up in the front seats."

No one could save me. Will noticed that my classmates were staring unblinkingly at us and turned away from me, publicly severing ties to save his own butt. He moved up two seats and sat with a pair of fourth graders, who turned away

in disgust as he leaned over, hawked up a loogie, and let it dangle precariously from his lips before sucking it back up.

It was a sunny day, but I prayed for rain. I prayed that my mom or Will's mom would pick us up at the bottom of Summit and I'd be saved. I stood up when the bus reached my stop, and my entire class leaped off the bus, hooting and hollering. It occurred to me that I could have stood up at any of the four stops before mine—they would have exited the bus, and I could have simply sat back down and waved at my would-be assassins from safely behind the back window. Will pushed me forward.

"It's too late," he whispered. "Make sure you don't talk to me when we get off."

But then I stepped off the bus to deafening cheers, and almost fell over in surprise. Mark Steeley clapped me on the back, then shot me in the face point-blank with a rubber band. I yelped but then realized this was a primitive form of affection.

"Congratulations, Nick," Ellen said. "Doesn't it feel neat?"

"Huh?"

"We always go to the winner's house on Friday, to play with Marvin."

I felt relief for a few seconds until I realized I hadn't been invited to join in on the celebration the previous two Fridays. I felt lucky and depressed. Suddenly they were talking to me, and I felt nervous again.

Will rejoined the pack once he realized I wasn't about to get mugged. He clapped me on the back, and though I

wanted to tell everyone how he'd ditched me, it felt good to have him around. The road we lived on, Summit Drive, was in the shape of an upside-down horseshoe plastered to a hill. We both lived at the top. Ten minutes later we reached my house. The front door was unlocked. My mom was still at work. The crowd followed me through the hallway and into the kitchen.

"Weird furniture," Craig muttered, pointing at the Korean heirlooms: ancient wooden chests with pearl swans inlaid into the sides, a couple of traditional brush paintings hanging on the walls.

"Come on, we don't have all day," Steeley whined.

"What now?" I asked stupidly.

"Take him out, Nick," Ellen said. "We pass him around and pet him for ten seconds each. We go through the line twice, and then we put him back in the cage."

"Um, okay," I said, and opened the top of the cage. I reached in and pulled him out, but rather than pass him off to the first set of greedy hands I suddenly felt the urge to make the most of the moment. I no longer saw Marvin as the wizened, gray-whiskered class mascot beloved by generations of third graders but as a trophy.

"Come on, pass him, Nick," someone shouted.

I lifted Marvin up, mimicking Björn Borg when he first raised the Wimbledon trophy. My dad and I had watched him play tennis on TV. I copied Borg by kissing Marvin's belly before raising the hamster again and facing the students, pretending they were photographers. A couple of kids laughed, egging me on. When I raised him a third time Marvin decided

he'd had enough and peed down my outstretched arm. I looked up, and upon realizing urine was dripping down my forearm, I immediately dropped him. The hamster fell like a lead pellet. His feet didn't even twitch as he smacked hard on the linoleum floor. The impact was so loud it stunned everyone in the room, including me. For a few seconds no one breathed. Steeley bent down and poked the hamster with his index finger. Marvin's back made an audible clicking sound.

"Eeeewww, his spine's completely broken, you can feel it," he said, sickly pushing against Marvin's back. A universal gasp passed through the kitchen. Steeley looked up at me. "He's dead."

A stunned silence. I started edging backward out of the kitchen, but everyone's eyes refocused on me so I froze. I looked at Will to save me.

"Nick killed Marvin," he uttered. I felt like strangling him.

"The urine . . . it burns," I pleaded helplessly, holding out my wet, pissy hands as an alibi. Ellen screamed, and then everyone else screamed, and Craig shouted, "Let's get out of here!" and everyone poured out the front door in a uniform stampede. Mark Steeley was the last to run out of the house. Just like the final moment of *An American Werewolf In London*, when David Naughton, starring as the werewolf, peered at Jenny Agutter through sad, human eyes right before attacking, Mark turned and gave me a sympathetic look. He was the only kid besides Will who wasn't horrified or later traumatized by the hamster's death, and he never shot me with rubber bands again. I had gained his respect.

❧ ❧ ❧

The problem was that back at school on Monday no one, including Mark Steeley, would talk to me, and I continued to get ignored. For the next six months I focused on my art skills during recess and quickly became an expert at drawing dragons and mansions while everyone else played Four Square and mastered Lemon Drops and Around-the-Worlds. I taught myself calligraphy during indoor recess one rainy day. I even started collecting stamps. By springtime I was at an emotional low point. Having been ostracized by everyone except Will for the hamster incident, I was even more desperate to make friends. Will and I walked home from the bus stop every day with Paul Turgess and Mitch Wertz, who lived a few houses down from us, but I didn't feel like I was really friends with them, because we never talked during school. Paul was a sickly-looking kid with perpetually flushed cheeks. Mitch was chubby and wore thick plastic eyeglasses.

We barely talked on the walk home from the bus stop, either. It wasn't until the first Monday in April of that year that I broke through. I was watching them kick a pebble up the hill, wondering if they'd ever invite me to join in on their fun when Mitch asked me out of the blue, "Are you Chinese?"

I sighed loudly.

Paul and Will gaped at me.

"My parents are from Korea," I replied.

"Is that in China?" Paul asked.

"Sort of." I wasn't sure. Aside from my looks, I'm hardly

Korean. Although my mom cooks ninety pounds of rice a week and the kitchen perpetually reeks of kimchee, the only food I eat willingly is McDonald's or George's Pizza or junk food from 7-Eleven. My favorite television show when I was little was *Alice*. I've never set foot in the old country and my parents never taught me how to speak Korean. As a result, whenever they lapse into their native language to discuss ways to punish me, it sounds like two birds coughing.

"So you must know tae kwon do? My older brother is a brown belt," Paul said.

"Yes," I answered quickly. "I also know kung fu."

They were immediately convinced by the proof of my eyes.

"Teach us!" they cried in unison.

They probably assumed all Asian people are born with martial arts skills already infused in the brain. Maybe I told them that. We agreed that the lessons would be given in my backyard after school on Thursdays. It was still chilly outside, yet they insisted that they should wear pajamas as uniforms to the lessons.

"Wear whatever you want to the lessons," I sighed. They stared at me, waiting for more words of wisdom. "Just make sure to bring your hearts."

Mitch stopped me when we reached his house.

"Teach us something now," he said.

"I can't. I need time to prepare. The first thing you have to understand is that kung fu isn't something you can just explain. It's going to involve hard work," I said, cribbing fragments of my tennis instructor's weekly spiels.

"We understand," they replied, already a trio of loyal robots.

And this began my two-month career as an eight-year-old kung fu instructor. Renfield had given me the keys to popularity. Or so I thought.

I walked into my house that day feeling powerful, but that night I couldn't sleep, remembering that my mom could catch dragonflies by grabbing the wings, while I fainted if they buzzed by too close. I'd never been in a physical fight my entire life. I couldn't even swim. I bawled for a good half hour before finally draining into sleep. The next morning my new plan was to simply stay home from school. I'd convert the bedroom into a bubble; Principal Wallesy would come over, witness me laboring for breath, and tearfully agree to have my assignments sent home to me. I considered admitting the truth for maybe two seconds, but even then I knew that the truth is never an answer.

At the bus stop the next morning I got the feeling that they had forgotten everything. Mitch and Paul were climbing trees while Will sat on his backpack, occasionally bending over and bracing a hand on the curb; he believed he could feel the vibrations from the approaching bus. When we arrived at school, Paul and Mitch hopped off first and sprinted for the playground to squeeze in a couple of minutes on the swings. Will ran after them without saying goodbye.

"I'll see you at lunch," I called out to him. He stopped.

"Hey, Nick, can you teach me to throw a Chinese throwing star? I know you're Korean and all, but I'm sure you know better than I do."

"Of course. I don't have any on me, but I'll teach you how to throw one eventually," I lied, and it felt harmless and silly until he reached into his back pocket and produced a rusted metal throwing star. I gawked at it. "Where did you get it?"

"Found it in the woods," he said. Will found a lot of things in the woods.

"Swell." I barely managed to breathe as I walked into the classroom. I could feel him staring at my back as I pulled the door shut with my left shoe. I sat at my desk, drawing a big black circle with a Ticonderoga #2 pencil. I filled it in, kept working at it until the entire page was shiny black. Then I wrote sentences in the black spot so no one else could read it. *I don't know how to kung fu. I am a liar. I wish I knew kung fu.*

At recess I tried to forget the mess I was in. I was standing on a half-buried tire in the playground, pretending I was on a raft surrounded by killer whales, when I had my first epiphany ever. It was so simple. I slapped my forehead. Whoever had invented kung fu had had to start from scratch. Same with tennis or making mittens. In order for something to exist, someone had to first create the process. I didn't know kung fu, but neither did they. I would simply improvise my own version of martial arts. I would make it all up.

A tingling sensation formed at my fingertips. An imaginary warrior now stood before me. I watched in slow motion as the warrior tried to kick me. "Okay, now in the movies they block these kicks," I whispered to myself. I made a swiping motion with my right hand. I made up rules, and to my surprise they made perfect sense. *The key to blocking your opponent's kick is to move faster than the kick itself.* I made up more rules. Someone had to shout for me to come inside after the recess bell had rung. Students back in their classrooms were pointing at me as I ran through the double doors.

❧ ❧ ❧

My confidence only grew. I had seen plenty of *Kung Fu Theater* movies on channel 13. This proved to be a distinct advantage—for example, I knew that the moves in martial arts were always named after an animal or an insect. My dad had had me convinced I was going to become a pro tennis player someday, and up till then I'd believed him wholeheartedly, but as I continued developing fight moves and my own combat philosophy, my day-old epiphany only made more sense, and I wondered if kung fu was actually my true calling.

On Thursday afternoon the four of us walked ceremoniously up the hill from the bus stop. Mitch and Paul eventually couldn't contain their anticipation and ran ahead to don their pajamas and makeshift headbands. Will kept pace with me. I had transformed from a mere neighbor to someone he revered. I could feel him watching the way I walked. He was analyzing my every movement in an effort to glean something.

"I already knew you were Korean," he said. "My dad told me. I just forgot. Why didn't you tell me you were a kung fu master?"

"I try not to talk about it because it's not something I practice anymore."

"Have you ever killed anyone?"

I suddenly grabbed him by the collar, pulled him over to the curb, and looked around frantically for a few seconds. Sweat actually dripped from my nose.

"I'll kill you if you tell anyone."

"I knew it," he whispered.

"It's not something I'm proud of."

"Tell me about it."

"It was in the black forests of Korea. He was a hunter. It was self-defense."

"Why did he attack you?"

"I was wearing a tan coat. He thought I was a deer."

"Didn't you say anything? He just kept attacking?"

"Once a hunter makes up his mind . . ." My voice cracked, then trailed off.

Mitch and Paul shouted from up the road. They ran ahead to my house, their white headbands waving in the wind. They were barefoot.

"Do I have to take my shoes off, too?" Will asked, instantly alarmed.

"No, but don't tell them it isn't a rule," I said, and we both laughed.

"You're sneaky," he said.

❧ ❧ ❧

We sat in a small circle on the grass just off the porch, having a roundtable discussion on the theory and practice of kung fu. At first I was jarred by their questions, but slowly I regained confidence, realizing anything I said would be taken at face value.

"So what you're telling me is ultimately I can kill anything I want with barely any effort, right? I mean, that's the point, after all," Mitch said, his hands folded contemplatively under his chin.

"You got part of it right. Are you guys listening? I'll explain it one more time." I sighed dramatically. "Yes, kung fu is about killing things—of course it is, since you're dealing with so much power, power that normal people don't even know exists. But it's not really about being able to kill."

"It's about defending yourself, right?" Paul said. He acted so damn authoritative since his older brother was a brown belt. I laughed at him. Mitch and Will joined in and Paul blushed.

"Nope. It's about being able to *seriously hurt* someone. If you turn it up a notch, you can kill, but then you go to jail. Most of what I'll teach you is illegal."

"You promise to go all the way? You'll teach us how to kill? It's our choice, right?"

"I can't *not* teach you how to kill, but it isn't worth it if you don't see the purpose behind all this." I was getting frustrated. They were so young.

"The purpose is to seriously hurt, not kill, but we could if we wanted to," they chanted in monotone.

"Excellent."

"My brother says tae kwon do is about finding out who you are and gaining confidence and self-respect," Paul said.

"Tae kwon do is a lot of things," I said. "But back in

Korea it's considered the babiest form of martial arts. You teach it to little kids. You can't kill someone with tae kwon do. In Korean it means 'feel good, do.' "

"Shut up, Paul," Will said savagely. "Nick, we're all for the kung fu, man."

"Good," I said. An hour had passed.

"I have to leave in a couple of minutes," Mitch complained.

"Tomorrow I'll start teaching you stuff, but for now, I'll demonstrate something," I said, brimming with confidence. "Will, please stand up."

He didn't budge.

"Promise I won't hurt you," I snickered.

He hesitantly lifted his body off the ground. Mitch whistled.

"Now, so you all can understand, or even begin to understand, we'll do this at one one-zillionth the speed. Will, pretend we're in space, and take a swing at me. No, too fast, slow down, there, slower, good. Now watch my hands."

I started waving them in small circles and rubbed my elbows across my chest real fast. Eventually Will's fist floated into orbit, and I slammed my right hand and then my left into his wrist. He shrieked and frantically waved his hand, watching it turn bright red.

I bit my bottom lip to keep from shrieking myself.

"That's self-defense," Paul exclaimed.

"No, if that was tae kwon do, it would be self-defense, but this is kung fu, and if we did this at real-life speed, Will's hand would have been chopped off," I shouted.

"*Serious hurt,*" Will murmured.

"This is so cool," Paul breathed.

"That's all for today. Go home and think about what I've told you. I don't expect all of you to return tomorrow," I said, turning from them and heading up the porch steps. In the sliding glass doors I could see their reflection as they walked off, inspecting Will's red hand. Someone down the street was practicing the flute. I waited for my grin to dissipate.

"Hey, guys," I called out. They stopped. "What I just showed you, the demonstration with Will?" I waited. They nodded. I had them. "It's called . . . the Hummingbird."

"Is that because you move your hands so fast that—"

"Silence!" I screamed, pressing a finger to my lips.

They walked off in a collective daze.

As the weeks passed, I started to seriously consider the possibility that I was a born kung fu master. The nobility of this mission grew inside me, and I felt humbled by my own presence. My pupils called me Sensai Park, and I referred to them as *dojokill*, real fast and guttural, which I told them was Korean for "kung fu student." After teaching them the Hummingbird, I taught them their first kick, the Triceratops—where you kick someone in the dick and then execute two mini kicks to each side to deflate their balls. Then I taught them their first punch, called the Whale's Tail, which no one really got the hang of. It was complex—

a stiff, open-palm punch followed by a raking motion down the chest with your fingers to push the enemy's guts backward; in theory it causes irreversible internal trauma. They couldn't figure out the timing, or if they did get the timing right, their raking motions were pitifully weak. That day I had them each do twenty knuckle push-ups on the lawn as punishment.

As their learning progressed, I took a backseat in the demonstrations. The newer moves I was devising were harder to execute. At the end of the second month of lessons I taught them a scissors kick, where you lie on the ground playing dead, and when your would-be assailant walks by you swipe from opposite ends at his torso—if you do this in real time you can pretty much halve him.

At no point did any of them seem remotely skeptical. I realized I was blessed. They were the best type of student: attentive, hardworking, eager to learn more. One Sunday afternoon, unbeknownst to Mitch and Paul, I taught Will how to use his throwing star. He got a headache realizing how off he had been, simply chucking the thing like a Frisbee. He had no idea you have to grasp a throwing star with just the thumb and pinkie. I offered him a soda when he couldn't quite get the distance down. My dad watched from the upstairs window with a puzzled expression on his face.

"I should go," Will said. "Thanks for the soda."

We shook hands.

"I didn't just give you that soda," I replied. "You *earned* it."

He smiled gleefully and ran off. I sat down on the porch.

I felt older and wiser. My knees even cracked. I heard my dad's footsteps behind me.

"What were you doing?"

"Hey, Pops. Oh, nothing—I was just teaching Will how to use his throwing star."

"But you don't know how to use one," he remarked. He stuffed his hands in his pockets and stared at me.

My face boiled, and I shook my head. "Dad, we *all* know how to use one."

He smiled crookedly. Then his face hardened a little.

"It's not good to lie to your friends."

I didn't say anything.

"Let's play tennis," he suggested. "You should be concentrating on tennis."

"Things are changing," I said. A breeze shushed through the trees, and I watched a clump of recently mowed grass roll across the yard. "I don't know how much longer I'll be playing tennis, now that my kung fu career's taking off."

I was realizing this as I said it, and it almost made me cry.

"Just get your things," he said, and walked inside the garage.

I had started playing tennis, along with soccer and basketball, after school once we moved to Renfield. Soon it became obvious that tennis would be my main sport, but now the way of kung fu seeped into my tennis lessons. On the tennis court I made chopping sounds when I worked on my backhand slice approach, and in the bedroom I'd pretend to hit a kick serve, which ultimately provided the groundwork for my most lethal move, the Nail in the Coffin. If done properly, you could move someone's brain down into his left foot without changing his outward physical appearance for eight seconds, before his body caved in like an accordion. I vowed never to teach it, though; it was far too lethal. I started planning my adult life. I'd play pro tennis and use the accumulated prize money to open a kung fu academy. Will would be my business partner. Life and the future were starting to make perfect sense, and each day I woke up with a renewed vigor.

Word spread around the playground that I was teaching my neighbors kung fu, and soon others wanted to receive instruction. Even Kent Cole—the biggest kid at Crying Stream Elementary—wanted to become my disciple. At the start of every recess I'd give my new friends a short lesson behind the jungle gym, in an attempt to maintain a level of secrecy. Glenda Berrenger and Missy Means saw us one day, sat down on the grass next to my invisible dojo, and pretended to have a picnic. Within seconds they forgot about the imaginary picnic and were instead gazing at me with googly eyes. I told myself to stop bathing in the girls' admiring stares because it made me forget where I was in the lesson. I was foolishly risking teaching something wrong, which, given the delicate finesse necessary to produce these brutal fighting techniques, could have proved disastrous.

Within a week I had over a dozen pupils standing before me in the now traditional hexagon formation, and eventually I had to employ Will and Mitch as assistant instructors. At first I was hesitant to loosen my grip on the reins. I felt like the general of a small but potent army, and I had no desire to relinquish even a fraction of the attention I was now receiving, but as I watched Mitch and Will teach others how to perform the Triceratops, I could feel their hearts pounding with confidence, and it was at this point when I realized the true message of my kung fu: ultimately, it was my moral duty to instill this confidence in my students. It was the first time in my life I'd ever given back, and I found that helping others was almost as satisfying as helping myself.

❧ ❧ ❧

On the first of June, Mitch's older brother, Joe, knocked me temporarily unconscious in under two minutes of our unofficially sanctioned Renfield Battle of the Martial Arts—held in their basement. Will and Mitch cried foul and insisted that the fight wasn't over, because it was the cement floor, not Joe's reverse kick, that had dropped me. They demanded a rematch.

"Shasta," Joe shouted through gritted teeth. "Mom's gonna ground me for life. Here, Nick, wrap your head with this towel to stop the bleeding. Paul, get some water."

"I'm fine," I said. My voice was shaky. "It's a good thing we stopped, though. I didn't realize how high up your floor is." My lungs felt like they had collapsed.

"Rematch," Mitch hollered. "Rematch rematch rematch!"

Joe patted me on the back and ran upstairs. I felt like booting.

"Listen, guys, this was good for me," I said, choking back tears. "Because I know now that I'm out of shape—I've focused unselfishly on teaching you guys things, and my skills have diminished. I think we should stop for a while so I have time to get back into killer condition."

"How long will that take?" Mitch whined.

"A year, maybe. I think my head cracked a little."

"We know enough to kill people, though, right?" asked Will.

"Yes," I murmured. "You and Mitch and Paul are now the most dangerous *dojokills* in Renfield. But you must use these skills wisely." For the first time in two months I realized what a sham I was. Telling them they were actually dangerous was like telling them they were invisible. "But promise me you won't use these skills on normal people. Only during extreme situations."

"Of course," they said, but they were looking off into space.

My head wasn't cracked, and I never told my parents about it. I had a thick bowl haircut at the time that hid the gash. It scared me, because I'd pick at the scab in my sleep until it bled again, and I would wake up feeling wet behind the ears and my face would be webbed with blood. I'd have to throw out the pillowcase in the morning. I couldn't go all out in tennis after school because running full speed made me dizzy.

A few nights after the fight my mom and dad lugged a humidifier into the bedroom and showed me how to refill it with water. My dad was still wearing his yellow hard hat. He worked at an elevator test tower during the day, and the hat was required of all engineers on the site, but my dad also wore the thing anytime he did chores around the house and when he mowed the lawn on weekends.

"It's so dry up here—it's not good if you keep getting bloody noses. We're running out of sheets that don't have your blood on it," my mom said. Her hair was in curlers, and she was wearing her white nurse's uniform.

My dad stared at me through beady eyes. I looked away.

"It's nobody's fault," I whispered to the wall. "It's just dry in here."

"Are you picking your nose? You have to try to stop," my mom scolded.

In fact, I was picking my nose quite a bit in those days. All they had to do was turn over the curtain next to the bed to see.

"I'm sure this machine will help," I said.

They left the room. I sat next to the humidifier and sniffed in the jet-stream fog for five minutes before remembering that I wasn't really having nosebleeds at night. With one final shot of hope, I karate-chopped the humidifier with a stone fist.

It hurt like hell.

two

Paul and Mitch (the only *dojokills* besides Will who hung out with their sensei outside of group lessons) simultaneously moved to Renfield Hills, the richest part of town, a month before third grade ended. They were inseparable, and apparently their parents were, too.

I remember praying that all of third grade had been an elaborate setup for a huge surprise birthday party at the end of the year. It wasn't. Luckily, at the eleventh hour I got a phone call out of the blue from Paul, who invited me to a sleepover at his new house. I accidentally mentioned my ninth birthday. A few minutes later Mrs. Turgess got on the line and suggested we celebrate it at their house. I covered the mouthpiece and asked my parents. They weren't thrilled with the idea. I noted that we had nothing planned, and since they both worked it wasn't even feasible to have a party at our house.

My parents suggested inviting friends over on the weekend after my birthday, and I cringed for three reasons: first, I was a little kid, and there was no way in hell I was celebrating my birthday *after* my birthday; second, now that Paul lived in a mansion I desperately wanted to explore every corner of it; and third, whenever Will came over my mom would humiliate me by cooking one of her hybrid meals. She had a habit of mixing American and Korean food together, like serving cheeseburgers with a side of rice doused in ketchup, or spaghetti and meatballs with diced kimchee to spice it up. Will dry-heaved the day she made him a grilled cheese sandwich, replacing the bread with gim (dried seaweed wrap). My personal least favorite was her notion of Korean pizza. The thought of my new friends possibly being exposed to such horrors made my stomach turn over. In my opinion they didn't need any more hard evidence that I was Korean. So I lied and said the Turgesses had already bought decorations.

"You're our only child, we should celebrate your birthday together," my mom said. "I don't see why you can't have a party here."

"I've never been inside a mansion before," I said.

"Yes, you have, in Maine that one time," she countered.

"That doesn't count. It was a restaurant."

"Didn't you get sick?" my dad added.

"It was food poisoning," I said, practically in tears.

They eventually decided I could go. I informed Paul.

"We'll go to the surf store in Simsbury," he said. "I might buy a skateboard."

Paul and Mitch were the best-dressed students at school, in my opinion. They always wore surf and skateboard clothes. Every Monday at school Mitch would wear his fluorescent green Jimmy Z sweatshirt, and I'd get hypnotized staring at it.

"Is that where you get all your clothes?" I asked.

"It's the only place around," Paul said. "You could use some new threads."

I blushed. Up till then, my favorite outfit had been a ratty Izod tennis warm-up. It was green and blue terry cloth. Mark Steeley sometimes wiped his boogers on my sleeve and defended himself by claiming I was wearing a towel.

"See you tomorrow. Don't forget to bring your bathing suit," Paul said.

I couldn't believe my luck. I knew from my eavesdropping sessions that Paul's mansion had been designed by his parents, and not only did it have an in-ground pool and hot tub, but there was also a bowling lane in his basement. He'd told his parents that the bare cement room was boring without a bowling alley, and the following weekend his parents had had a guy come in to take measurements. Apparently they never used the thing. He also had a pool table and a dart board, a zillion Nintendo games, and a pantry full of SpaghettiOs.

My house, on the other hand, had nothing fun to offer. We had a skylight in the master bedroom, but the glass was so cloudy you could barely see out of it. We had a Coleco Adam home computer in my dad's study, but no games for it. In fact, I wasn't even allowed to touch it. And from the back porch you could see this very same rusted metal water tower through the trees, which made our property look ten times poorer.

For dinner my mom served *dubu jige*, a spicy tofu soup loaded with little copper-colored fish, and a side of french fries. I swirled the cloudy soup with a spoon and finished the fries, and then sat still, grimacing as my parents slurped the soup through their teeth like a pair of baleen whales.

"What are you bringing to the party?" my dad asked.

"It's my birthday. I don't have to bring anything," I explained.

"You should bring something, since you're a guest," he said.

"I could fill a Tupperware bowl with the leftover *dubu jige*," Mom suggested.

"Paul doesn't eat minnows," I said. "Don't worry, I'll think of something."

My mom sighed.

I paced back and forth in my bedroom for nearly an hour but couldn't think of anything to bring to Paul's house. Finally I ran across the street to ask Will for advice. He was sitting on the back porch, throwing sticks at his two elderly, perpetually salivating sheepdogs, trying to get their attention. They always reeked of wet fur and had the saggiest balls in the history of canines that would visibly bang against their heels as they walked painfully across the front yard, and they perpetually bit at people because they were going blind.

Will's house was bigger than mine. The living room was two stories with a ceiling fan and numerous skylights. Will's dad ran a beer distributorship, and his mom was a blond former pageant winner with a Barbie-doll body. They drove matching kit Porsche 944s with Chevette engines. Hers was powder blue, his was hunter green.

"Guess what—I'm invited to a sleepover at Paul's new mansion tomorrow night!"

"Can I go?" he asked.

"I'll ask them," I said. I hadn't considered the fact that Will wasn't invited. "Can you think of anything I could bring as a present?"

"You could bring me," he said, unblinking.

"I'll try," I promised. "I have to bring something cool, though."

"Follow me," he said.

His parents were in the kitchen sipping cocktails with Jefferson Airplane blaring in the background, so we easily snuck upstairs and crept into their master bedroom. Will motioned for me to take the clock off his mother's antique hope chest, and then he lifted the lid. I nearly dropped the clock when I saw what was inside: stacks and stacks of *Playboys*. On the cover of the top magazine was a photo of a blond girl holding a magician's hat over her chest. She was beautiful. I didn't realize it at the time, but this was the moment when I finally discovered my life's true calling: girls.

Will grabbed that issue and another, then closed the lid.

"Your mom looks at *Playboys?*" I asked.

"These belong to my dad. She doesn't know he keeps them in here."

"How do you know?"

"Sometimes he looks at them on the back porch, and when she comes home he runs upstairs and puts them away." He slipped the issues down his pants and showed me how to walk backward out of the room, rubbing my feet on the carpet to erase any tracks. Then we bolted for his bedroom, and I slammed the door behind me.

"We did it," he said, and we shook hands. "You have to take me."

"I'll ask, but I really need those *Playboys*."

"You can't borrow them unless you take me."

"Listen, I'm sure they've seen one before. I've seen plenty of *Playboys*." I started walking toward the door in slow motion, waving goodbye as if I was in orbit.

"Fine, see ya."

I stopped.

"Please?"

The sound of breaking glass, followed by giggles downstairs.

"Okay," he said. He wrapped the magazines in newspaper and sealed the package with duct tape. "You can't open it until tomorrow."

He handed me the package, and we shook hands.

"Let's play," he said.

He opened his bureau and pulled out a G.I. Joe toy figurine, still encased in plastic. It was Lady Jaye, one of two female characters on the show. She had red hair and was my favorite character. I started brainstorming how I could distract Will and steal her for myself. Will started playing with his tank, smashing it against the wall, chipping the plastic barrel of its cannon. I turned Lady Jaye over and read her bio. She had graduated summa cum laude from Bryn Mawr in the late sixties, and her specialty was the crossbow.

"Put her against the wall—I'm gonna ram her with my tank," Will said.

I immediately shielded Lady Jaye. She was only plastic, but it just seemed wrong.

"Give it back," he said.

"Let's do something else," I said, still holding Lady Jaye behind my back, which rendered me defenseless, and Will immediately shot me with a fist version of the Triceratops—one punch to the dick and two mini punches to deflate the balls.

I gasped. Tears immediately plinked onto the hardwood floor, and I desperately clutched at my jewels. I almost threw up because I could actually feel my nads deflating. I reached inside my underwear expecting to feel fluid or blood, but my legs were dry.

"Nice execution." I barely managed to get the words out. Through blurred vision I saw that Will was thrilled with my analysis. As the pain dissipated I realized he had just clocked me in the nuts for no good reason. "I get to punch you back," I said.

Will's face changed.

"No way."

"I won't ask Paul if you can come tomorrow night," I said.

We stared at each other for a few minutes.

"Okay," he relented. His eyes turned softer, almost wet. "Nick, you're a kung fu master. You could kill me."

"Do you remember anything I told you? I taught you the power to kill so you would never have to. Now just try to relax."

Will started sobbing without producing any tears, and eventually he stood up so his balls were level with my nose. I wound up and punched him as hard as I could. He fell back, banging his head against the radiator before collapsing in a heap on the floor. It was comforting to see him writhe in pain, knowing the worst was already over for me. I told him to just try to breathe, but he was crying too hard to hear me.

"I'll call you later," I whimpered, and stood up. I couldn't stand completely upright; it felt like my upper body was connected to my thighs by taut rubber bands. I edged out of the room with my teeth bared and limped my way home.

🍀 🍀 🍀

The next day I packed quietly and called my dad at work to let him know that Paul's mom was coming to get me. He had left some emergency money in an envelope upstairs on my desk. I fingered through the bills. About ten buckaroos. Not bad, but it felt even better when I added the sixty I'd already skimmed off his wallet the night before in preparation for the big shopping spree. I waited downstairs, doing math in my head, making guesstimates on how much clothes seventy bucks would get me.

A car horn honked.

"Hello, Nick," Mrs. Turgess said. "So nice to finally meet you. I can't believe we lived on the same street for a full year and never got to meet each other." I shrugged and shook her hand, then got in the backseat with Paul and Mitch. Paul quietly explained how we weren't allowed to say *sucks* in the car (toward the end of third grade it had became our favorite word), or at least anywhere near his mom. She was a devout Catholic.

I said hello to Mitch, then opened my backpack and took out a Walkman. A verbal agreement between us was that in exchange for their clothing tips I'd introduce them to my music. I had discovered WESU, Wesleyan's college radio station, by accident one night. I taped hours and hours of it, and within a month I had a shoebox full of mix tapes. My parents were impressed that I did this on my own, and bought me cases of blank cassettes to support my new hobby. At the end of the school year I brought some mix tapes for show-and-tell, and Paul and Mitch were the only ones remotely interested. As Mrs. Turgess drove us back to Paul's house I introduced them to some songs. Paul listened to Echo and the Bunnymen's "Do It Clean," and then Mitch shook his head to XTC's "Respectable Street." Paul and Mitch pressed their ears against my headphones and tried to listen along to the Clash's "White Man in Hammersmith Palais."

A few minutes later we turned onto Renfield Hills Road. I'd driven through the neighborhood with my dad a couple of times on Sunday afternoons, and though the houses only made me more aware of my own living situation, I loved staring at them. The houses ranged from Colonial mansions to modern spaceships that stretched over a couple of acres apiece. The modern houses boasted multiple bulbous skylights, sharp roofs, rectangular shutterless windows, and impeccably trimmed sod lawns. My house, on the other hand, was undoubtedly the smallest house in town. Correction: it was tied with the replica next door. I hated it; a generic green Colonial filled with other people's dust and grape jelly stains on the kitchen Formica. The front yard was yellow (fittingly), despite various contracts with chemical lawn companies, and most frustratingly, it wasn't as big or fancy as everyone else's.

Mrs. Turgess pulled into the driveway, and I could barely contain my excitement. Paul's new house was humongous. We headed upstairs. Paul's older brother, Brian, was gone for the week at a lacrosse camp. They both had their own private bathrooms in their bedrooms, and in the upstairs loft there was a foosball table and a Ping-Pong table. I'd never picked up a Ping-Pong paddle in my life, but since I already played tennis I handily beat both of them. They called me a natural. I blushed.

The house even smelled a little different from mine—rich and American instead of poor and spicy-cabbagey. The carpet was cream-colored and so deep my toes disappeared into it. Like Will's house, most of the rooms had high ceilings. I folded my hands together when they weren't looking and prayed thanks for having had the foresight to celebrate my birthday here. I wondered if I was going to grow up shorter then everyone else because we had such low ceilings.

We went down to the kitchen to get something to eat. The silver refrigerator had an ice cream maker built into the freezer door. I begged Paul to show me how it worked.

"It's a pain in the butt," he said, kicking the shiny door.

"Why don't you boys play outside? I have some cooking to do in here," Mrs. Turgess said. She looked worried. We filed out through the garage. Mr. Turgess was waxing a mustard-colored BMW 325i. He'd wipe at a spot, stare at it, then wipe it again. Paul rolled his eyes. We sat on a boulder at the edge of the driveway.

"What are we doing?" I asked. "Are we gonna look for mica or something?"

"We're just sitting," Paul said.

"What are you talking about? Shouldn't we be looking for mica?"

Mitch threw a pebble at a passing DeLorean. Paul yawned.

"Let's go swimming in your pool, then," I suggested.

"You haven't seen it." Paul frowned. "It's tiny, and the water's always freezing."

"What about bowling in your basement?" I asked.

"The scoring's all confusing if you have three people," Mitch said.

"Then let's go back up to your loft and play foosball," I said.

"It's boring to hang out in the loft," they both replied.

"But I've only been in it once," I said, pretty sure I was on the verge of spazzing out. Paul yawned again.

"Trust me, there's nothing to do around here," he said. "This place sucks."

🍂 🍂 🍂

For dinner we ate SpaghettiOs with meatballs, and garlic bread that Mrs. Turgess heated up in the microwave in order to keep it chewy. Afterward we were still hungry, so she made us grilled cheese on the Jenn-Air. I scarfed down glass after glass of powdered Gatorade. I felt sorry for my mom, the way she slaved away in the kitchen only to create awful excuses for meals compared to Mrs. Turgess, who never broke a sweat and easily made the best dinner I'd ever eaten in my life. Eventually we went into the living room to watch *Battle of the Network Stars*. I sank into the cream-colored sofa and practically had to wade out. Paul's parents abruptly left the room. The steps didn't creak once as they went up the stairs to the second floor.

"Hey, guys," I said. They looked over at me. "I have a surprise for you."

Their faces lit up.

"When we go to sleep I'll show you," I teased them. Mitch threw a pillow at my face. The tassel at the end poked me in the eye, and I howled. Paul's expression changed, so I shut up. For the first time all day I worried neurotically that they didn't like me, and my left eye started twitching like crazy.

"Okay, Les!" Mr. Turgess hollered behind me, dimming the track lights. Mrs. Turgess walked into the room slowly, carrying a Fudgie the Whale cake with nine candles on it.

I was shocked. I had completely forgotten about my birthday.

"Make a wish," they said. I had nothing to wish for—everything was perfect. I stopped feverishly twirling my hair and let out a sigh.

The cake wasn't very good, but afterward everyone handed me a present! Mitch gave me a Body Glove mock turtleneck. I couldn't say anything; I was all choked up. Paul gave me a friendship bracelet he had woven himself, and his parents gave me a new soccer ball—a hand-stitched Adidas Azteca. I knew from visiting Soccer Plus in Unionville that the ball was really expensive. Everyone gave me a group hug, and it made me feel like an orphan.

By the time we set up sleeping bags in the loft it was too late to play Ping-Pong or foosball, so I just rolled a foosball across the table, turning it into a game, seeing if I could roll it all the way across without touching a player.

"So what's the surprise?" Mitch asked.

I reached into my backpack, pulled out the package, and slid it across the carpet. They stared fearfully at the duct-taped package. I nudged it closer.

"Go ahead, open it," I said, and watched Mitch grab it and tear the paper apart. When they saw what was inside they were too stunned to move.

"Where did you get these?" Mitch whispered.

"You have to be careful," I said. "They're old issues from the seventies, but in mint condition."

Paul tiptoed over to the door and made sure it was locked, then hopped back. Mitch turned to the first page of photos. A brunette with gigantic bazookas smiled at us as she lounged on an orange beanbag. Paul and Mitch giggled and pointed at the naked woman as if they were embarrassed. I felt like I couldn't breathe; I'd never seen a naked woman before. We took turns holding a flashlight and stared at all the pictures. Paul turned the pages too quickly, and I wanted him to slow down but didn't want to sound bossy. They lost interest in the magazines after only five minutes.

"There aren't that many pictures," Mitch complained.

"Where's your Walkman? I want to listen to your tapes," Paul said.

"Are you blind?" I asked both of them.

Mitch went to sleep a minute later, and Paul put on my headphones and closed his eyes. I went over to the door and rechecked to make sure it was locked, then crept over to the far corner of the loft, away from Paul and Mitch. They were already snoring, whereas I felt like I was going to have a heart attack from all the sugar I'd ingested. My mom didn't keep sweets in the house; the only way to get a sugar fix at home was to OD on Flintstones vitamins and wash them down with a glass of maple syrup.

I twisted the flashlight on and opened one of the magazines. My hands were shaking. I pulled out the centerfold. Miss January had straight black hair parted down the middle and the longest stomach I'd ever seen. Her breasts were shaped like bananas. I traced them with my fingers. I brought the paper to my nose. It smelled like cake. Her smooth skin looked so creamy it had a calming effect on me, like cottony snowflakes falling in November. I felt delirious and destroyed at the same time.

I wanted desperately to meet Miss January and touch her skin. All of a sudden I felt an uncontrollable desire to lick the page, so I did. The words on the back of the page showed through. I gently nursed the wet spot with my shirt and smelled the page again. She was lying in a bed with deep red satin sheets. Above her was a framed painting of an early president. I closed my eyes and pretended I was a white-wig-wearing judge back in the olden days, coming home from the courthouse. Miss January took my wig off, placed it on a desk next to an antique musket, then opened my black robe and disappeared inside it. We started levitating and glowing. In real life I turned over onto my back and stared at the stucco ceiling. I discovered that I could picture her perfectly without looking at the page.

"Memorize *all* the pictures," I whispered to myself, holding my hands as if praying. "So that they're always with you."

Before I knew it my calculator watch read 2:30 a.m., and I was still wide awake. The life I'd had before discovering girls seemed like another century, and the kid I'd been before tonight felt like another person.

I gladly let him go.

It wasn't until the sky started to lighten, the first birds began to chirp, and the flashlight was fading, giving off a dim yellow light, no longer a beam, that I finally decided to crash.

♣ ♣ ♣

I was nudged awake at dawn. I woke easily because it was so cold, but my eyes felt like logs and I couldn't feel my left arm, which was sore from holding the flashlight in an upright position all night. I immediately remembered the centerfold and wanted to sneak a look, but Paul said no, and made me hide the *Playboy*s in my sleeping bag. We went downstairs. The inside of the kitchen was blue and stiff. Mrs. Turgess was cocooned in a terry-cloth robe. She greeted us quietly and told us she was about to make breakfast. We sat down on stools at the bar in a corner of the living room and waited.

"This fall you should get off at our bus stop and play with us," Mitch blurted out.

"Okay," I said, trying not to blush as I felt a delicious chill run through me.

As promised, when we went back into the kitchen, we walked into a room full of wonderful breakfast smells. Paul's mom made the best omelets, heavy on the American cheese. The bacon was extra crisp, even brittle, and it broke apart inside my mouth. We gulped down tall glasses of apple juice and devoured buttered toast and then collapsed on the dining room floor for twenty minutes, unable to move.

Then Mr. Turgess drove us over to the surf store in Simsbury. The store was huge inside, with skateboard decks and surfboards hanging on the walls. Paul helped me pick out three T-shirts.

The shopping spree wasn't as exciting as anticipated. In fact, everything—even the cake and my presents—took on a muted glow in my memory compared to Miss January and the rest of my new, naked women friends. Paul inspected a couple of decks but couldn't find one he liked. *Who cares?* I thought. I suddenly felt ridiculously antsy because I wanted to look at the magazines again. Bells rang as I anxiously pushed through the glass doors.

🐾 🐾 🐾

The moment we pulled back into the driveway is permanently burned into my memory. Mrs. Turgess was standing next to the garage with her arms crossed.

"Paul, get inside the house right now!" she shouted, her face bright red.

I froze. Paul got out of the car and followed his mother into the garage, and I could hear her scolding him. Mitch looked at me and shrugged. Mr. Turgess sat in the car with the door open, his palm resting on the handle. He couldn't decide whether or not to investigate. Paul stomped out of the garage.

"Those aren't mine!" He was glaring at me. I felt a sinking feeling.

Mrs. Turgess walked over to the car. She seemed to be refusing to look at me.

"Jim, why don't you take Nick home? Paul has to get ready for catechism."

Mitch and I ran upstairs to grab our things. I reached in my sleeping bag for the *Playboys*, but it was empty. Mitch gasped. The magazines were resting in plain sight on top of my knapsack. I glanced out the window and saw Mrs. Turgess explaining everything to her husband. Paul was talking, too, pointing up at the loft. I ducked out of sight and groaned.

"What should I do?" I asked Mitch.

"Nothing," he replied. "She found the nudie mags. This is bad. It's too late."

"Am I in trouble?"

"I bet Paul is. Thank God I'm not him. You shouldn't have brought these here."

"It's not my fault. Will made me," I whimpered.

I packed the *Playboys*, and when Mitch wasn't looking I stole a Ping-Pong ball and zipped the knapsack shut. We went out the front door. Paul was standing next to his mom with his hands jammed down his front pockets. He wouldn't look up at me. Mr. Turgess started up the car. I got into the backseat. Mitch stood next to Paul.

"Mitch, your mother wants you to go home now," Mrs. Turgess said.

He glared at me for a second before walking down the driveway. I waved at him from the backseat as Mr. Turgess pulled out, but he didn't see me. The drive home was torture—Mr. Turgess didn't say a word the entire time. I felt immense guilt asking him to pop the trunk when he dropped me off so I could get my presents. He said "Happy birthday," but there was a trickle of something in his voice that made me redden. My dad appeared in the doorway, wearing an aquamarine tennis warm-up; the bottoms of his sweatpants were tucked into a pair of white tube socks. He waved at the car. Mr. Turgess waved and smiled brightly at my dad as I went inside. The gifts were heavy.

"They got you that ball?" he asked, handling the Azteca. "It looks expensive."

"Where's Mom?"

"Work."

I plopped down on the sofa in the living room. A spring went boing.

"How was your weekend?" he asked.

I gave him a wink. He went to the kitchen. The house felt cold and damp and smaller than usual. He returned carrying a square vanilla cake with a single candle on it. My mom must have baked the thing at dawn before going to work. He lit the candle, and I blew it out without making a wish. He cut a slice. The last thing I wanted to do was eat cake. My teeth still felt gray from the eight pounds of sugar I'd ingested the night before. But seeing how crappy the cake looked, and picturing my mom baking the cake before work in her nurse's uniform, made me pick up the spork. My dad was watching intently, barely blinking. I sporked a bite. It was stale already, and I closed my teeth on a pocket of flour. It tasted awful, but I ate the whole thing. My dad handed me a box wrapped in Christmas wrap. I shook it and immediately knew it was a new pair of shin guards.

"Happy birthday," he said. "Are you happy?"

I looked at him, thinking about Paul's new mansion.

"Yes. Thanks for the cake," I said.

"Nine years old. It's going to be a good year." He looked longingly at the garage door. "Well, I should do some work. I'll be in the front yard if you need me."

I took a sip of milk. It was warm. The milk left waves on the insides of the glass. I could hear my dad bump into the wheelbarrow outside. I sat there with the lights off. When I felt up to it, I carried my presents upstairs to the bathroom and tried on the new clothes in front of the mirror. I considered the stolen money I had spent. I thought about Mrs. Turgess finding the *Playboys*. I pictured my mom at the convalescent home that very second, helping an old person roll to dinner. A good person would return the clothes and apologize to anyone who would listen for being such a spoiled brat. But I knew I would never do that. Useless air fizzed out of my lungs as I stood there in my new clothes.

The awful feeling lingered, and eventually I was staring out the window, listening to my dad rake up the lines of recently mowed grass. I was trying to identify what exactly made me a bad person. It wasn't necessarily a bad thing that I'd brought the *Playboys*, was it? Maybe it was all the clothes I'd bought. Or the cake my mom had made before work. At the very least I knew that hearing my dad rake only accentuated the guilt. So I put on my hooded sweatshirt and went downstairs. My dad was surprised to see me.

"Do we still have that extra rake?" I asked.

He smiled, took off his yellow hard hat, and pointed at the garage. I went inside, grabbed the second rake, wiped some old leaves off the broken tines, and went to work. It was getting colder, but the harder I pulled the rake through the grass the more I perspired, and soon I'd warmed up. I kept at it. It wasn't much, but it felt like something.

three

The summer before fourth grade Paul brought Mitch along to his parents' new summer cottage in Nantucket, and they stayed there for most of July. They sent me a postcard in the mail. Will came over, and we read the postcard a couple of times out loud before he suddenly ripped it up out of jealousy. We got into a huge fight, and it was almost an hour before we made up.

I spent the rest of summer taking tennis lessons at Farmington Farms Racquet Club, playing with Will, and every night before going to sleep I'd lock the door and stare at the *Playboys* until my eyes got sore. Will forgot about letting me borrow them, and I was afraid he'd ask for them back, so I never mentioned them to him again. Aside from Miss January, who was by then my imaginary girlfriend, I got bored staring at the same pictures over and over. I got so bored I actually started reading the articles. The night before fourth grade started I stumbled over the words *blow* and *job*. What the heck was that?

My obsession with Miss January didn't let up in the slightest as the months passed; in fact, it only grew with each passing day. I'd create scenes in bed using my hands as puppets and bending my knees so the down comforter morphed into a mountain. I pretended Miss January was facing me at the edge of a sheer rock cliff as a dripping orange sun set, and then I smushed my hands together, twisting to accentuate the passion of our kiss. I'd eventually flick off the light and think about how much life had changed.

A year earlier, I'd been so nervous about going to a new school I could barely sleep the night before classes started. Now I could barely close my eyes because I couldn't wait to sit with Paul and Mitch at lunch. I pictured them calling me over to sit with them, then introducing me to their new friends from Renfield Hills. The next day, more people would call my name, and I'd actually be forced to make a choice.

My desire for popularity was as ever-present as my desire for female companionship.

I giggled myself to sleep.

🐦 🐦 🐦

My fourth-grade teacher was Mr. Weller, the one male teacher at Crying Stream. He was a huge silver guy who always wore dark blue suits. He had a roaring laugh, and immediately all the guys loved him and all the girls were afraid of him. He had been in the Navy for forty years before becoming a teacher. He came up with nicknames for all the students: Mark Steeley became Tinman, Ellen Gurvey was Princess, Alicia Bolis—twin sister of Trina Bolis—became Barbie, Paul Turgess became Lollipop because of his rosy cheeks, Andy Cordello—who played the trumpet—became Andy Cordello the Trumpet Guy, and Kevin Ellis was Loggersly, which no one understood, but he was the teacher's pet, so it was assumed Loggersly had been a redheaded private during the war or something.

My nickname was Charlie. I didn't know why, but I liked it.

Mr. Weller sat down on top of his desk one afternoon and asked us what job we wanted to have when we grew up. No one raised their hands.

"This isn't for gold stars. Just say the first thing that pops into your head," he said. "Tinman, how about you?"

"I want to race cars," he said. "And be a fireman, like my dad."

"You can't do both," Ellen scoffed.

"He can have whatever job he wants," Weller told her. "What job do *you* want?"

"I want to become president," she said.

"The first woman president, eh? I wouldn't put it past you, Princess."

What was I going to say? It had to be something exciting. No one else played tennis, so becoming a pro tennis player wouldn't impress anyone. Kung fu instructor? Just saying *kung fu* made me recoil at this point.

"I want to be an astronaut," Loggersly shouted.

"You'd make a good astronaut," Mr. Weller said, patting him on the head. "How about you, Charlie?"

Everyone stared at me.

"Charlie's the Karate Kid," Tinman said, and I smiled. Then he made the martial arts whine, and everyone laughed.

"Ah so, ah so," Loggersly said, bowing to me with his hands folded together. He did circles in the air with one hand, then the other. "Danielson, wax on, wax off!" Mr. Weller giggled, mimicking his motions, then noticed my face was purple and told him to knock it off.

"Your father's an engineer, right? That's a great job to have. This country needs more engineers. Anyone else?"

A dozen hands went up.

"I don't want to be an engineer," I said, waving my hand.

I didn't have an alternative answer ready, so my mind raced. Mr. Weller sat at the edge of my desk and waited. I grew so frustrated I saw green and red splotches in my vision. And then it came to me.

"I want a blow job," I blurted.

Mr. Weller's jaw dropped. The students looked at each other, puzzled.

I got the feeling that this was no ordinary job.

♣ ♣ ♣

That year we switched classrooms in the afternoon from Mr. Weller to Miss Hamilton. She was teaching us fractions, but

I never paid attention to the lesson. Perfecting drawing dragon eyes in my notebook was much more interesting. One day when I glanced up, Miss Hamilton was no longer wearing any clothes; instead, she was standing in front of the class totally naked. I looked at the other students. Tinman was diligently scratching his left arm in the same spot over and over, while Princess was writing down numbers in her notebook. I looked back at the teacher, and she was still buck naked.

Holy moley.

Her arms and her thighs were tan like her face, and she kept making hand gestures and pointing at the numbers on the chalkboard behind her. For a few minutes it felt good to see her naked, but then it got annoying so I shut my eyes tight for ten seconds in order to squeeze the image out. But the dark screen in my head showcased Miss Hamilton, too; she was waving at me, and her breasts were all jiggly. I opened my eyes. She was still unclothed in real life. I tried to focus on anything but her. The way Loggersly's sickly snot eggs hung from his nose like threats. Missy Means's brown hair, with a purple plastic barrette holding a messy clump of it above her head. Andy Cordello's calculator-shaped handwriting. The rest of the afternoon my head ached, and I couldn't wait to escape the classroom. I bumped into the wall next to the door on the way out.

I met Will in the bus line and we had a chuckle about something, but when I stepped up on the bus Martha the bus driver smiled, and she too was completely naked. For some reason her enormous, saggy breasts lacked nipples. I pinched my forehead as Will pushed me to the back. I must have looked like I was in severe pain, which I was, because Will shook my shoulder. "Are you okay?"

"I have a headache," I replied.

"Here, hurry up and take one," he said, offering me a red Pixy Stix. Will could be intensely caring sometimes. I tore off the top and poured the red powder onto my open palm, then buried my nose in my hand and inhaled with two sharp snorts. It made me cough. Once the red powder was in my nostrils I wiped at the excess powder stuck to my cheeks, then stuck my sweet, crystallized fingers in my mouth while simultaneously snorting the already inhaled powder deeper into my brain. It caused a momentarily pleasant jarring sensation.

"Feel better?"

"Much," I answered. "Thanks."

"I have something to show you when we get off the bus," he said.

Will was about to give me information interesting enough to forget about girls for the rest of the day.

I successfully avoided looking at Martha as I stepped off the bus, but in the side mirror I caught a momentary glance of her rubbery breasts. I shook my head. The bus drove off. He whipped out a handful of blue index cards.

"What are these?" I asked, leafing through the deck.

"I busted the lock on a cardboard box in the principal's office during detention."

"You stole these?"

He shrugged. I glanced at the first card. Across the top it

read: *Alicia Bolis*. Neatly printed under her name was her room number, her teacher, and then a series of comments, followed by dates, written in different colored pens. *Mousy twin, friends with Glenda Berrenger, 3/8. S+ student, good at art, 9/14.*

"All the cards are like that. They talk about us," Will said. A car turned onto Summit, and we turned away as it passed. I cradled the cards inside my jacket like I was shielding a gun. We sat down on the curb and riffled through them.

"It's different handwriting on the cards," I noted. "Look at the dates—some of the comments are from last year and in different-colored pen."

"Tinman," Will said. "Read his."

I found Tinman's card. I recognized Mr. Weller's handwriting at the bottom.

Real firecracker. Good athelete, 9/5. Poor math skills, no discernible writing skills, but good at leading the class. Already popular, 9/10.

"Do the teachers decide popularity?" Will asked.

I was stunned at the notion.

"I don't know."

"Read another."

Missy Means. Already a manipulator (indoor recess queen), 12/3. Cruises socially, but has trouble with fractions. Possibly dyslexic, 2/7.

"What's dyslexic?" Will asked.

"I think it means she's good at cursive."

Mitch Wertz. Average student, but likable. Attached to Paul

Turgess, 3/12. Typical Renfield Hills kid. Probably be president of high school, 4/9.

My desire to live on Renfield Hills tripled that second. I picked up Beth Linney's card. She was in Mr. Weller's class, too.

Hard to figure out, 1/19. Keeps to herself, but socially savvy, 2/15.

"I hope my card says that," I said. "Where's mine?"

"It's not there. I couldn't grab all of them. He'd notice."

"What about yours?"

"Give them back," he said, reaching for the cards, but I pulled back.

Next thing I knew he was chasing me up the street. I cut into the woods, and luckily his asthma suddenly attacked, so I was able to put some distance between us. I cut back onto the road and lightly jogged ahead as I fingered through the stack searching for his name. He collapsed onto the curb just as I found it.

"'Will Fahey,'" I read aloud. "'Typical ADD Ritalin chewer. Bad influence on Asian kid. Nick Park's mom requests they not be in the same class, 3/2. Troublemaker, 4/12. Poor student, plus learning disabilities. Probably flunk HS.'"

He stared at me. A breeze passed, so his face was blocked by the tall weeds for a couple of seconds, but when the breeze died down I realized Will was crying.

I ripped up the card.

"I don't care," Will said, sniffling.

"What's ADD?" I asked.

"Huh?"

"What's Ritalin?"

"Vitamins for my sickness."

"Can I try some?"

"Your mom hates me."

"She doesn't," I said quickly.

"What does HS stand for?" he asked.

"I don't know. High school?" I guessed, and immediately realized I was right.

Will tried to pick up the scraps of the card, but a breeze blew them across the road. I watched him chase the bits; he looked like a decapitated chicken chasing nothing. I helped him gather up the remaining pieces. A scrap was stuck in a tangle of dandelions.

"That's why we're never in the same class," he said.

"Guess so. But we're best friends," I offered.

"I hate your mom," he said.

"Me too." Though I'd never really hated my mom before, I believed it wholeheartedly. "She's a terrible cook."

"I *hate* her food," Will sniffled in agreement.

We walked up the hill. Will took back the remaining cards and stuffed them in his backpack. My nose was tingling from the Pixy Stix, and I ran inside to get a drink of water. From the kitchen I could see Will walking through the woods to the side of his house. I sat at the kitchen table for a few minutes, thinking about the card, and how it had labeled me as the "Asian kid." I spent five minutes trying to figure out why the label bothered me, but then realized I was missing *Transformers*, and stubbed my toe running blindly into the living room as I pulled my Smokescreen print T-shirt over my head.

❦ ❦ ❦

Will called that night. Actually, he phoned twice. The first time my mom answered and he immediately hung up. I waited by the phone upstairs until it rang again, and quickly picked it up. My mom got on the line after about a minute.

"I'm on the phone," I shouted.

My mom remained silent on the line.

"It's Glenn," I lied. I could hear the television from downstairs through the receiver. "Get off the phone, Mom."

"Who's Glenn?" my mom muttered in a defeated tone before finally hanging up.

"I hate her," were Will's first words.

"I do, too. More than ever."

"You didn't tell her about the cards, did you?"

"Of course not. It's a secret, right?"

"Right."

"Oh, okay. I won't tell anyone."

"What did you want to explain today? When your head hurt."

"Oh, that. I can't stop picturing Miss Hamilton naked," I said. Will was silent on the other end, and I immediately regretted saying it.

"Are you serious?" Will started laughing.

"And the bus driver," I blurted.

Will snickered, sounding like his old self. I started mistrusting him again.

"Now we *both* have secrets," I reminded him.

"See you tomorrow," he said, and hung up before I could remind him a second time.

❧ ❧ ❧

Midway during math class the next afternoon it started again. My head ached, and I winced through an hour of watching Miss Hamilton's Jell-O-like breasts and groaned in pain while she wrote fractions with her squirmy butt in my face. Something was seriously wrong with my eyes. I glanced over at the door. Will was standing in the window, pointing and laughing at me. The students started noticing him. Miss Hamilton walked toward the door, and Will ran off. My face was flushed, and I was certain he was going to shout that I was in love with her or something.

"Who's that?" Ellen asked no one in particular.

"That's Will Fahey. He's retarded," Missy Means explained.

"No, he isn't!" I shouted.

The entire class craned to look at me. My eyes welled up a little, and I focused on the chalkboard, at Miss Hamilton's nipple-deprived breasts, until everyone turned around again. I heard Missy whisper to Ellen, "They're best friends," and I pretended to draw a dragon on the top right corner of the textbook. It felt weird defending Will while at the same time wanting to Whale's Tail him. I wiped my eyes when no one was looking.

What confused me about involuntarily visualizing Miss Hamilton naked was that she wasn't even pretty. Her nose was pointy and her frizzy hair always looked sweaty, but I couldn't stop picturing her naked. I also couldn't stop picturing Martha the bus driver naked every time I stepped on the bus. I was a perverted Superman. As the bell rang I silently vowed to stop staring at the *Playboys* at night in order to get the rest crucial to curing me. I glared at Miss Hamilton's breasts and shook a fist at her bare butt as she faced the chalkboard. I knew in my heart I'd beat this disease.

❧ ❧ ❧

Will and I didn't talk on the bus ride home that day. We snorted our Pixy Stix in silence, then stared out opposite windows. The silence felt like an apology, and I was tempted to say something comforting to him, but I wanted him to apologize first. As we stepped off the bus, Will screamed, "Nick Park loves you, Martha. He thinks about your boobies all the time!" Then he shoved me off the bus, and I fell onto my palms, scraping them. Martha stared at me as she turned the wheel. The bus pulled away, coughing up two distinct puffs of black smoke.

"Son of a booger," I gasped, and dove for him. He ran up the road and out of harm's way. "I'm going to get you!"

I chased him up the hill. He was prepared this time and took two puffs from his asthma inhaler as he ran. I stopped running. He turned around and walked toward me cautiously. I pretended not to be mad so that when he got close enough I could give him the Triceratops. I casually stared at his dick and balls, lining them up in my sights.

"We're even," he said, holding his hands out.

"No, we're not! I didn't do anything."

Will gave me a puzzled look. Then he shrugged. I tried to kick him, but he easily dodged my attacks. How depressing. Student defeats master. I growled and futilely lashed out at him, and he started giggling, realizing his combat superiority. Eventually I stopped. Will started dancing in circles around me, chanting that he was now the best kung fu fighter in the world. The grin on his face made my blood evaporate.

"Missy called you a retard in math class after you left," I muttered, walking past him. It felt awful and soothing simultaneously. He started bawling in front of me, for the second time in two days, and I reasoned it was his vitamins making him cry like that.

"Now we're even," I said.

four

At the time what scared me the most about my uncontrollable habit of visualizing grown women naked was the fact that no one else in my grade was even remotely interested in girls at all. I was ten years old and already obsessed with girls while all the other boys were still daydreaming about being able to fly or shoot lasers out of their foreheads and didn't have the slightest clue about the female species; in fact, most of them actually hated girls. Paul and Mitch refused to sit next to them at lunch, and Will threw rocks at the Bolis twins during recess. It was just another way I was different from the other kids in Renfield, and it only caused me further anxiety. All the boys hated Barry, the one kid who played with girls at recess, and parents at our Renfield Termites soccer games jokingly referred to him as the "gay kid." I was already the lone Asian kid—I didn't want to also be considered one of the gay kids.

Luckily, in the spring the guys in my grade started coming around, and my worry that this obsession with girls was some sort of abnormal disease began to dissipate. At recess once a week all the boys would cut away from kickball and corner Livia Streehorn by the swings and make her show us her boobs. I remember she was abnormally developed for a fourth grader, with what I considered at the time to be ridiculously full breasts. The boys would laugh and run away when she flashed us—meanwhile I'd simply fall over in the dirt, gasping for breath. Livia would cackle and start riding the swings. She didn't seem to mind showing everyone her goods. I was always the last one to falter back to the kickball game, like a wounded infantryman returning from the front lines.

Around this time, I mentally relaxed and let my ridiculously enlarged pituitary gland go berserk. Sure enough, within weeks I became the youngest kid ever to jerk off in the history of mankind. When it came to matters of love and making myself shiver I was always an accelerated student. One afternoon I was lying sideways on the carpet reading the latest issue of *Motor Trend* magazine, trying to memorize the engine performance statistics for the latest Lamborghini Countach, when I leaned over to take a sip of Juicy Juice and felt the tingling sensation for the first time.

"Hello?" I asked out loud.

My brow furrowed, and I waited for it to happen again. After a minute I took a few more sips of Juicy Juice, figuring perhaps it was this particular flavor that tickled my nether region. Twenty minutes later I finally felt that odd twinge again and realized it was the friction from the carpet making me feel giddy. I continued to make myself feel giddy all weekend. At school on Monday I listened attentively to every conversation around me and discerned that no one else knew this magic trick, which meant I had no one to consult with on the matter. As a result, I was ridiculously paranoid about jerking off. Writhing in bed, I'd picture ghosts or spirits all around me, pointing transparent fingers at me, shaking their heads in utter disgust. The ghosts would embarrass me so much I'd have to pull the covers over my head, even though it made it hot and difficult to breathe.

♣ ♣ ♣

In addition to my brain and body going through the changes that most boys would typically experience years later, elementary school also only continued to influence my racial identity. I was the only non-Anglo-Saxon student in suburban Connecticut at the time, and my teachers gladly did their own part to mold me into the ambivalent monster I am today. Remembering grade school now only makes it more clear how much my teachers *did* screw me up. I was already leery of being referred to as the "Asian kid" so it probably didn't help to be deemed the main exhibit in the now-defunct Immigrant Fair toward the end of fifth grade.

The fifth-grade Immigrant Fair was an assignment in humiliation for me. We were each told to bring in a plate of food representative of our heritage that our mothers had prepared the night before. Even though I was just a naive ten-year-old, I somehow knew to fear this day. Sure enough, Miss Grant stood before us and said, "Nick Park is our true immigrant, being the one student who is a purebred in his ethnicity. Most of you children are a quarter German, a quarter Irish, and so on. Since Nick is the only student here who is one hundred percent something else, he gets to describe his food last." This was the first time as far as I can remember that an adult had verbally made a public reference to my ethnicity.

Jefferson Kaminsky brought in angel ear cookies, which didn't seem all that Lithuanian, and Princess brought in a pumpkin pie her mom had bought at the Finast grocery store. She was supposedly a direct descendant of George Washington. Sometimes when we recited the Pledge of Allegiance in the morning the guys in class would face her and not the flag as they lip-synched the words. The pumpkin pie was a big hit, as were the angel ear cookies and Mitch's tube of German mustard. Paul supplied the saltines for Mitch's mustard. Alicia Bolis brought in a bowl of borscht, and Miss Grant passed out plastic spoons so we could try it. I figured she'd forgotten about me and my pure-bred food, so my shoulders relaxed a little.

"Okay, Nick, it's your turn," Miss Grant said. She curled a finger at me, and I shuffled to the front of the class carrying a brown paper bag. I was humiliated even before Tinman and the rest of the guys started snickering. Miss Grant rambled on about how I had come from a very far-away place, and the students gaped at me. I squinted my eyes at Miss Grant in an attempt to blast her to bits with a death ray.

"Personally, I love Korean food. Has anyone here had it before? Probably not, since Nick's the first Asian, to my knowledge at least, to ever live in Renfield."

The night before my mom had filled Tupperware bowls full of kimchee and rice. The smell alone would have killed my classmates, so I hid the bowls under the living room sofa and stuffed two boxes of Kraft macaroni and cheese in my backpack. I silently prayed my thanks that I'd had the fore-sight to avert further humiliation. I placed the brown paper bag on the desk in front of me. It looked like a bomb.

"Go ahead and open it," Miss Grant said, her eyes sparkling.

I opened up the bag and took out the unopened boxes of macaroni and cheese.

"That's not Korean," Tinman shouted.

"My mom didn't have time to cook it," I whispered.

"What's this?" Miss Grant asked as she walked over to the desk. She picked up the boxes with both hands, examined them with a perplexed expression on her face, shook them like maracas for a couple of seconds, then placed them back on the desk. "A sense of humor is a sign of intelligence, but we already knew that about you, Nick. Now, we don't have much time, so where's the real food?"

"That's it. That's what my mom makes," I said. Technically it was true, only usually she threw out the cheese packet and instead added chopped-up *bulgogi*, *kung namul*, and hot bean paste.

Miss Grant's face turned red.

"I'm going to call your mother tonight to see if you even told her about this," she whispered in my ear, then turned to face the students with a lively smile. "For the rest of class, children, you are free to talk quietly among yourselves!"

Everyone cheered.

🐦 🐦 🐦

Fifth grade was a big year for me—as well as being publicly outed as a Korean, it was also the year I finally fell for a woman my own age. On the second-to-last Monday of the school year Amber Milwood tagged me out in kickball during recess. I could have sworn she put in a little extra push when she touched me, and I immediately developed a crush on her. That night, I sniffed the left sleeve of my Niagara Falls sweatshirt and was positive I smelled her. I nearly fainted a few days later when I found out my mom had washed it.

For the rest of the week I spied on Amber constantly, and during recess I tried to impress her with my kickball skills, but the added pressure made me flub easy catches, and I failed to kick a single home run. At first this was frustrating, but eventually this was exactly what made me feel totally normal for the first time in a long while. It was comforting to know that I could fall in debilitating love with a girl *my own age*, and shortly thereafter I was finally able to stop seeing Miss Hamilton naked nonstop, as well as Martha the bus driver and all the other older women in my life. I found it refreshing to see Martha the bus driver every morning and afternoon, fully clothed from mullet to steel-tipped shit-kickers in various shades of denim, and I always greeted her with a sincere wave and smile.

Sometimes at night I'd wear my Niagara Falls sweatshirt and re-create in slow motion the moment when Amber first touched me.

I made a few more pitiful attempts at conversation with Amber but quickly gave up trying to talk to her and instead relegated myself to admiring her from afar. It wasn't nearly enough, and as the end of elementary school and graduation day loomed nearer, the big question for me was whether or not I'd be able to get Amber to sign my autograph book. It was a custom for the teachers to let the fifth graders roam the halls all day signing each other's autograph books on the last day of school.

To have Amber Milwood's autograph became my main goal in life.

🐜 🐜 🐜

When the day finally came it was cloudy and threatening to rain. Will and I blew bubbles with the sample bubble makers the teachers had passed out. After the ceremony we sat on the grass by the funnel-ball hoop and watched everyone make the rounds, trading autograph books. The night before my dad had driven me to CVS to pick one up, and now it rested in my back pocket like a guilty confession. I didn't want anyone to sign it other than Amber. Paul and Mitch came over and asked if I wanted their signatures, and I politely said no. They looked insulted. We sat together at lunch and played on the Renfield Termites travel soccer team on the weekends, but ever since Paul and Mitch had moved and Miss January had entered my life we definitely weren't as close. They grimaced at Will, who had his eyes closed and was obviously on another planet or something, ferociously giving himself a shoulder hicky.

Amber was standing with her friends in a circle, laughing over what other students had already written, other boys. Mrs. Fahey hollered for Will from the parking lot. She was wearing a pink tube top and a miniskirt, and I gladly pictured her nude, feeling none of the head pains I got from picturing Miss Hamilton or Martha the bus driver. Will turned to me. "See ya later," he said. We shook hands, and he ran off. Loneliness obscured me again as I sat by myself on the grass away from the rest of the students. I prayed for my mom to show up so I could go home, too. I stood up and almost left before I pinched my leg. No. I was going to do this. I wasn't going to wimp out.

I nearly threw up.

When I was done leaning over the grass, spitting, I ambled over to Amber. She was wearing a red dress with miniature black Lab puppies stenciled all over it. My legs practically buckled with each step. I stood behind her for a minute before Beth Linney noticed me and tapped on Amber's shoulder. She turned around.

"Nick."

Her voice was soft and willowy.

"Hi," I squeaked. I held out my autograph book. "Would you sign this?"

"Okay," she said, holding a hand out.

I abruptly rammed it back down into my pocket, realizing she might think it was weird no one had signed mine. For that matter, it was still covered in plastic.

"Give it to me, I'll sign it," she said, gently taking it from me.

I opened hers up, and there were only two pages left. All the multicolored pages were folded diagonally, making it puff out like an Oriental fan.

"No one's signed yours," she said as she peeled off the plastic wrapping.

I found an empty page toward the back of her book. It was green. My mind was blank. I casually lifted the back end of the previous page. It read:

> Roses are red, violets are pail, see you next year in the middle school jail.
>
> —Kent Cole

It was poetry. It was genius.

"Maybe you should save this—there are only two pages left," I said.

She laughed.

"Just write your name if you can't think of anything."

I signed my name and folded the page. Then I hastily opened the page and encased my signature in a sloppily drawn heart before shutting it again.

"Here you go," she said, and we exchanged autograph books. "Have a great summer."

She ran off and rejoined her friends. They started prancing around in a little circle like clay reindeer. I stood up and lumbered over to the parking lot and huddled behind a brown van. I opened the book and turned to the first page. It read:

> *Dear Nick. Have a nice summer.*
>
> > *Love,*
> > *Amber Rhodes Milwood*

I leaned against the back tire of the van, unable to breathe. I held the spot on my chest where I figured my heart was. She had used the word *love*. She had called me *dear*. My cheeks soon ached from giggling too much.

After I regained my composure I parked my butt on the curb. A line of cars, all navy blue with tinted windows, formed at the exit, and I watched everyone leave. When the parking lot was empty I lay on my back and closed my eyes. I pretended I was holding hands with Amber at the firemen's carnival, our cheeks bearded with partially melted cotton candy. Eventually a car horn honked. I looked up and saw my mom waving from inside her brown Chevy Citation. She was wearing her starchy white nurse's uniform, and her face looked worried. I walked over to the car. My mom leaned over and rolled down the passenger-side window.

"Sorry I missed your graduation," she said. I stepped inside and shut the door, and we drove off. "How was it? I'm late for work. Did everyone else's parents come?"

"It was good," I said. "Not everyone's parents came to the ceremony."

She kept glancing over at me as she drove, so I rambled on about the ceremony. I didn't mention or show her my autograph book. I kept talking and she kept nodding, but neither of us was really listening, because I was daydreaming about Amber and she was thinking about work.

SUNDAY
10:49 AM

I can hear the faint bleat of trumpets in the distance as the high school jazz band starts practicing "Pomp and Circumstance." It's almost 11 a.m. and I can't believe they haven't sent the rescue dogs out yet.

Through a break in the trees I can see my parents, maybe a hundred yards away, watering the garden in an attempt to perk up the flowers for graduation pictures.

Things changed drastically once I got to middle school because that's when classmates started having co-ed parties on the weekends; as a result, popularity suddenly became an even more serious issue in sixth grade. Renfield Middle School drew its students from the two elementary schools in town, Crying Stream and Lowell. For some reason I seemed to be the only one left off the invite list to the first co-ed party of the fall. It was all the more frustrating considering the fact that I was the only sixth grader who truly appreciated girls in the first place (aside from maybe Kent Cole, who had a deep voice and ball hair by the fourth grade). I'd descended into social Siberia sometime during the first week of middle school and had no idea how I'd gotten there.

This is, apparently, the theme of my life.

five

On the first weekend of sixth grade Tinman ripped off the Bolis twins' bikini tops at Princess's pool party, and practically every guy in the sixth grade witnessed the boob fest but me. Typical. I heard the story the following Monday. I was sitting at lunch with my soccer teammates: Mitch, Tinman, and two kids who had attended Lowell Elementary across town— Keith Kagis and a burly kid named Rollo Tivares. Since Paul was best friends with Mitch he got to sit with us, too. Everyone who had tried out for the middle school soccer team the first week of school made it, except Will. Mitch was retelling the story because I'd asked him to, and at first I didn't believe him, but everybody's face looked serious.

"None of the girls would swim at first," Mitch said. "They were complaining that the water was too cold, so only me and Tinman were swimming. Everyone else sat at the edge of the pool, dipping their feet in the water, tossing pennies at us."

"Did they toss pennies as a reward?" I asked Mitch.

He frowned at me for a second but soon realized I wasn't kidding.

"Quit asking questions," Keith hissed. "You're like Rollo's little brother."

I shut up. It shocked me that someone I just met a few days ago could snap at me so comfortably like that. Since he was the biggest in the group, he immediately became the leader, while everyone else became his loyal subjects.

"Me and Tinman were *diving* for pennies," Mitch explained. "Anyhow, Tinman gets it in his head that he's a shark, and he starts swimming around the edge of the pool with his hand sticking up out of the water."

"Like a fin," Keith added to me, then hummed the theme to *Jaws*.

"Yeah, I got it," I snapped back at him. Everyone laughed, and it felt good to gain revenge, but then I realized I was the butt of the joke.

"Suddenly Tinman grabbed both Bolis twins' legs," Mitch continued, "and pulled them off the edge and into the deep end."

Tinman's eyes lit up; his hands made motions, reenacting the experience.

"At first they were embarrassed, but then they started swimming around, and I dove under them, came up between 'em, and ripped their bikini tops off!" Tinman said a little too loudly. All our faces turned white. I glanced over at the pretty girls' table. The Bolis twins were laughing and looked far from traumatized.

"The pool had lights along the bottom of the wall, pointing up, so you could see everything like it was daytime," Rollo said proudly, as if he'd installed the lights himself.

"What did their boobs look like?"

"They were perfect," Mitch drooled. "Man, Nicky, you missed it. Imagine four perfectly round oranges."

"With little cherries in the middle," Tinman added, and we all laughed. "I wanted to dive in and squeeze 'em."

"How long did you get to look at them?" I asked.

"What do you think? A couple of seconds, not even, and then they covered themselves, and then they went underwater and put their tops back on," Keith said.

"That's not very long," I said.

"Two seconds, three. But they were the longest seconds of my life," Mitch said.

He high-fived Keith and then Paul. Then everyone except for me went around high-fiving each other, overcome with pride and joy.

"Why didn't you keep pulling their tops off?" I asked Tinman.

It seemed like an obvious question, but everyone looked at me like I was an imbecile. Tinman shook his head, offended.

"I'd like to see you do it," he said.

The bell rang, and everyone bolted except Mitch.

"You can get me invited to the next party, can't you?" I asked Mitch.

"I can't invite anyone. They're strict about the lists, Nicky," he said. I gave him my doe-eyed look. "I'll try, okay? But I can't promise you anything."

"Thanks, bud." I sighed. "I wish I'd seen it. Tell me again about their boobies."

"What's there to tell?"

"Were there freckles? Were they tan or white? Did they have hard nipples? Were they quarter-sized, pink or brown—"

"Jeez, Nick, it happened fast. I don't know—want me to draw you a picture?"

We both laughed, but I handed him a pencil. He started sketching on the table. He drew two stick figures and then four big circles.

"That looks like a jumbo jet," I said.

Mitch tossed the pencil over his shoulder.

"And all the girls watched, too?" I asked.

"They were mad at first, shouting at Tinman. Missy jumped into the water and guarded the twins while they put their tops back on."

"Were the twins upset at all?"

"They were crying, and when they got out the girls gave them a big group hug."

My throat knotted up.

"That's so sad," I said in a moment of tenderness. "I would've protected them."

"Would you protect them if it meant you wouldn't get to see their boobs?"

"I don't know," I answered. Mitch eventually left, but I didn't notice because I was now daydreaming that I had been at the party and dove into the pool and blocked everyone's view as the Bolis twins put their tops back on, and later when everyone lost interest in the spectacle the twins led me by the hand behind a big tree and as thanks for my chivalry took turns lifting their bikini tops, letting me lick their shiny boobs clean of chlorine until I passed out, mildly poisoned but bug-free.

❧ ❧ ❧

That Friday afternoon I sought Mitch out by the lockers before final period. I glanced at the wall clock. The weekly party was in five hours and twenty-three minutes. I caught up with Mitch as he was heading with Kagis and Paul for the stairs.

"Oh, hi, Nick," said Mitch.

"So what about tonight?" I asked.

"Oh, yeah—good news. Listen, I asked, and they said maybe next time," he said.

"Who's they?"

"The eighth-grade lax guys. It's their party," Mitch said. "The last one was overpacked, actually. I gotta make the bus."

Mitch and Kagis walked off, whispering to each other. Paul lingered for a moment, smiling awkwardly. He said goodbye, then ran to catch up with them. I knew Mitch was lying. He'd never even asked if I could go. I knew the party was going to be at Missy Means's house, so the lacrosse player excuse was a lie, too. At the same time, all this lying seemed like a nice gesture. He cared about me. I shuffled back through the doors and into the hallway. A few students scurried by to catch their buses. The sound of engines sputtering as the last buses exited the parking lot. I leaned against the lockers and let my body slump down against the wall. My back caught against a combo lock, and I let out a squeal. I sat against the wall and stared out the rectangular windows. It was fittingly cloudy outside. Then I realized it was Plexiglas, and probably sunny. Still fitting.

❧ ❧ ❧

I think I had some sort of important moment that Saturday when I woke up and turned on the TV. It was depressing, but I realized I'd outgrown cartoons. I failed to rouse interest in *The Snorks* and went back to my bedroom. I prayed I hadn't missed another party. What had I done to have God punish me like this? How did I not deserve to see the Bolis twins' boobs? I was dying to see them. I knew that no one in my grade could appreciate their boobs as much as me. It was clear that God or perhaps Satan was testing me, and it was my mission to figure out why.

There was something obvious I was missing. I suspected there was a clue to my loserdom somewhere in my bedroom. I panned the walls, but nothing stood out. I fingered through the winter shirts in my closet. Aside from a couple of sentimental favorites, at that point my wardrobe was no different from that of any of the popular kids: Polo and Gap rugby shirts and a couple of L.L. Bean checked sweaters. My tape collection lined the bookshelves. I had the most unique tape collection in Renfield, which wasn't a plus, but it certainly wasn't a negative.

"I'm fricking cool," I said to myself. "Why doesn't anybody notice?"

I continued investigating the room for clues. I scanned through a five-subject notebook from fifth grade. The first day of each class was respectable from an academic standpoint—I'd scribbled down notes and quotes from the teacher, a promising start to the semester. The rest of the pages, however, were filled with pictures of helicopters and dragons and my autograph. Four pages in a row in the social studies section were completely blue with ink. Apparently I had spent entire periods scribbling mindlessly into the page until every white space was taken up. The pages were curled and stiff with dry ink, and when I held the notebook in the light at a certain angle I could make out words and phrases and names inscribed secretly in the blue ink. *I love Missy Means. I hate Tinman. Missy Means's boobies. Give me your boobies. Licky booby. Boobalicious.* On another page was a series of drawings of Missy's breasts hidden in the blue ink. There were so many pairs of honkers it looked like the linoleum pattern downstairs in the kitchen, and it hypnotized me after a while.

"I'm an idiot," I said to my reflection in the closet mirror.

What alarmed me were those dragon drawings. Only nerds drew dragons. I thought about what I had been denied: a three-second view of the Bolis twins' boobs. My mind raced with a million composites of what their chests might look like. It wasn't fair! "No more dragon drawings," I said, and slapped myself in the face. "Seriously, Nick, you're not listening! No more dragon drawings, even in private. It's a small sacrifice for a greater good, and you know it." But deep inside me I still wanted to draw dragons; in fact, I suddenly felt the urge to draw one right then and there. I slapped myself again, only this time I accidentally clobbered my nose, and it started bleeding. I stared at my bloodied face. "Jesus, you *are* a loser."

Only I wasn't being serious. I knew the bloody nose was an accident. I was merely being infantile and feeling sorry for myself. I took off my left sock and applied continuous pressure to the side of my nose with it as I continued the investigation.

Ten minutes later the room was a mess. I had sifted through everything, even tried on a couple of my outfits to make sure I didn't look like a poseur. I couldn't find anything wrong with me. Aside from the dragon-drawing addiction—which, like my eyesight, was correctable—there were no aspects of my persona in general that warranted elimination. I stared at my profile in the closet mirror for a couple of minutes before crossing out the final entry on my list of theories.

Possible Reasons Why I'm Not Popular
1. ~~Outdated wardrobe~~
2. ~~Too smart~~
3. ~~Addiction to drawing dragons~~
4. ~~Unsubtle public nose picker~~
5. ~~Scoliosis?~~

I sat down on the bed, utterly defeated.

Out of the corner of my eye I saw it. How had I missed it? My body tensed. Clouds must have rolled in front of the sun, because at that moment the room darkened a little. I turned on the lamp and shivered. I could see my breath. My stomach growled and my knees felt shaky, but somehow I managed to walk across the room to the bookshelf. My head was level with the blinding yellow of the trophy collection, but my hands reached for the plastic picture frame resting on the shelf below.

The picture was of Will and me sitting on the curb before a Renfield Termites travel soccer game. He was wearing the most repulsive Jams shorts with little cartoons of calculators sprinkled all over them, and smiling like he'd never seen a camera before. I was smiling too, thoroughly oblivious to the truth:

I was a loser because of Will.

Social leprosy wasn't my fault; it was *Will's.* How could I have been so blind? Intelligent thoughts flowed freely into my brain, and the picture of understanding grew clearer with each passing second. I examined the photo again. He was such a dork. All of a sudden I remembered that on the first day of school an eighth grader had circulated a list of all the remedial kids during lunch, and Will was on the list. I'd consoled him for hours without ever really thinking about it. He *was* remedial!

"And I let you into this house," I screamed at his goofy mug. I shook the plastic frame as if it was his neck. "You even slept over seven times!" I whipped the frame against the wall; it bounced back harmlessly but nearly poked my eye out. Kodak Will stared up at me from the carpet. The sheet of plastic covering the photo had cracked, so we were split apart by a jagged line. I took this as a sign from God. "So be it," I said softly. My rage subsided, and it occurred to me that I now knew the key to gaining popularity.

All I had to do was ditch Will.

To celebrate, I spent the next twenty minutes sitting next to the phone with the white pages in my lap, prank-calling various hot girls in my grade and shouting, "Vagina!" into the receiver before hanging up. Then the phone rang, and I jumped five feet in the air without using my legs.

❧ ❧ ❧

At school the following week it took way more effort than I anticipated to phase Will out of my public life. It made me feel guilty, but I made it up to him when no one else was around. It was a dangerous game. For example, I'd ignore him when he called my name in the halls, and dart into a classroom so no one would see us together, then later I'd track him going into the bathroom and sneak inside after him. I'd invite Will to hang out at my house after school, then fake an extended piss by cupping my mouth and making a hissing sound. After he left I would wait an extra minute before exiting myself.

A month later I was miserable. The absence of Will in my life made my soccer friendships feel all the more incomplete, but not enough to make me want to patch things up with him. I just needed to stay the course and remain patient. Ditching Will had failed to change my social status, however, and I considered the possibility that my theory was wrong. I was about to realign with him out of sheer boredom, but then the freckly bastard started ignoring me back.

Around that time something happened that triggered a chain of events that would cause me to look at my popularity situation in an entirely different light. One Friday I was called from pre-algebra class down to the music room to see the band teacher. Mr. Mazursky greeted me, led me into a tiny office, and closed the door. He was a bald guy with a gray goatee, horn-rimmed glasses, and a tan blazer with brown elbow patches, and he topped off this ensemble with a pair of used red-and-green bowling shoes. I'd never noticed his shoes in regular band before. He closed the door behind me.

"Nick, I've heard quite a bit about you this summer from the Crying Stream band teacher. He says you're something else on the alto sax."

"Maybe."

"I want you to try something for me, okay? Do what I do," he said, and started clapping like a European. I clapped in unison, and couldn't help but laugh. He laughed, too. "Now tap your foot like this," he said, tapping on the first beat and in between the second and third beat. It took me a few tries, but pretty soon I was doing it. I chuckled to myself and focused on my feet, my hands; the percussion I was creating.

He was right. I was a musical prodigy.

"Okay, you can stop now," he said.

I stopped.

"That was very good. You're a natural. Do you know what that was?"

"No."

"That," he said, placing an arm around my shoulder, leaning in so I could smell the Listerine on his breath, "that, my young Nick, was . . . *jazz*."

"Oh," I whispered.

"I'm the bandleader of the middle school jazz band.

Every December we perform with the high school jazz band at Jazz Fest, which raises money for college scholarships. I've never gone into it with a star saxophonist, and I'm wondering if you think you have what it takes to lead us to victory."

"Victory?"

"It's unspoken, but the high school band teacher, Mr. Spagnoss, and I have a friendly rivalry going. I think this might be the year my band outperforms his."

"Because of me?"

"It's been twenty years since we performed 'Harlem Nocturne'—you know, the theme song to *Mike Hammer*? That's the greatest crowd-pleaser I've ever known."

"You think I could do it?" I asked, even though I already knew the answer.

"I know you can play it. You're a born jazz musician," he said, staring up at the fluorescent light blinking above us. "Practices are an hour before first bell, every morning. Can you make it?"

That I didn't agree with, but he looked so excited, and I figured maybe this was a way for me to stand out among the uninviteds. Maybe I could become a saxophone star and become popular that way.

"Okay," I said.

I returned to science class and promptly ruined my lab partner's experiment. We were melting glass rods over a Bunsen burner, creating eyedroppers, and I melted all of his successes into pairs, thinking this was the right thing to do. I didn't care when the teacher started yelling at me, because I was thinking about Mr. Mazursky's proposal, and wondering what the odds were that the Bolis Boob Fest could happen a *second* time.

✦ ✦ ✦

That night I told my parents over dinner everything Mr. Mazursky had said, only I embellished it a little because that was how I operated back then. Outside, a dog howled.

"He says I'm the greatest musician to walk through the doors of Renfield Middle in over seventy years," I gushed, incapable of stopping for a breath. "And he thinks I can bring glory to the middle school jazz band because I'm the first student to ever display the potential to perform 'Moonlight Rascals' at the Live Aid benefit in December."

"Nick, this is wonderful news," my mom said. "I knew you had a talent in you."

"He's already a tennis phenom," my dad said, winking at me.

"In music. I knew you could do something with music."

"He said I'm the best he's ever heard," I said. "And he's heard everybody."

"I told you Nick was special," my mom chided my dad, and he shrugged. It was surprising to hear that my mom considered me special. She never watched me play tennis, and used most of the air in her lungs to criticize my study habits despite the fact that up till then most of my homework assignments had involved drawing with colored markers.

I turned to my dad.

"You didn't think I was special?" I asked.

After dinner I went outside to juggle the soccer ball. I should have been working on my left foot, but I could juggle like a fiend. As I bounced the ball off my knees a hundred times apiece before switching to my puppies, I thought about Mr. Mazursky's comments. Could I really bring glory to the jazz band? Would it possibly bring me—

"Why haven't you returned my calls?" Will asked, startling me. "Are we, like, in a fight or something?"

"What up, dude?" I said, but couldn't hide my nervousness. "Don't be silly."

"You're trying to be friends with the soccer guys."

"They *are* my friends."

"*I'm* your friend. Are you ditching me?"

I looked at the woods.

"You do stupid things in school," I blurted. "It makes me look bad."

Will reacted as if he'd gotten shot.

The moon and sun were both in the sky, and I pretended we were on an uncharted planet. Will picked up my soccer ball and started heading it, a sign of forgiveness. I swiped the ball, started dribbling around him. "Come on, steal it," I said. Will took two steps and kicked the ball as hard as he could, just missing my shin. The ball landed in the woods. I wanted to shove him for nearly kicking me, but his eyes were shaking. He walked away. I stayed motionless. I waited for him to stop or at least look back. His head eventually disappeared down his driveway, and I realized I hadn't been breathing.

six

Within a week I hated playing in jazz band. It wasn't the music—I actually enjoyed playing the songs (which weren't jazz, really), and it was obvious I was the best sax player. But—although I quickly became Mazursky's pet and the rest of the band wished they were me—it didn't feel like progress because I realized that the seventh and eighth graders in jazz band were a bunch of nerds. So nerdy that Andy Cordello the Trumpet Guy was—if you were forced to rank them— one of the *cooler* kids in jazz band. I already had this whole Will friendship to overcome, and though I figured I was probably the coolest person in the band compared to those losers, I still knew I had to publicly distance myself from them at all costs.

♣ ♣ ♣

On the night of Jazz Fest, I was putting on my suit when my mom entered my room. It was snowing outside, had been since the morning. She was dressed in a black evening gown with thick shoulder straps and a line of beads cut diagonally across her chest like a sash. Her face was ghost white with pancake makeup. It was weird to see her all dressed up like that. Even after she'd gotten home from work she'd often leave her nurse's uniform on—sometimes to spice it up she'd wear a homemade pink shawl over her uniform.

"Do you want to practice?" she asked.

"No, I'm ready."

"Could I hear you play your solo?"

"Really?" She had never asked to listen before. Unlike my dad, who had taken up Ping-Pong when I couldn't stop talking about it and took me to the tennis courts or the driving range sometimes when he got home from work, my mom—when she was home—usually slid into the indentation shaped like her body on the living room sofa, where she knitted and watched *Falcon Crest* and read Jackie Collins paperbacks until around two in the morning before finally falling asleep with the lights on. She sat down at my desk. I closed my eyes and added vibrato in all the right places and really gushed up the solo. I couldn't wait for the general public to catch a whiff of my talent. When I finished I noticed she had her eyes closed and was tapping her feet and nodding. She opened her eyes, and we smiled at each other.

"I knew you were a musician. You've always had a good ear. When you were three years old I'd play Mahler's Second in the living room, and you'd wave chopsticks like a conductor for hours. You never missed a beat. If only you practiced more, you could get a music scholarship to Juilliard someday," she said, handing me a five-dollar bill.

"What's this for?"

"A present. Do a good job." She quickly left the room.

I finished putting on my tie, gagged, and walked out of the bedroom soon after, flicking off the light with a downward swipe.

It was still snowing when we left the house, and the roads

were slushy. The speedometer crept up to ten and hovered. My body writhed in pain from being forced to travel so slowly. My dad was visibly grinding his teeth, and my mom was bracing her forearms against the glove compartment as if we were about to wrap around a tree. A car passed us on a wide turn, and it made my dad nearly lose control of the car even though we were completely safe. It reminded me of the time I had ridden on the handlebars of Will's Mongoose dirt bike and forced him to crash for no good reason. I shuddered at the thought that this fear of everything might be hereditary.

They dropped me off at the front of the high school, and I ran into the lobby. I made my way through the mass of parents in the hall. Strangers patted me on the back. After a minute of being randomly touched I noticed Mitch and Paul, jumping and waving behind the crowd. We tugged our way toward each other.

"What are you doing here?" I asked, high-fiving them.

"Renfield Termites always stick together," Mitch said.

"Thanks, bro," I said.

I felt pumped. I took out my sax and let Paul hold it. He pretended to play, closing his eyes and shaking his head. When I left they bowed as if I was royalty.

"Nick," Mr. Mazursky said as I finally entered the band room. He was wearing a dark green corduroy suit with red elbow patches that matched his bowling shoes. The four strands of hair on his head curled into sweaty circles like a stringy pretzel. "Tonight's the night."

"And tomorrow's the day," I replied, laughing, but he didn't laugh back, so I started coughing violently.

"Could you feel the buzz in the audience outside?" he asked. "They know something special is about to happen."

A pair of electric eels were circling my stomach, but his mood encouraged me.

"We're going to kick butt," I said, and we high-fived. I had the solo down pat. Actually, it was ridiculously easy, I just played the melody to the song for two minutes. Then I had a twelve-measure solo, not improvisatory, and it was simple enough that I could focus on adding flair to it, bending the notes a little. At the last rehearsal even the drummer, who was in competition with me since he had a big solo in the middle of a decidedly cheesy version of Herbie Hancock's "Rockit," had nodded in deference to me when I finished.

We were up first. Our set would be twenty minutes long, and then for the rest of the night we could either hang out and watch the high school jazz band or go home. Since my parents were there, I was stuck for the duration. I placed my sheet music on the stand, even though I didn't even bother using it. The other sax players sat next to me, adjusting their stands. The drummer sat down on his stool, and the snare rattled lightly.

The cafeteria was all dolled up. It was impressive. Huge papier-mâché snowflakes dangled from wires tied to the girders above us; the near wall held a huge banner that read JAZZ FEST—A NIGHT OF JAZZ; three tables draped with red paper tablecloths held bowls of punch, trays of hors d'oeuvres, and a huge pyramid of green apples. The one non-elderly lunch lady had been forced to work that night, wearing a black blazer over her daytime uniform and gripping a stack of plastic cups as she stood still next to a glass bowl of eggnog. She looked suicidal.

Mr. Mazursky stepped up to the podium and gazed out at the band. His face looked professional. He took off his glasses, dabbed at his eyes, then looked at us again. "Make me proud," he mouthed to us. One of the trombonists elbowed me in the ribs. Mr. Mazursky nodded at the people who stood by the doors, waiting to open them, and then shouted, "And a three and a four and a—" and bam, we were playing a medley of Joplin ragtime tunes.

As the adults and the little kids filed in they clapped and pointed at us. Camera flashes went off, blinding me, but I knew all the songs by heart, so I just closed my eyes and played along. We really were the best middle school jazz band ever. Mazursky looked like he was staving off a crying jag as he waved his skinny baton at us. Now and then he turned to wave at the crowd and gauge their reaction; he'd turn back with a crazed smile on his face.

My parents stood in a corner, taking pictures. They were a tag team, my mom snapping away and my dad preparing the next roll of film, ready to take the camera. I was getting antsy to play the solo, psyched to bring the house down. I winked at Mitch and Paul, who were standing next to the food tables, munching on chips. Finally we finished playing "Rockit," and Mr. Mazursky turned to face the audience. The drummer took this opportunity to punch me in the shoulder.

"Bring us home, Nicky," he said. I nodded.

"I'm on it, motherfucker," I replied.

"Ladies and gentiles, how are you doing?" Mr. Mazursky asked, his voice high and cracking. People cheered. "Well, I have to say you all look so lovely tonight. This has always been a special occasion, but I wanted to point out something before we play our last piece."

My throat started feeling funny.

"Tonight on lead alto sax we have a very special player. He's only a sixth grader, but he's probably the best dang sax player we've had in all my years at Renfield Middle School." A lady cheered. It was my mom. "His name is Nick Park. Music must be serious business in the Park household."

My throat was closing up. I tried to breathe, and it tickled my mouth and made me cough. My dad waved. I took evasive action and started breathing through my nose.

"Anyhow, I wanted to take this opportunity to thank Nick for giving me the greatest gift ever, the chance to perform 'Harlem Nocturne' for you lucky people. It's a dream come true. So let's hear it for Nick Park and the middle school jazz band!" Mazursky cried.

Then we were forced to stand up and bow. I was choking to death but managed to smile. We sat down, and the audience hushed. The drummer started tapping the high hat cymbal and the opening strains of "Harlem Nocturne" started humming through the trumpet and trombone sections, and then it was my turn to shine.

I started playing the melody. My throat had shrunk by three-quarters, so I couldn't get all that much air into the mouthpiece at first, but I could at least hear each note. Thank

God. My throat started opening up as I adjusted to the circumstances. I just closed my eyes and played. There was a tap on my shoulder, but I ignored it. When my solo came up I executed it perfectly, managed some vibrato on the long notes, not quite as fancy as when I performed for my mom, but it was serviceable. With the constrained air supply, I was doing an admirable job. With my eyes closed it grew easier to play, to create, to feel the jazz pulsing through my body.

When the song ended, I opened my eyes. There was friendly applause, but it was scattered. My parents were gaping at me. Strangers smiled almost apologetically at me. Mitch and Paul were pretending to slash their throats with plastic knives next to the food table. Mr. Mazursky was staring at his feet, and his face was turning red. His hands were shaking so much the plastic baton waved all over the place. The drummer was the first to stand up, and then we all hurriedly grabbed our sheet music and filed off the stage to mild applause. I stared at my feet as we walked through the cafeteria to the exit doors, wondering what had gone wrong.

When we reached the hallway my throat immediately opened up, and I sighed.

"What was that all about?" I asked Andy Cordello.

"Are you joking?"

"No. Everyone seemed a little reserved at the end, don't you think? Maybe Mazursky exaggerated about this song bringing the house down. Or do you think he tired them out with that speech? Did he make them clap too much at the beginning?"

"Do you even know what you just did?"

I stopped. He was looking at me as if I was on the opposite side of a glass partition and we were talking into red phones.

"What happened?" I asked. My throat had closed up again, so I barely squeaked the words out. His eyebrows were arched in a funny way.

"Nick, I could barely hear you. I bet no one in the audience could."

"What?"

"It was as if you were pretending to play or something, I don't know. I tried to tell you—I tapped you on the shoulder, but you didn't pay any attention. You were playing triple pianissimo, so we sounded terrible."

I waited for his face to betray him, but then Mazursky grabbed me from behind.

"You," he said. "Is this some sick joke?"

"Mr. M., I just found out that—"

"What's wrong with you?"

"My throat closed up. I tried to play as loud as I could."

He just stared at me for a couple of seconds. "You don't deserve to enjoy the rest of tonight."

"But—"

Mr. Mazursky stomped off. Before turning into the bandroom he smashed his baton into a thousand shards against the brick wall and let out a strange, savage yelping sound, as if he was a bear caught in a trap. I was now alone in the hallway.

I got my things together, and as I left, my bandmates waved at me gloomily.

"Stay chill, Nicky," Andy Cordello the Trumpet Guy said.

"What are you talking about? He made us sound like shit," the drummer snapped.

They were still arguing as I exited the room. I wondered how I was going to explain to my parents that we had been banished from the premises. I walked halfway down the hallway before noticing that my mom was already waiting for me at the other end.

"Your father's getting the car," she said, and disappeared from view.

Problem solved.

I jogged to catch up with her, but when I turned the corner she was gone. The sounds of the high school jazz band filtered through a crack in the double doors as I left, and to add insult to injury I could hear a great sax solo and the crowd whooping it up. My mom was shouting at my dad inside the car. He got out and started wiping snow off the back window with a curled-up road atlas.

"I think I might have messed up," I said.

"Guess this means you'll just have to focus on tennis," he said.

My mom was staring straight ahead out the windshield, unblinking. I got in the backseat and blew hot air in my cupped hands, and we drove off.

seven

I brought my alto sax to school the following Monday but spontaneously skipped jazz band practice. All morning I had a stomachache thinking about it, but then Mr. Mazursky ignored me when we crossed paths after lunch, and I immediately decided to quit jazz band forever. This would be a turning point for me. Will ignored me the entire bus ride home, and when we got off he ran ahead. He glanced back a few times to see if I was chasing him, and I pretended I was staring up at something really cool in a tree. Using peripheral vision, I watched him disappear around the corner, and then I resumed walking.

After dinner I casually mentioned to my parents that I'd quit jazz band. I figured they wouldn't care since they still seemed humiliated about my bomb at Jazz Fest.

"What?" they asked simultaneously.

"It's no big deal," I said softly. "Everyone's doing it."

"Quitting becomes a habit. You're only in sixth grade—that's far too young to be quitting things. Seung, talk some sense into the boy." She resumed reading a trashy paperback, but I could tell she wasn't really reading it because her mouth was twisted into a sideways comma and she was staring straight at me.

"Now, there really is no excuse," my dad said, clapping me on the shoulder. "You will focus twice as hard on the tennis court from now on, okay?"

I nodded fervently. My mom rolled her eyes at him.

"Why are you encouraging him? Today it's jazz band, tomorrow he'll quit tennis, and before you know it he'll be selling drugs. I saw a segment about this on *West 57th*."

"Nonsense, and besides, he wasn't even that good at the saxophone!" My dad broke out in laughter, and I laughed with him for a few seconds before realizing he had just pissed me off. "Honey, it seems clear he doesn't like to play. He should focus on what he's good at, and he's good at tennis."

They had a stare-down. It was gripping.

"Well, you just make sure he gets that tennis scholarship to Stanford," she threatened, and left the room. A few seconds later she started chucking plates and bowls into the sink and watching them shatter to make herself feel happy.

🌱 🌱 🌱

When I got home from school that Friday my mom informed me that I was grounded for the weekend (not that I had anywhere to go) for quitting jazz band. That was also when my mother handed down the ultimate punishment: "And you're coming to church on Sunday." Apparently Reverend Su had told my parents that the kids my age had started meeting in the basement after the service. My mom felt it would be good for me to interact with them— "They're known for never giving up." Incidentally this little visit to church became quite an eye-opener for me.

We used to attend West Renfield Baptist Church on the other side of town. I never listened to a single sermon, and

Sunday school was a joke. The only thing I liked about it was that I'd always fake a stomachache and excuse myself so I could have first dibs on the doughnuts in the kitchen. We went regularly for three years. Then one day my dad got severe hemorrhoids, and as a result, we didn't go for a month because the doc warned that sitting on the wooden pews would aggravate his tags. What ultimately pissed my parents off was that the church immediately sent letters nagging us about missing two weeks of donations, as if that's all we were good for. As a result, my parents started regularly attending the Korean church in Granby.

I'd been to the Korean church a few times back when I was in elementary school. I hated going, and not only because it was a long commute each way. First of all, the sermon was in Korean. I don't speak Korean except for a couple of swear words I learned from my parents, since they only talk to me in Korean when they're pissed off. Second, you don't get to stuff your face with doughnuts at the Korean church. And that's what church, to me, is all about. You torture yourself for forty-five minutes, but then you're rewarded for your sacrifice with delicious cinnamon-powdered doughnuts and all-you-can-drink orange juice in tiny paper cups. At the Korean church, they always feasted after the sermon as if they'd starved all week. There was a huge, elaborate Korean meal, but since I hated Korean food I never ate a thing. Early Sunday morning my mom would make dozens and dozens of egg rolls and wrap the platters in tinfoil. The car would reek of egg and beef, and the smell would literally cling to my clothes for days.

"No, thanks, I'll pass," I replied, but she had already walked into the bathroom and started curling her hair for work.

♣ ♣ ♣

By the time I woke up Sunday morning my parents were already dressed for church. I picked out my salmon tie, shaped like the fish. I knotted it and then scrunched my shoulders into my old blazer as I ran down the stairs. My mom had bought it right before my first growth spurt, and now it took considerable effort to push my arms through the sleeves. My wrists and forearms showed, so I looked like Crockett on *Miami Vice*. My mom frowned at my appearance.

"We should get you a new suit," she said.

"I don't plan on making this a regular gig," I warned her.

I put on my Docksiders, slumped in the backseat of the car, and started listening to my Walkman. The Velvet Underground's "Pale Blue Eyes" played in my ears. Forty minutes later when we pulled into the parking lot I pretended to snore, hoping they'd let me just stay in the car and catch some Z's. My mom pinched me on the cheek.

"Jesus," I said, rubbing my jaw.

"Don't say the Lord's name in vain in a church parking lot," she snapped.

The church was built into a hill, so the parking lot was sloped. A group of Korean people stood outside the main entrance of the church and when they saw us they began whispering to each other. It was bizarre to see so much black hair in one place. I lagged behind my parents as we approached them. A tiny woman hopped over to us.

"Welcome," she said. "Is this Nick?"

"Nick, do you remember Mrs. Lee?" my mom asked.

"Nope," I replied.

My mom glared at me. I cringed, anticipating another pinch.

"I knew you when you were just this tall," Mrs. Lee said, holding her right hand below her knees.

"I don't think I was ever that short."

"Nicholas, surely you remember Mrs. Lee," my mom repeated.

"I don't recognize any of you people," I said honestly. They all looked the same to me . . . utter strangers.

A man shook my hand. The rest of the group surrounded us.

"So this is the tennis phenom? You're so tall!" the man said.

Everyone nodded.

"I guess," I said.

"Nick, this is Mr. Lee," my mom said.

"Remember Sunny and Grace?" Mr. Lee asked. I shook my head. "They'll be downstairs after the sermon. You are very handsome, Nick."

He grasped my shoulders and laughed.

"He's big, too."

"Jesus Christ."

My mom pinched me again, this time on the elbow. She didn't know that the elbow is the one spot you can pinch as hard as you want. I held my elbow out, inviting her to pinch it again, but she ignored me.

We met up with some more people sitting in the pews. Practically everyone's daughter was named Sunny or Grace, and every son was Billy or Franky. No one else was named Nick. I wondered if Koreans emulated Italian Mafia families on purpose.

Finally the reverend began the Korean sermon. I looked at my parents and shrugged. A lady instantly appeared at my side and handed me a small transistor radio with earplugs. I put them on. A man was translating the sermon into English; his voice boomed through the earplugs, and I winced. I looked behind me; the translator was a miniature guy with silver hair huddled next to a metal box like a Korean Wizard of Oz. He suddenly hacked and coughed and gagged for twenty seconds into the microphone before starting again.

He could barely speak English. Or rather, he didn't know any verbs. I sat there grimacing at his wholesale massacre of the English language, but then I noticed that kids my age were listening intently to their headphones as if the guy made sense. My parents smiled admiringly at me, assuming my furrowed brow meant that I understood the sermon. The translator paused, then said, "Don't bed with unhappy thought. Unhappy thoughts rot bone marrow." An old lady in front of me turned around and noticed my tie. She quickly faced front again. Maybe my salmon-shaped tie was an ancient Korean Mafia message. "Tonight, old lady, you'll be sleeping with the fishes," I whispered. I turned down the volume dial on the small transistor and fell asleep easily.

❧ ❧ ❧

After the service ended, everyone migrated to the lobby. Three women stood like an assembly line in the kitchen, methodically emptying Tupperware filled with Korean food onto hundreds of plates. I inspected the selection of sweet *bulgogi* beef and egg rolls, praying for a small cardboard box full of Munchkins. Surely, I figured, not every lady here had had time this morning to prepare elaborate platters of *mondoo* and *gim-bop*, but woefully there weren't any store-bought doughnuts, only the pistol's retort of a dozen rice cookers clicking at once and the familiar reek of homemade kimchee.

"Nicholas, come here," my mom instructed.

My parents were standing next to the reverend and his wife and daughter—who looked my age. She was thin and had long, black hair. Her eyes were smaller than mine. This moment sticks out because she was probably one of the first girls I had no physical interest in, and this confused me.

"Nick, this is Peggy, Reverend Su's daughter," my mom said.

"Hi," Peggy mumbled. I shook her hand. It was clammy and pink.

"She's going to take you downstairs where the kids get together," my dad said.

"No, you don't have to," I told her.

"Come on," she said, pulling me away.

I followed her down a spiderwebbed passageway and

through a room that was bare and blue. The dust made me sneeze. I was allergic to the place. We entered the basement. The light was blinding, and as my eyes adjusted the door closed and I found myself surrounded by at least twenty Asian teenagers. Most of them were high schoolers. The guys had overtly penisy-looking step haircuts, which for some reason didn't look as cool as they did on my Renfield friends, while the girls all wore scratchy-looking cotton dresses and had straight black hair that almost looked blue. Everyone seemed to lack discernible eyelids. Actually, the sight of these weird-looking Korean teens compelled me to pray. I thanked God for making me good-looking (relatively speaking). The walls were covered with rotting wood paneling, and the orange carpet smelled of mildew. It felt like I'd been transported to Seoul back in the seventies. In my head I heard the faint strains of Foghat's "Slow Ride" sung in Korean by a gay tenor with excessive vibrato. I could feel the difference between me and the rest of them.

"Everyone, meet Nick," Peggy said uninterestedly.

"Hi, Nick," they recited in unison.

"Hi," I said, and I noticed that my voice sounded so American.

A chubby girl introduced herself as Grace Kim. Aside from Peggy, Grace was the only other person in the basement around my age. Everyone else went around introducing themselves to me, and I said hi to four more Graces and three Sunnys.

"I can't believe Nick Park is actually at our church," one of the Graces said.

"Why can't you believe it?" I asked.

"You're from Renfield, right? Don't you go to a white church?"

"I haven't been to any church in years," I replied. Hearing her say "white" made me wonder if she secretly thought she was black. Confusion loomed over the surface of her moon-shaped face.

A pimply Korean guy walked over to us. "I'm Franky." He held a hand out, but mine was sweaty, so I pretended I didn't notice. His smile flickered. "Me and Sunny go to K.O. together. Peggy goes to Renbrook, and Grace is at Westminster."

I was usually shy anytime I met someone, but for some reason I didn't feel shy at all around these strangers, yet I still felt out of place. I slid into a seat, but then everyone sat down cross-legged on the floor, so I scooted off and sat on the floor, too.

"I went to Jimmy Choi's party last night," one of the older Graces said. She frowned. "It was really boring."

I rolled my eyes. No one saw me, so I rolled them again.

"He's a senior, right?" Sunny asked.

"Yeah. He's depressed because he got deferred early admission to Harvard."

Everyone murmured softly. One of the Sunnys leaned over toward me.

"You bored yet?" she whispered.

I nodded.

After five minutes of sitting silently, listening to their lame conversations, I realized I was surrounded by a bunch of nerds. I could tell just by looking at them that they didn't go to parties in their towns. I gathered from their conversations that they hung out exclusively with other Asians and studied all the time and played in school orchestras and probably regularly read passages from the Bible for fun. The guys in the room didn't look like they played sports. I started feeling claustrophobic.

"Peg, you should invite Jimmy's brother Eric to the barbecue," one of the older Sunnys suggested. Peggy looked over at me.

"Nick, we're having a barbecue after church next week. You should come," she said. "We're gonna play volleyball in the parking lot."

I pictured these pitiful nerds trying to play volleyball for a couple of seconds. They were bumping into each other and falling over in my head.

"Yeah right, I'm sure that would be a blast—*not*," I muttered, looking at my shoes, and when I looked up I saw a dozen slanty eyes glaring at me. I noticed for the first time how much more intimidating slanty eyes were when they glared than regular eyes. Which explained something! I must be more intimidating than I thought.

I was probably grimacing at them, because they eventually stopped trying to involve me in their conversation. I heard the sound of thudding footsteps above and envisioned my parents upstairs, frothing at the mouth because they were so excited to be conversing in their native tongue.

"So how many other Asian kids go to Renfield?" one of the Graces asked, trying to be nice I think.

I made a zero sign with my hand, nervous to attempt speaking even English.

"I figured as much," she said. "That explains why you're whitewashed."

The air changed as everyone sucked in a little of it. I was confused for a second but recognized the uncomfortable silence.

"Huh?"

"You're a banana," she continued. "White on the inside, yellow on the outside."

Yellow on the outside? I needed to find a mirror. Was the color of my skin altered under these fluorescent lights? I always thought I looked nothing like other Asians. How depressing.

"What do you mean?" I asked.

"It's the way you dress. The way you talk. Everything about you," she said.

"I don't know," I said for no reason.

Banana? I felt dizzy. What did this mean? I also always saw myself as different from everyone else in Renfield since I was the only Asian kid, but I'd never considered the possibility that *they* noticed that I was different, too. Did everyone in Renfield see me as a banana? Did my classmates see me differently than they saw themselves? I guess my consciousness about my race took on a whole new meaning to me at this point.

"Are you okay, Nick?" the oldest Franky asked. "You look sick."

My face felt like it was turning red. According to art

class, if my skin really was yellow, that would mean my face was actually turning orange. I was confused.

"I just remembered, I have a poster due tomorrow," I lied.

They resumed talking. I glanced at my Swatch.

"I have to go," I said apologetically.

"It was nice to meet you," Franky said. "Don't forget to bring sneakers next Sunday for volleyball!"

I shook his hand and left. My parents were waiting for me in the parking lot. They smiled apprehensively as I approached. I waved at them.

"How was it?" they asked in unison.

"Great. I'm a changed man. Let's get the hell outa here."

"Yahoo," my dad said, giving me a thumbs-up sign. "We should have taken you to church a long time ago. These children are a good influence.

"Reverend Su says the children get together during the week, too," he added.

"We asked the Lord to forgive you for quitting jazz band," my mom said.

"*Gracias*," I said, staring at my reflection in the rearview mirror.

"You're not going to quit anything again, are you? You've learned your lesson?" she asked. "In order to succeed in life like these children, you must always strive to persevere and always try harder, no matter what."

"Say no more," I said. "My quitting days are over."

"Hooray!" they both shouted.

The roads were mostly empty, and the stoplights were all

blinking yellow. I popped a mix tape into my Walkman and "When I Grow Up" by Michelle Shocked started humming through the headphones. It started raining as we got on I-84. The speedometer plateaued at forty. We eventually got off the highway, and as we neared home I started to try to picture myself as my classmates might see me. How could they possibly see me as a banana? I didn't look anything like other Asian kids. Seeing them up close in the basement proved it. They looked like foreigners. I didn't, too, did I? Did my own friends not see the real me? Were all white people blind? When they looked at me did they see what I saw when I looked at the basement Koreans? It wasn't inconceivable. I now had a new theory as to why I wasn't invited to parties, and it had nothing to do with Will or the jazz band nerds.

I realized that I wasn't popular because of my ethnicity.

The notion that my race had something to do with my lowly social status had crossed my mind before, but I'd always come to the conclusion that it was impossible. I figured that there were two reasons why my being Korean wasn't the reason I was considered *not* party-worthy. First of all, no one at Renfield Middle ever outright used any racial slurs—that only happened when strangers from other towns noticed me at the movies and at fast-food restaurants. That was the only real way I could tell when someone realized I was Asian—I'd get slurred. Second, Mitch was Jewish, and no one seemed to care, so I figured it wasn't race. I couldn't believe that I might be wrong on both counts. I remember that what scared me most was the fact that—if this was true—there was nothing I could do about it.

This was the moment when I realized I'd been wearing the wrong prescription eyes all along. I was just starting to see how messed up I was. It was definitely feasible I was this oblivious about how others saw me. How did I desperately want brown hair and not expect others to notice that mine was black? I'd been walking around with blinders on. As my dad pulled into the driveway I started realizing just how deep-seated and unconscious my self-hatred and desire not to be Korean already was. It wasn't *normal* to have an incomprehensible hatred of pandas, Laundromats, and anything silk.

I sat in the backseat with my hands folded together and my eyes shut.

"Look, he's praying," my mom whispered, but I ignored them. It wasn't really a prayer, more like a wish: *Let me wake up tomorrow the same person I thought I was this morning. Just Nick. Please be wrong about this*, I silently pleaded with myself.

But if I wasn't, what then?

SUNDAY
11:14 AM

From the sound of it rehearsal has just ended. I can hear dozens of car horns honking and I can just picture the caravan of sunburned seniors exiting the parking lot in a slow procession. Girls lazily waving at each other out of moonroofs, football guys leaning on their horns, pumping their fists at the school. Maybe there's been a pileup.

Now that rehearsal is over, I have to admit a part of me is really stuck in the past tense, wishing I could simply redo last night. I kick at the fence that surrounds the water tower and melodramatically shake my head. Eighteen years to build up to a one-night performance that will scar me for the rest of my adult life.

eight

By the fall of seventh grade I was so obsessed with Beth Linney that I commissioned Wesley Lipkitz—already a burnout at age twelve because he didn't play any sports—to take secret pictures of her in the hallways of Renfield Middle School. I had no other choice. The blockade to our love was being popular: Beth was, I wasn't. The key was to be patient, because at this point I'd resigned myself to the fact that there was simply no way I'd become popular in the near future.

My awkward stage had coincided with my discovery at the Korean church that I was a banana, and by the time seventh grade started I pretty much hated how ugly I had become. I had awoken to the universal ugly phase everyone goes through, but mine was a worst-case scenario. I was at Defcon 1. I was gaunt at a meager 115 pounds. My arms were so skinny and my chest so narrow I looked like a stick drawing of a human being. My eyes were tiny (but not slits), and my eyebrows were set far above my eyes. I couldn't understand why they looked so different from my friends' eyebrows. I tried on a million pairs of shades at Caldor, trying to find a frame that would cover my eyebrows. My mom assumed I just loved shades, and thought she was helping things by making sure my next pair of eyeglasses were prescription sunglasses. For six months—until I "accidentally" broke them—strangers at the mall referred to me as "the blind kid."

After being labeled "yellow on the outside" I started conducting a homemade test where I drew a line on my forearm with a yellow highlighter to see if they were right. I figured if I couldn't see the line, then the prophecy had come true. I'd think about the term *banana* lying in bed at night. Historically, maybe Asian teens were always nerdy, and so everyone assumed that all Asians thereafter were nerds, too. Were the soccer guys blameless? It wasn't their fault that it was hereditarily embedded in their heads to think I was a geeky loser. I just needed to show them times had changed, or that I was an anomaly, or the first of a new breed of cooler, party-going Asians, or something like that.

But back to my repulsive face. Student photos for the yearbook came about unannounced in the fall, and in addition to wearing an ugly sweater I also happened to give a queer smile, and it horrified me months later when I realized in the bathroom that this was the same expression I have when taking a shit. I prayed that my face would radically change in the future. In the meantime I had no choice but to hibernate. I deemed this a temporary phase to lie low and conduct research. My goal was to learn as much about Beth as possible through the only means with which to get closer to her: illicit head shots.

The requirements: Wesley Lipkitz was not to tell anyone about the nature of these pictures; he could not disclose the name of the client for whom he was taking such pictures; he was not to approach me or attempt to engage me in conversation except after school in the woods behind my house. Wesley's one request was that I provide payment for the film upon receipt; costs would cover the expense of the film, the developing, and a five-dollar charge for services rendered. I countered that it would make more sense for me to examine the photos first. Out-of-focus photos would lower the service charge, as would unidentifiable photos. Though I requested certain photos focus on Beth's body (for example, at least two shots of her butt), it had to be clear she was the subject in every shot.

When he tried to object to such specifications I had to remind my stupid, temporary compatriot that I knew things, many things that would convince his parents to go through with their threats of military school. It was well known that he was a minor oregano dealer at Renfield Middle. "But I need more," he griped after a silence had passed. "I want Eric's Game Boy."

At the time, the Nintendo Game Boy was still in the prototype stage and not yet available for sale in the United States. It could be purchased only if one's parent went on a business trip to Japan. And only one student in Renfield currently owned a Game Boy.

Eric Louie.

Of the 332 students who formed the middle school student body, one in particular far outweighed everyone else. Consistently topping off at more than three hundred pounds on a five-foot-eight-inch frame, Eric Louie, a fellow seventh grader, was almost wider than he was tall (at least to the naked eye it seemed so). His daily uniform consisted of a bright blue jean jacket with two AMOCO—ALWAYS THE RIGHT OIL patches sewn into the shirtsleeves, and matching size 72 dark blue jeans. He always wore the same faded green baseball cap with the John Deere insignia. His hands were doughy, impossibly thick, and strangely underdeveloped. His index finger seemed no longer than my own pinkie.

Eric had a slight gland problem. He perspired approximately two quarts an hour (guesstimated). The mere shifting in his seat after second homeroom bell brought forth a torrent of sweat down the back of his already damp denim jacket. His brown bangs were always matted black against his forehead. The Game Boy looked like an inefficient gray pebble when held in Eric's massive hands. He was obsessed with it and took serious pride in his ability to beat anyone at Tetris.

One day Eric was engaged in an arm-wrestling match, the latest craze to sweep the testosterone crowd at Renfield Middle. A group of maybe twenty guys regularly showed up to watch the contests. The highlight that morning was the match-up between Eric Louie and Scott Timber, the class wimp, who moved like he was made of rubber. Surprisingly, they were evenly matched. Twelve minutes elapsed. A puddle of sweat had not only formed on the desk but spilled onto the floor. Bubbles were forming on Eric's hand from the exertion.

I knew the window to do the deed was closing. I squeezed my eyes shut for a moment.

"Timber's getting tired," Rollo said, pointing at Scott's red face. "That's the chink in his armor, man, no endurance. I want to switch my bet!"

My face flushed at the word *chink*, and I froze. Even though no one looked at me, I felt a strong sense that they were at least thinking about me after Rollo said it. I walked behind Eric, mock-cheering him on like the others. I got down on my knees. Everyone was hypnotized as I casually slipped the Game Boy out of Eric's backpack and hid it under my shirt. I grabbed my belly, faking a stomachache, and left the room. A twinge of guilt set in, but I dissolved it by imagining Eric laughing when Rollo said "chink." It worked, even though I knew Eric was a nice guy and would never laugh at something like that. Without looking I turned the Game Boy on; through the cotton fibers of my shirt I heard a tiny ping.

I played Tetris all night. By the time I went to sleep the game had taken up permanent residence in my mind. As I lay in bed the shapes would fall like snow from the stucco ceiling. The characters in my dreams moved in the same fashion as the blocks. Everything in the waking world the next day took on a different kind of precision. I could see pockets of space that I wouldn't normally have noticed, openings while walking; I'd rotate three times counterclockwise in order to slide into an empty seat during homeroom. Movement in general felt either agitatingly slow or frighteningly fast. My fingers ached at night from playing too much and in the morning from not playing enough.

♣ ♣ ♣

One day that week—about twenty minutes after I got home from school—the doorbell started ringing like crazy. I peeked out my bedroom window to see who it was. The top of Lipkitz's greasy head shone up at me. I paced the bedroom for a minute and then ran down the stairs. Through the front window I could see a paper bag clutched in his hands, and my heart somersaulted. I put down the Game Boy and headed to the front door.

I stepped outside, closing the door behind me. I didn't want him to even entertain the notion of coming inside. He was lower on the social totem pole than me, and interacting with him could possibly make me more of a loser.

"Where's the Game Boy?" Lipkitz asked.

My mind drifted for a few seconds upon hearing the name. Imaginary blocks started falling jerkily from the trees, coming haphazardly to a rest under the canopy of branches. A cat meowed.

"I don't have it yet," I lied.

"Eric told me he lost it two days ago. I know you have it."

Bastard, I thought. *He's gone and talked to the robbed himself!*

"It's very safe. I had to stash it. You'll have it tomorrow, Friday. Are those the pictures?"

"Not until I get the Game Boy."

"Never mind the Game Boy. You'll have that for the rest of your life."

"You'll have these pictures for the rest of your life, too."

"I don't need them. I was just curious about something. I feel like inspecting those pictures, to see if my theory holds true."

"What's the theory?"

I was suddenly outraged that a loser like Lipkitz would think to challenge my lies.

"I'll get it to you by Friday," is all I said.

"Here," Wesley said, handing over the paper bag. "You better not screw me over, Park. I mean it."

"Yeah, okay, sure."

I stalked inside and slammed the door, shouting, "Sucker!" at the closed door, squeezing the paper bag in my right hand. Then I quickly opened the door and repeated the promise. Friday.

♣ ♣ ♣

I locked my bedroom door and set the lamp down on the carpet next to me. I sat cross-legged in the middle of the room and peeked inside the paper bag. Even though the face I saw was orangeish from the light through the paper fibers, I immediately knew it was Beth's. My heart fluttered. I reached in and pulled the photos out, praying that there would at least be one decent shot.

The pictures had turned out better then anticipated. Who knew Lipkitz was such a talented photographer? Almost all twenty-four photos were perfectly in focus, centered, and well lit. Beth by the water fountain. Beth at her locker. Beth at her locker wearing a different outfit from the other locker picture. Beth holding a lunch tray, waiting for the line to move in the cafeteria. Beth talking to other students out in front of the school by the flagpole. Despite his rather lackluster attention to atmosphere, the delicate sensibility of Lipkitz's photos was irrefutable. I shouted an inhuman celebration from the pit of my stomach. I shadow-boxed. I sang.

I held up my initial favorite: Beth standing by herself at the water fountain, her right hand still pressing the button on the side, her left hand holding her hair back to avoid the water. Closing my eyes with the picture stenciled on my brain, I made her lips move; her hair fell out of her left hand

and her brown eyes stared unblinking. I opened my eyes and looked at it again. I glanced tenderly at Beth's expression, almost hoping it changed in those brief moments. But she was still curiously staring at the lens, almost surprised. About to be surprised.

I put the photo down.

❧ ❧ ❧

I dissed Lipkitz all Friday at school and balanced pleasure with guilt for another week, until the day I received an annoying phone call. Lipkitz was livid that so much time had passed since his delivery of the goods, and he demanded the Game Boy. I seethed. I had been so happy. I had photographs of Beth in my possession. I owned Tetris. There was an untouched four-pack of Duracell double-A batteries on my desk.

Technically, Lipkitz held the upper hand. He had done his duty and now was demanding what was rightfully his. Well, disregarding the really rightful owner, Eric Louie. I even decided to be fair, and reversed it so I was wearing Lipkitz's shoes. If he denied payment after I did such a chore, I would definitely be pissed, too. However, Lipkitz was a total loser. I had friends (at least during the week). His cooperation was a pathetic attempt to forge a friendship with me because I held higher status on school grounds. Did Lipkitz's loser status trump the fact that all decent men stand by their promises? It took me only thirty seconds to decide. Easing my conscience was the fact that I was under the spell of Tetris and surely couldn't be held accountable for whatever I might do.

"Sure, I'll get it to you soon, pal. I need to get batteries for it. It's only fair you have fresh batteries," I told him, fingering the unopened package of Duracells on my bed. This shut him up. I could feel his face smiling as he hung up the receiver.

🍂 🍂 🍂

I was sitting on the sofa in the living room after supper that night. It had been a fairly crappy supper, but I was sensitive to my mom's ego. I even waited for her to go to the bathroom before I scraped the lamb egg rolls dunked in applesauce into the trash. I thought about Beth. My guilt over subjecting her to spy photography was dissipating, but I couldn't stop worrying that something so secretive had to come out eventually. I had commissioned a loser to shoot a secret roll of film of the girl I loved. The photographer, Wesley, did not know the subject, Beth, though he did know that she probably thought little of him. That's what worried me. Wesley knew he was a loser. Sometimes losers feel they have nothing at stake and don't worry about repercussions since they can't sink any lower. The fuse on the bomb was lit. I could sit and do nothing, but it would eventually explode, and the blast would vaporize me into oblivion. Or I could dive on it now, deflate its power by minimizing the potential blast area, and maybe survive. Did heroic soldiers who dove onto grenades survive? Did they ever do it to save themselves? It didn't seem likely. I worked my brain into knots. Eventually I came up with a plan.

First, I had to decide which photo I liked least. An almost impossible challenge. After a couple of hours, I settled on a blurry water fountain photo. I turned the picture over and with a red pen wrote:

Beth,
>   To love a rose is to never stop dreaming, and in the cold blue steel of night, I think of you.
>   —Wesley Lipkitz

I read it ten times out loud, and it made me tremble. It seemed unfair that Beth would think that Wesley created it. I considered writing a crappy poem so that I could use this one when the opportunity presented itself, but I found it impossible to lower my standards. I placed the photo in an envelope and sealed it, cutting my tongue.

🍂 🍂 🍂

Monday morning. The trap was set. I took a position adjacent to Beth's locker and casually BS'd with a classmate I'd corralled to provide cover. As I pondered aloud what the social studies assignment was, Beth appeared and opened her locker. She took out the envelope and looked around. I stared at my shoes. She opened the envelope and turned the photo over. Her cheeks took on a rosy hue. Suddenly I spied Wesley walking down the hall. I prayed for Beth to stop Wesley. She did! They were now talking. I immediately walked toward them. As expected, Wesley collared me and nearly threw me to the ground.

"You jerk, what are you trying to pull?" Wesley screamed.

"What? What's going on? Oh, hey, Beth," I said.

"Nick." She said my name! "Did you write this note?" Beth held up the photo. I suppressed a blush.

"What's that?" I asked, pleasantly surprised at how casually it came out.

"Screw you, Nick. Beth, he made me take that picture so he could whack off to you, and now he's trying to frame me. This is bullshit."

"Could somebody please explain to me what's going on?" I shouted, throwing my hands up in the air.

Beth looked at both of us.

"Leave me alone," she said, and dropped the photo and walked away.

I watched her leave. Was she addressing me, too? I gritted my teeth, which was a good thing, because at that moment Wesley clocked me upside the head.

"What are you, psycho?" I shouted repeatedly, hoping Beth would hear. But she was out of sight at this point, so I stopped shouting.

"I hate you," Wesley said, and walked away.

Now I was standing in the hallway with everyone looking at me and the photo of Beth on the ground. I couldn't think of anything to say that wasn't incriminating, so I decided to chase after Beth. I turned the corner and saw her at the end of the corridor by herself.

"Beth," I said, panting slightly.

"What do you want?"

"Look, I talked to Wesley and figured this whole thing out," I said.

Second period had started, so the hallway was empty.

"Turns out he really likes you. I walked by, and he tried to pin the blame on me," I said. "I feel bad for the kid. He doesn't know you at all, does he?"

"I remember when he took those pictures," Beth said. "He said it was for the school yearbook."

"Really?" I couldn't help feeling impressed with Wesley for a moment. *Clever alibi*, I thought. Then I tried to appear confused by vigorously shaking my head. "Anyhow, I hope you don't think I asked him to take those pictures or anything, because that shit's just crazy."

"I know. It would be," she said. "It's scary that he'd do that. He doesn't even know me."

"I almost feel bad for him," I replied quickly.

"It really freaked me out."

"But you know, Beth, if a psycho was going to take pictures of someone in this school, I can understand why he'd pick you," I said.

She stared at me.

"You know, this is the first time we've ever really talked since middle school started," she said, then immediately blushed at the statement.

"I know. I'm grateful Wesley's a psycho," I said quickly.

We both laughed.

"Don't call him that, it's mean," she said, still laughing.

"Yeah, well, anyhow, I'll see you around," I said, walking away.

♣ ♣ ♣

Later that day I realized a miracle had occurred. Since my conversation with Beth, we kept crossing paths between periods, and she said hello every single time. In fact, it seemed that maybe she was warming up to me as the day wore on. Her hellos developed into short yet sweet sentences, like "Hey, stranger," and "Hello again." I felt as if no one went to the school but us, and in the bathroom I mimicked the Heisman Trophy stance before coming out.

"What's going on, Long Duk Dong?" Kagis asked as I emerged from the boys' room. I blushed. He was standing with Paul by the water fountain. "You have a perma-grin on your face."

I wanted to tell them about how Beth was talking to me, but since I barely knew Kagis I didn't trust him. His eyes were as creepy-looking as Tinman's. Besides, there were people around—the bathroom door opened and closed behind me.

"I'm just in a good mood, that's all," I said.

Kagis and Paul laughed.

"Hey, great news, everyone—Nick's in a good mood," Kagis hollered. He shoved me playfully into the lockers. "Anus."

They walked off. I wanted to check my hair before I saw Beth again, so I pushed open the bathroom door once more and stepped inside, at which point Wesley Lipkitz delivered his second cold-cock of the day—this time into my gut.

Wheezing, I went down. And then a sweaty hand picked me up by the collar. It was Eric Louie. I'd never been this close to him, and smelled for the first time the awful BO Eric's mealy skin gave off.

"I want my Game Boy back," gurgled Eric.

"Fuck you, Nick," said Wesley.

"If you don't return it tomorrow, I'm going to crush you," said Eric.

"Fuck you, Nick," Wesley repeated; it sounded as if he had a string dangling from his back. I was surprised at Eric's strength; he was slowly choking me to death, and I wanted to deck him in the face, but somehow the thought of my knuckles coming into contact with Eric's sweaty cheek repulsed me into submission. I wished I had a bat or a crowbar so that I wouldn't have to directly touch Eric's skin. I was dropped onto my knees.

"Here's so you don't forget," Wesley said, then kicked me in the face.

Due to the direction and force of the blow, I ended up staring at the ceiling. The fluorescent lights flickered erratically. The tiled walls looked wet. I rotated my head, and the sand on the floor, accumulated from hundreds of sneakers, ground into my matted hair. I stumbled over to the sink and washed my face. I stared at the mirror and noticed a pimple above my lips. I regretted ever stealing the Game Boy. I should have stood firm on the fee for the pictures. Then I assured myself that Wesley Lipkitz was going to get his in due time. I forced myself to laugh. I sounded like a hyena, I thought. Then I realized I hadn't the slightest clue what a hyena sounded like. A sixth grader walked into the bathroom, saw my bloody face, and backed out. I thought about Beth. Regardless of the pain my head was feeling from the kick and the ache in my stomach from getting punched, I decided this was all worth it. I knew this was all happening because of love.

I guess I should have given up the Game Boy.

nine

Since I had figured out that I was a loser because of my godforsaken race, I made it a goal to improve my overall look, or at the very least make a concerted effort to disguise or compensate for my ethnicity. It was gradual, but by eighth grade I was becoming a pro. I started wearing baseball caps to school, and found that if I lowered the brim enough, nobody could see my Korean eyes. It was 90 percent a mental thing; I kinda knew they could still tell I was Asian, but I thought that if I made it not so glaringly obvious they'd perhaps notice it less.

That winter all the popular guys in my class started wearing flashy ski jackets to school. It immediately became my deepest desire to own a flashy ski jacket, too. By looking the part, maybe they'd just let me into parties by default. Renfield Middle let out early the Friday before Christmas for winter break, and over dinner I explained the merits of Thinsulate and Gore-Tex to my parents. They listened intently, nodding in agreement. As I rambled on about the importance of warmth in general I happily pictured myself wearing a new Spyder ski jacket just like Mitch's, only in a different color.

"The winters in Renfield are brutal to begin with, and meteorologists suggest it's only going to get worse," I said, looking at my hands, clenching and unclenching them in front of me. "You're right, of course, layers do help, but only Thinsulate, a material NASA helped develop, can decisively defeat the bitterness of New England winters. At school Mitch sometimes complains he's too hot because his jacket's so warm. Kagis's hair is always sweaty when he shows up in homeroom."

"But you don't even ski," my dad said.

"Are you listening? They wear these jackets to school. I'm talking about being able to walk from this house to the bus stop without the risk of hypothermia. It's not too much to ask. We should all get new ski jackets."

"It's too expensive," my mom said. "No jacket's worth that much."

I frowned.

"Staying warm doesn't come cheap," I chided her. "And the price is nothing if you consider how long these jackets last. Thinsulate is what they build F-16s with. I could wear it through high school, maybe even college, too."

"You're only thirteen. You'll outgrow it in six months," my mom said.

I hadn't considered this fact.

"I'll still wear it," I insisted, and turned to my dad. "I just want to be *warm*."

"Maybe for Christmas we can consider—"

"I'll be dead by Christmas," I snapped.

We drove to Clapp and Treat in West Hartford. The ski store was having a sale, so my green Spyder jacket actually cost a little less than anticipated. I convinced my mom to buy a Gore-Tex ski hat for herself. It had little mooses stitched across the front. The next morning when I woke up I immediately put my jacket on and showed my parents how warm I was. "See?" I asked my dad. "Feel the back of my head. I'm actually fucking *sweating*."

"That's great, Nick," he said. "But you really have to quit cursing."

That was the first step in looking cool. During winter break I also got fitted for contact lenses, but none of the fanfare I anticipated followed when classes resumed in January. For that matter, no one even seemed to remember that I used to wear eyeglasses in the first place. That day Mitch appeared at my locker after homeroom.

"Is Glenda in your third-period class?" he asked. "I'm going to ask her to Class Nite."

"But it's not until the end of the year."

"Everyone's asking everyone already. You better hurry up, Park."

I couldn't believe it. Mitch said goodbye and walked away, and I just stood there, caressing the soft Thinsulate insides of my Spyder jacket. At the end of middle school there was a big banquet called Class Nite where the eighth graders and their parents sat in the cafeteria and watched a slide show of middle school. Academic awards were handed out—it was kind of an informal graduation ceremony—and then the parents left and there was a big dance, the only dance where you could bring dates.

An all-new problem for me.

Throughout the day word spread each time someone new asked a girl to Class Nite. Glenda said yes to Mitch. Tinman asked Missy Means at lunch. Kagis got set up with Alicia Bolis. Trina Bolis said no to Paul, but then he got asked by Beth Linney. (That was disappointing—even though she never talked to me anymore, she was the only hot girl I'd thought I had a slight chance with.) By the end of the week everyone on the soccer team had secured dates. Most of the pretty girls were taken, and I was pretty much the only stag left in the forest. I gave up hope that I'd ever be able to land a date.

Since I never went to any parties or hung out with girls at all outside of school, my nightly fantasy became increasingly unrealistic. Before going to sleep I'd spend an hour making out with the pillow, pretending it was one of the girls from school. I'd close my eyes and pretend a volcano had erupted, but we were too engrossed in our lovemaking to notice, and the orange lava would cover us and kill us and decades later tourists would visit the spot and point at our blackened forms and take pictures, saying things like, "Now that's what I call true love. Doinking each other's brains out even as the pyroclastic flow vaporizes their genitalia."

♣ ♣ ♣

By mid-May, three weeks before Class Nite, I'd decided to just bag going altogether. I was walking past the art rooms after lunch, feeling aimless and crappy, when Maggie Shaughnessy approached me for the first time in my life. She smiled at me. My body felt like Jell-O, as if my bones had suddenly disintegrated. It took considerable effort to force my jaw muscles to produce a greeting.

"Hello, Maggie," I finally said, all soft and scratchy—my sexy voice.

She was generally considered the best-looking girl from Lowell Elementary, and even the most pro–Crying Stream guys had to admit that she pretty much blew away the Bolis twins *combined,* looks-wise. She had brown hair and glowing green eyes and almost powdery, white skin. Did every other guy at Renfield Middle feel Maggie's power this close? I'd had plenty of crushes by then, but as Maggie's green eyes trained on me for that first time, everything I knew to be true about life immediately turned false.

She was otherworldly.

"So do you have a date for Class Nite?"

"I'm probably playing a tennis tournament," I said quickly.

I couldn't believe she was about to ask me to the dance! I felt dizzy.

"Paige Cooper doesn't have a date. She mentioned you at lunch."

They sat together at lunch, along with Missy Means and the Bolis twins. It was arguably the hottest lunch table, pound for pound, in the history of mankind.

"What? Really?"

"Would you ask her?"

"Would she say yes?"

"She wants to go with you."

"Yeah, but does that mean she'll say yes if I ask her?"

"Well, it means she wants to go, so I guess so."

"Does she just want to go, or does she want to go with me? Those are two totally different things. One second you're asking me to ask her, the next I'm asking you if she'd say yes and you go, 'Uh, I guess so.' I don't understand."

"Are you going to ask her?"

"Would you ask her if you were me and you heard from a girl like you that someone like Paige was interested in someone like me?"

I was freaking out because I'd never asked anyone out before to anything. I was an asking virgin. Still, the panic was outweighed by the sheer excitement that a fairly hot girl wanted to go to the dance with me. I couldn't believe my luck. A few minutes earlier I had been feeling sorry for myself, and now not only had I secured a date to Class Nite without having to do anything, but Maggie Shaughnessy herself had approached me about it. Then I felt bummed for a few minutes: for a flicker, I had thought Maggie was asking me out herself.

As I walked to class I gave Paige some thought. Why would she want to go with me? Was my popularity ranking subtly rising without my knowledge? Or maybe she wasn't as cool as I thought? Why hadn't anyone asked her to the dance yet? Had her stock gone down as a result, and would that reflect poorly on me if I agreed to go with her? This was getting complicated. Ultimately, I decided it could only help my cause, and I reveled in the luxury of not having to worry about a date anymore.

❧ ❧ ❧

That night I sat by the phone, trying to call Paige. She had wavy brown hair, and at one point or another I had imagined banging her. That didn't mean much—I fantasized about banging everyone (except for maybe the Korean church girls). *Just call her.* I picked up the phone. *She'll say yes.* I compared this task to having to call Maggie out of the blue and asking her instead. It wasn't even comparable, and it brought things into perspective. This was a cakewalk by comparison. The first night I got as close as positioning my body near the phone. I even touched the receiver once, but the cold plastic chilled my fingertips.

The next night was the same deal. It wasn't until the third night that I was actually able to bring the phone up to my ear and start dialing. The seventh number became the new stumbling block. After an hour my ear rang from the bray of the electronic phone lady admonishing me to hang up and try again. This was too damn hard. What I needed was reaffirmation. It had been three days since my talk with Maggie. Maybe Paige had been asked already. Maybe she'd changed her mind. I had passed her in the halls seven times since, and the last time she'd only smiled without saying my name. Perhaps the window of opportunity had passed? I'd decided only a fool would call her without an up-to-date report.

The following morning I waited for Maggie outside the art room. I spent a couple of minutes staring at the latest batch of cheesy student murals that never made any sense whatsoever. Finally I tapped on the glass and waved at Maggie. She put on her jean jacket and came out into the hallway.

"Are you going to ask Paige out or what?" she asked.

"Listen, I was wondering about our talk last week," I said.

"I figured you forgot, or didn't want to go with her."

"Yeah, it slipped my mind. Why, does she still want to go?"

"Are you going to ask her?"

"I don't know. Does she still want to go?"

"Just ask her, Nick. Jeez."

"I might be playing in a tennis tournament. I have to wait and see. But if I were to call, say—oh, I don't know, like tonight, you think she'd answer yes?"

"I told you yes already."

♣ ♣ ♣

Three weeks later and less than half an hour before Class Nite began I locked the door to my bedroom and sat cross-legged next to the phone. "Dammit, you're going to do this." I calmly exhaled and picked up the phone. The number was committed to memory by now. It started ringing. I smiled and patted myself on the shoulder. This was another turning point in my life. The phone kept ringing. I glanced at the clock. I didn't give up hope. I kept track of how many times the phone rang in her house. Apparently her family didn't own an answering machine. When I reached thirty I finally hung up. My dad honked the horn.

The parking lot was practically full when we arrived. I noticed most of the parents were dressed casually, while my dad was wearing a blue suit and my mom wore a red dress with matching high heels. My mom patted me on the shoulder and smiled warmly. I could tell how proud they were of me just by looking at their eyes. My dad immediately approached the one black kid in my grade, Monty Banks, and feverishly shook his hand. I was feeling good about my parents, grateful for their birthing me, but these pleasant thoughts evaporated immediately when I saw them standing next to Monty.

"It is such a pleasure to meet you," he said to Monty. "Nicholas, come over here. Can you believe Eddie Murphy came tonight?"

Monty laughed out loud, but I knew my dad was being serious.

"Okay, that's enough," I hissed, yanking him away.

My mom chased after us. Monty was slapping his knees.

"Can you believe it, a superstar actor like him?" my dad asked. He glanced back at Monty with a look of pure awe. "At Renfield Middle School. The Beverly Hills police officer. Does his son go here?"

"Are you serious?" I screamed as I pulled him away.

"That's Monty Banks. I've played travel soccer with him for five years now. We had dinner with his parents!"

"That's Monty? Wow, he's really grown."

"You're unbelievable."

"But he has a mustache."

"What the fuck would Eddie Murphy be doing here?"

"Nick, please don't curse," my mom whispered, looking around to make sure no one had heard me.

"Don't talk to anyone else," I said. "I'm warning you."

My dad kept craning his neck to look at Monty, not quite believing me. I winced every time I heard Monty laugh. I prayed he wouldn't tell anyone. This was worse than the time someone had insulted Monty at a soccer game and my dad approached Mr. Banks at halftime and kept asking him, "Seriously, what is a jungle bunny?" Actually, everyone laughed then, too. The Bankses are incredibly tolerant people.

The slide show was stupid. Mostly it was pictures of the popular kids posing with Mr. Roberts, the hip social studies teacher all the popular girls had a crush on. His shtick was that he wore cashmere V-necks every day as if it was his uniform. There was a photo of him surrounded by the cool kids pawing at his supersoft sweater, and in the background, blurry, was me, running toward the camera. "Lean on Me" played over the sound system. The last slide, a close-up of Missy Means proudly holding a shark-shaped felt pillow she'd stitched in home economics, slowly faded, and then the lights came back on. The audience cheered.

Mitch and Paul walked over to me and my parents.

"Hey, Mr. Park," Mitch said.

"Hello, Meech," my dad said.

I flinched. Mitch and Paul laughed; they thought he was hilarious. His accent sounded more pronounced around my friends. Maybe I'd just never paid attention when he talked to them. I shook hands with my parents and watched them leave.

"How's it going, Meech?" Paul asked, giggling. He reached for his inhaler after laughing for ten seconds. He had asthma, just like Will, and was always sucking on that inhaler. I wondered if it gave him a buzz—a treasured secret among asthmatics. I've since tried it and all it did was make me cough.

Eventually everyone else's parents left, the lights dimmed in the cafeteria, and ten seconds later "Turning Japanese" by the Vapors erupted over the sound system. Someone shouted my name, others giggled, and I attempted to make myself disappear. It didn't work, but I did feel a buzzing sensation in my nose and ears.

It was a relief I hadn't asked Paige to be my date, because once the lights turned out in the cafeteria it dawned on me that I didn't have a clue how to dance. Kagis and Tinman could do all the cool dance moves. Rollo did the Worm to Thomas Dolby's "She Blinded Me with Science." The Bolis twins moved together like an Olympic synchronized swimming team, and Maggie looked like she was twenty the way she moved her hips. Even Mitch was a good dancer; being slightly cherubic, he just made his face and body vibrate madly like the guy in the video for "Beat It" and everyone cracked up. I wanted to mingle with the soccer guys, but they all were dancing with their dates. I didn't want to be a fifth wheel, so I approached Will. He was wearing a rubbery looking T-shirt with a tuxedo drawn on it, and pretending his body was stuck to the wall like in the Rotor ride at Riverside Park. I laughed at first, then looked around to see if anyone could see him acting like a dork. I looked back at Will. He had stopped dancing.

"Hey, neighbor," I said.

He didn't reply, but he also didn't tell me to get lost, so I stood there next to him without saying anything. Will started hopping in place, in time to the music.

Monty Banks walked by and pasted a hand on my shoulder.

"Your dad's a riot," he said before slinking off to the dance floor, doing the King Tut and the moonwalk to perfection. The crowd cheered.

Kagis walked over to where my back was pressed against the wall next to Will a couple of minutes later.

"Check it out, Glenda Berrenger's wearing a red dress," he said. "That means she's got her period. Bummer, eh?"

"I didn't know that. Is that why they sometimes wear red pants, too?"

"Yeah, so they don't have to stress about bad drip control," he said.

We watched Glenda for a few minutes. I thought I could see that she was moving around real cautiously, as if she was afraid she was about to explode or something.

"So why aren't you dancing?" he asked. His date, Alicia,

was at the water fountain with a gaggle of pretty girls in frilly dresses.

"I don't feel like it," I lied. I started moving in a circle, pretending to hit forehands and backhands in time with Duran Duran's "New Moon on Monday." It actually felt cool in an epileptic kind of way. Kagis giggled.

"Are you playing air tennis?" he asked.

"It feels slick, though. Does it look good?"

"Actually, it does," he admitted.

He mimicked me as we danced along the wall for a minute before I realized he was messing around with me. The soccer guys and their dates were laughing and pointing. I punched Kagis in the shoulder, and he playfully punched me back. Will was still stuck to the wall, and his tongue was sticking out, so he looked like a scarecrow.

"Will's such a doofus," I said.

"Uh-huh," Kagis muttered. Alicia waved at him, and he walked away without saying another word. I drifted back to Will.

"This dance is boring," I told him.

"I'm huh-huh-having a blast," he answered quickly, pretending he was Max Headroom, and then turned so his back was facing me.

He had no clue how stupid he looked, but hanging out with him felt like the right thing to do. I sighed. I was a soccer guy, and here I was with Will the space cadet. We were the only wallflowers at the last dance of middle school. Unbelievable. A train formed during "Love Plus One" by Haircut 100. As the minutes passed I started getting into a serious internal debate about whether or not Will truly looked dumb pretending to be a scarecrow, but just as I was nearing an epiphany about myself the double doors opened and a stream of cold light seeped onto the dance floor.

Paige and her group of friends walked in. She looked beautiful. She was wearing a pink dress with angel hair spaghetti straps and white nylons that made her legs look like floured drumsticks. I suddenly felt absurdly fidgety. My Swatch read 10:38.

"Nick," a voice like a flute said. I turned around. It was Paige. "Hi."

"How're you doing?" I asked. My tongue was trying to choke me to death.

"Great. And you?"

"I was playing in a tennis tournament, so my legs are tired," I lied automatically.

"Oh, downer, I was gonna see if you wanted to, you know, dance."

"Actually sure, I can dance, Paige," I said, and she led me to the middle of the floor as the opening piano intro to "Against All Odds" by Phil Collins started playing.

I could smell her. My sweat merged our bodies, and my knees on occasion bumped into her thighs, making me feel all liquefied. I tried to sniff her neck as inconspicuously as possible. I panned the cafeteria and saw that Ellen Gurvey was trying to get Will to dance, but he was refusing to do anything but move around like a scarecrow, his arms askew. She was giggling and trying to push them back down. He looked insane.

"Why didn't you want to go to the dance with me?" Paige asked.

"I did. I called tonight, but you had already left."

"I thought you were going to ask me like a month ago."

The song ended, and everyone clapped. The DJ, a fat white guy wearing a pink satin bowling shirt, shouted into a megaphone, "Okay, people, it's time for your last dance of middle school. Congratulations, and remember to grab your yearbooks on the way out. This is rockin' Sammy Sam signing off!" Led Zep's "Stairway to Heaven" started playing. I expected Paige to say goodbye and walk away, but instead she just stood there, fiddling with the dozen black jelly bracelets dangling from her left wrist.

"Wanna dance again?" I asked.

It felt good to finally ask her to do something. She smiled.

"I promised Rollo a dance, but he looks busy."

We danced again, and it was even better then before. It felt amazing to rotate slowly and know that everyone was noticing us together like that. At one point she rested her chin on my neck, even though it was all sweaty, and when the fast part at the end of the song came on we detached like a pair of recently serviced bald eagles. We slinked away from each other. I resumed my post next to Will. We were both internally spastic from dancing, taking deep breaths. He suddenly squeezed my shoulder. Even though it was dark inside the cafeteria, I could tell this meant we were friends again. I made eye contact with Kagis, and he gave me a thumbs-up sign. There was something different in his facial expression. I was convinced it was because he'd seen me dance with Paige, so I looked cooler in his eyes. This was an important moment, and it would influence my actions in the future. I could tell that things were going to be different for me in high school.

ten

Right when I thought things were going to get better I was blindsided.

There was a heat wave that summer, so I spent most of my days at Will's house. He had central air, and we'd try to freeze ourselves to death by lying still next to the floor vents in the master bedroom. Eventually his mom would find us, notice the goose bumps on our legs, and make us go outside. We would impatiently boot a soccer ball back and forth in his backyard for twenty minutes before sneaking back in. One time we were lying on the floor next to his parents' bed when Mrs. Fahey came out of the bathroom wearing nothing but a towel around her head. Even Will seemed fascinated. She had heavy, swinging *National Geographic* boobs, a bit of a belly, and an acre of dark hair between her legs. Seeing a woman's body in the flesh for the first time immediately gave me a woodrow. She gasped, awkwardly covered herself, and screamed for us to get out. Her face was flushed, and I noticed little red splotches forming on her thighs.

After seeing his mom buck, Will and I went outside and

nervously juggled the soccer ball for a couple of minutes, not saying anything. Eventually she came outside with a pitcher of iced tea. She was wearing owl-rimmed sunglasses and a yellow cotton dress, and didn't seem mad anymore. I tried to picture Mrs. Fahey naked, but I involuntarily morphed her face into Paige's, and soon I was visualizing a monster hybrid of them with huge horse teeth and three nostrils. I hated when my brain did that.

We were training for soccer tryouts that fall. The high school coach had sent us letters, describing the winning tradition at Renfield High, providing a schedule of practices during Hell Week right before school started, and I made it my personal mission to make the varsity squad. I was nervous about going to high school, and my theory was that getting on the team might help my chances to make upperclassmen friends, and then maybe the girls in my grade would like me better.

Will and I would practice headers and trapping the ball all morning until we'd get sick of each other and I'd go home. I'd spend the rest of the day practicing tennis and loitering at Farmington Farms Racquet Club. I was partially sponsored by Yamaha at the time and even though I hadn't won a NELTA tournament in months, I had a high ranking and my game was still improving.

At night I'd sneak out the back way to smoke cigarettes with Will on the boulder in front of my house. His mom smoked, and I'd always punched him whenever he'd try to steal one when we were younger, but I was so bored I finally tried it. I realized how ignorant I'd been, chastising Will all this time when it was actually a great (albeit deadly) hobby. The neighborhood was always completely dark, and we'd stay silent, concentrating on smoking our cigarettes. Paul and Mitch were up at Paul's summer house in Nantucket. I heard that Rollo and Kagis were around, but I didn't know either of them well enough to call them up, so I spent every night with Will on that rock, puffing away.

One night in late June we sat on the boulder having inhalation contests. Will held the record so far; he could inhale as hard as he could for eight seconds, which made the burning orange tip look like a bird's beak. The abnormally dark stain of tobacco on his filter from inhaling so hard made me jealous.

"It's because you swim," I told him. "You have bigger lungs. You're like a fucking pearl diver or something. I wish I swam."

Will coughed, and clapped me on the shoulder, which jarred the image of Mrs. Fahey nude back onto my brain.

"Remember when we saw your mom naked?" I asked.

His eyes lit up.

"I porked her once," he replied.

"You are so lying."

"Okay, I didn't, but I have seen her naked a lot since then."

I frowned at him.

"Really! With my binoculars from the backyard. I saw my dad doing her."

I still didn't believe him, but I was overcome with a sudden desire to make love to Mrs. Fahey myself. I wondered if there was a chance she'd say yes.

"I want to see."

"They're my parents," he gasped, and mock-slapped me across the face. Then he motioned for me to be quiet, and we crept down his driveway and around the house to the backyard. The light was off in his parents' bedroom. We stood there for about twenty minutes, but the light never went on. I got crabby, whispered goodbye, and walked home, stopping at my secret bush to spray myself with perfume and gargle mint Scope with a tinge of dirt.

The next morning I woke up and for some reason felt compelled to look out the window. I gasped. There was a yellow moving truck parked next to Will's driveway. I sprinted across the street. Mr. Fahey was directing two guys in blue T-shirts across the yard as they carried the sofa to the truck. Mr. Fahey noticed me and smiled.

"Will's in his room," he said.

I ran upstairs and found Will sitting on his bed, playing with his old G.I. Joe toys.

"You want this?" he asked, holding up Lady Jaye. Even though we'd both stopped playing with G.I. Joes a few years ago, I nodded, and he tossed her to me. Her face was all scratched up, and she was missing her left foot. I stuck her in my back pocket.

"Why didn't you tell me you were moving?" I asked.

"I just found out," he said.

"You're lying."

His eyes twitched as he tried to think of a response.

"I just found out a month ago. Honest. My parents didn't know we got the house until last Friday, so I couldn't say anything."

I shook my head.

"Why are you moving?"

"My grandmother died. She was rich."

"But you're already rich."

"We're just moving to a bigger house. I'll still be in Renfield."

"Phew. Where are you moving?"

"Renfield Hills," he said, and I gasped.

It wasn't fair. He wasn't even friends with the soccer guys. Will would become cool simply by relocation, while I'd be left to wallow on crappy Summit Road by myself. Now pretty much everyone lived in Renfield Hills. The mass exodus—started by Paul and Mitch at the end of third grade—was now complete. I noticed a pair of Cabbage Patch Kids lying on top of a laundry basket.

"What the hell is this?" I asked, picking one up.

"I have to finish packing," Will said quickly, snatching the doll from my hand and tossing it in the closet.

"You should have told me you were moving."

"I'm sorry. Let's practice for soccer—I can always pack later."

"No, you can't," I said. "Play with your dolls in peace, you gaylord."

"Whatever, *kemosabe*," Will muttered softly.

I walked down the stairs and out the front door, on the verge of tears. I spent five minutes chucking rocks at his mailbox until the urge to cry subsided, then went inside my house. My parents were in the living room. My mom was lying on the couch as my dad putted golf balls into a coffee mug. I marched into the room, but they ignored me.

"The Faheys are moving," I announced.

"We know," my dad said without looking up.

"Why didn't you people tell me?"

"Thought you knew," he replied, lining up the putter.

"Can we move to Renfield Hills, too?"

"Nope," he said, and tapped the golf ball into the cup. "Hole in one!"

I sat down at the edge of the couch and pouted for a minute. They watched.

"I have no more friends around here," I said, finally.

"You can visit Will, and he can visit you," my mom said.

"Our neighborhood sucks compared to Renfield Hills," I said.

"There are starving people in Ethiopia right now," my dad said.

"Right, and they don't live in Renfield Hills, either."

"That's not what I meant."

"Are any of my grandparents dying soon?" I asked.

"Nicholas!" my mom screamed. "That's an awful thing to ask."

They talked in Korean for a few seconds, which was enough time for them to start shouting at each other. I got up to leave, but my mom motioned for me to sit. "Maybe we'll go to California someday and you can meet your grandparents. They're too old to travel, so you should visit them," she said.

"Or visit my parents in Korea," my dad added. "They miss you. Do you remember the one time you met them? You were maybe two years old."

"Yeah, that was a really great day," I said. "I think about it all the time."

"Really?"

"How the hell would I remember anything from when I was two?" I shouted.

"Calm down, Nicholas," my mom soothed.

My dad fiddled with the Velcro closure on his golf glove as my mom began cutting out grocery coupons and placing them in a white envelope. Eventually she looked up at me.

"Any thoughts, Nicholas?" she asked.

"Are any of them rich?" I asked.

They both laughed.

"Your father's parents live on a farm that harvests rocks," she said. "And we paid for my parents to come over to the States. We should have taken you earlier to meet them, but we're always so busy with—" She kept yapping, but she was totally missing the point, and I was in no mood to listen to her bullshit, so I went upstairs. I stared out the window, watching the moving people load the van. A few hours later Mr. Fahey pulled his Porsche out. Will and his mom hopped into the car. They were giggling about something. I turned my face sideways so I could see them for a few seconds longer, and then they were gone. The yellow moving van roared to life, and a minute later it drove off, too. I got on my tiptoes to see the roof of Will's house. Already it looked different.

❧ ❧ ❧

It took a week before my parents realized how miserable I had been since Will left. I moped around the house aimlessly and spent hours staring up at the stucco ceiling in my bedroom. They tried to motivate me to go outside, but I refused. At first I was being defiant, but soon I found that I couldn't move even if I tried.

After humoring me for a few days, my mom got fed up and forced me to go outside. She shut the door behind me and watched as I stood in the middle of the front stoop as if it was a raft, my feet unsteady. A bird chirped in the tree to my left. Eventually I stepped onto the yard barefoot in my pajamas and walked like Bambi out into the sun. The breeze died down, and moments later the sun graced my forehead with gentle heat. I stood in the yard for fifteen minutes, refusing to look up because I didn't want to see Will's old house or driveway. I could hear my mom sighing through the screen door.

My parents finally decided I was in dire need of companionship, and on my fourteenth birthday they got me a kitten. I pictured all those wiry Ethiopian kids with their own little kittens as a compromise—calicos and Russian blues with flea collars provided via airlift by the Red Cross. I may have been petty, but one look at my new friend and I was mad with joy. He was a tiny orange tabby with brown stripes on his tail that made him look like a mini tiger. I named him Boris, after Boris Becker the tennis player. When we got back from the animal shelter I converted an old shoebox into a bed using my old blanky, but Boris immediately leaped out of it and hid under my bed. I lay still on the carpet and stared at his glowing green eyes. Eventually he crept over, climbed onto my sunken chest, and went to sleep. I didn't move for an hour, listening to him purr.

That night I snuck out and smoked a cigarette on the boulder by myself, wondering what high school was going to be like. Hell Week for soccer was starting in two weeks. Although I was still fidgety, Boris had a calming effect on me, and I found that worrying about the future didn't seem so pressing anymore.

The bushes at the edge of the yard rustled, and Boris rushed over. I picked him up. His back was full of sand. I placed him on the grass and started walking in circles around him. He pivoted around to face me, like a hunter. I jogged to the front of the house. Boris chased after me. He crouched in the bushes. I pretended to not see him and walked seemingly unaware, employing peripheral vision. He attacked, then turned in midair when I faced him. The moon was still full, shining down on us through the bluish leaves. With a flicker in his eyes, Boris set up a fresh attack. I pretended not to notice him again. We did this for a while, just me and my new cat, running around in the front yard.

The next day it rained, and I spent the afternoon looking at my old *Playboys*. Since the three-dimensional girls in my life had developed I had decidedly less time for Miss January. I didn't notice Boris napping in the corner of my room when I started jerking off, and when he stirred I immediately pulled my shorts up. I felt sickened. I picked Boris up and scratched under his ears for ten minutes until I was certain he had forgotten the image of me spanking it. I cursed myself for corrupting a kitten. The sun broke through the clouds, and I was about to go downstairs for a snack when the phone rang.

"Is this Nick Park?"

"Yes, it is."

"Hell Week for soccer is coming. Are you ready for it?"

"Mitch?" I said, even though the voice was deep and unfamiliar.

"This is Giles."

"Oh, you're probably on the soccer team, right? I've been—"

"Are you ready for it?"

The sound of heavy breathing. In the background I could hear faint strains of Billy Squire's "Strokeman."

"I guess so," I said softly.

"Because there's still time to back out, you fucking gook," Giles hissed, and then the phone went dead.

I stared at the receiver.

It was at this moment that I realized that all of my problems up until now were nothing. Yes—being a Korean banana with no weekend plans and no hope of moving into a mansion with a bowling alley was no way to start high school. But apparently the soccer team wasn't much help, either.

SUNDAY 12:00 PM

The town fire alarm is wailing in the distance, as it does every day at noon. I lost so many wristwatches in high school that eventually I just stopped replacing them, so in the summers the only way I could tell it was time for lunch was by the noon alarm. Out of habit, my belly starts aching. To combat the hunger pains, I take brisk laps around the water tower and try not to picture food.

Sometimes I actually wish I was the dainty academic robot strangers often assume I am. Life would be so much less frustrating. Girls would be secondary to school, therefore I'd be immune to this heartache and humiliation, and last night would have never happened. Girls would just be obstacles I passed in the hallways on my way to a carrel in the library to eat my bag lunch in seclusion, and the prom would just be another Saturday night at home doing math equations for fun. I wouldn't be sitting here because I'd probably be rehearsing my valedictory speech, having spent the last four years focusing on homework and practicing the piano, destined to study engineering at MIT this fall, where in my freshman dorm room I'd have recurring wet dreams about porking an elf or something.

eleven

The frustrating thing about taking an honors course at Renfield High was that there weren't many good-looking girls in honors classes. Eighty percent of the reason I was considered the type of student who would take honors classes was because I was Korean, and Asian Americans have a reputation for being brainiacs. The other 20 percent was because of my well-publicized knack for making posters. I was so good that in eighth grade my social studies teacher submitted one to a national contest and I received honorable mention. It made the *Renfield News* and everything. As a result, during the summer before freshman year the guidance counselor insisted that I sign up for honors courses across the board, so I did.

My parents assumed I'd been hit by an intelligence ray as well, but eventually I proved them all wrong. At first this was a source of pride for me—I was almost defiant about how stupid (and therefore not nerdy or typically Asian) I was, but a month into freshman year I realized that I was on track to receive two C's and one D. When my parents saw my first few quiz scores they were upset but assumed I simply hadn't studied enough. Their faulty analysis proved to be a worthy alibi. There was a distinct possibility I *was* a genius; I just didn't apply myself. Then again, maybe I really was a moron.

This is why I started cheating incessantly. I was forced to by my family and my school just to maintain a shred of academic dignity. The night before a quiz I'd cut out a square of paper no larger than my thumb, then fill both sides with formulas or definitions and declensions using a mechanical pencil and a magnifying glass in order to write smaller. Spending hours miniaturizing the facts burned the formulas into my brain, so I rarely ended up using the cheat sheets. I reasoned I wasn't really cheating at all—I just preferred studying by writing information down on really small pieces of paper. During second semester I got caught peeking at crib sheets twice. In Latin class the teacher stood behind me for almost a minute before asking loudly, as if she was Gollum, "What has he got under his cupped hand?" I feebly replied, "He has nothing." She wrote a large X across my quiz and sat back down at her desk.

Luckily, cheating wasn't considered a serious crime at school. I only received two in-school suspensions. All I had to do was sit in a little cubicle just outside of the vice principal's office and whip up an essay about why cheating was bad. Since I wrote fast, the essay would be finished in five minutes and I'd spend the rest of the day staring out the window. I became a dedicated squirrel watcher. Not just during suspension, but all day, in every class, all the time. Soon I'd identified the four distinct families of gray tree squirrels on the school premises, and I even looked forward to the precise moment when the mother squirrel from what I had tagged the Tessio family would skip across the brick wall outside the window to root through the trash can by the entrance (11:42 a.m.). I felt like I knew these squirrels better than my own family, which wasn't entirely off the mark.

❧ ❧ ❧

I endured the bully Giles at soccer practice throughout the fall for one simple reason: Renfield girls loved upperclass soccer players, and I dreamed of eventually being a twelfth-grade soccer player, which I knew held serious cachet among the ladies. The previous year Renfield High's soccer team had been ranked number one in the USA Today national rankings, and this year the team had eight returning starters. Two of those were all-Americans, including last year's runner-up for Gatorade Player of the Year. The football team was a travesty, having failed to secure a winning season in over two decades. Meanwhile, the varsity boys' soccer team had amassed five class SS state championships in as many years, prompting newscasters and journalists in the state of Connecticut to regard Renfield's soccer team as a "dynasty," which, in all truth, it was.

It was a status symbol to date a soccer player. It was a status symbol to even be seen talking to a soccer player. It was a status symbol to wear a soccer player's varsity jacket. Come to think of it, I didn't really care about playing time or how the team was actually doing.

I did it all for the jacket.

It's silly how excited I was for it. But girls still couldn't care less that I played soccer, because nothing overrode the fact that I was a lowly frosh Asian guy. Besides, I only got to wear my jacket for two days. It didn't make me cry, but my throat knotted up when one day before homeroom Giles grabbed my jacket by the zipper and broke it, and then the next morning finished the job by literally cutting the hood off with a pair of scissors. I used to daydream about the chiseled me returning home from the army in ten years and visiting Giles at the local Sunoco and giving him a brain-damaging thrashing, which would land me twenty years in the stockade, then I'd get released, immediately track the now-vegetable Giles down, and beat the crap out of his catatonic ass all over again. But since I'm over him I rarely daydream about him anymore. Sometimes his face will pop into my head, but that's only when I'm doing push-ups or something.

The soccer coach was the freshman science teacher, and for the first couple of months he playfully picked on me, since Kagis and I were the only soccer players in class, and it was obvious the other students were a little jealous. I was the leading scorer for the junior varsity team and got to take the field with the varsity team at the end of blowout games. Then soccer season ended, and by late October I'd scored a 32 percent and 19 percent on the first two practicums of the semester, and the playful tone altered slightly. "Park, point out the cortex on the overhead," he said one winter afternoon. I walked up to the projection screen and stared at the image from the slide projector, feigning intelligence for about thirty seconds.

"Listen, I don't know if this is appropriate material for the students. I could show you where the cortex is, but it's kind of perverted," I said, shrugging.

"Maybe you'll crack open your textbook for the first

time in detention," he said. "I'd make you stand in the corner, but technically you're too old for that."

My mom was still at work when I hijacked the mid-semester warnings in the mail. I received warnings from all six of my teachers, informing my parents that I was failing their classes. Fortunately, parents didn't need to sign the slips so I crumpled them into five tiny balls and chucked them into the woods behind the house. Then I went into the woods, retrieved them, and threw them deeper.

❧ ❧ ❧

I'd always assumed Kagis was a meathead, but he turned out to be one of the top students in science class. It was also the one class I shared freshman year with Jaimy Ginsberg. She was a new student from Michigan and one of the only hot girls in the braniac courses. Her dark brown hair was cut short, and she had the most amazing bubble butt I'd ever seen. There were stools for seats in science, and when she leaned forward I could make out the perfectly symmetrical curve of both buns. When she'd turn around I'd pretend my contact lenses were irritating me and squint.

One day in November, the teacher showed everyone a picture of his wife, a forestry management worker, standing next to a tree she had bandaged, and I said, "Oh, stop, Jesus, please stop, you're giving me a woody dicot." No one laughed at that one, and I admit it fell far below my usual standards, but Jaimy rolled her eyes and said out loud, "Only Nick." Just that. Only Nick. This gave me hope, since I figured I was leagues more popular than everyone else in class except for Kagis, whom I felt I was tied with because we both played soccer.

Everyone kept the same seating arrangement except me because I was always late for class. One day toward the end of November I sat down on a stool in the back before realizing I was next to Jaimy herself. I'd never sat next to her before. I avoided looking at her, fearful she'd kindly ask me to move to another seat. I casually prayed for a miracle, something I could work with. The teacher started writing instructions on the chalkboard.

"Do you want to work with me on this lab?" Jaimy asked me.

"I guess." I tried to sound indifferent, but my voice cracked (it hadn't in two years), and so it came out "geh-hess."

The lab was a joke, which I was grateful for—I actually understood what was going on. It was a little experiment using microscopes, examining samples of blood for something. I focused extra hard in order to do it right and not prove to be an idiot. We exchanged few words during this part of the experiment. I feverishly thought of something witty to say, but my mind had turned to lead.

Then came a kiss from the gods. The teacher said, "Okay, which one of you is brave enough to draw your own blood?"

Instantly I raised my hand, even though the mention of blood made me dizzy.

"Park, you sure you can do this?"

"Of course," I said. "It's not dangerous, is it?"

"We've only lost two students to this experiment in over ten years," he joked.

Everyone laughed uneasily.

"Nick's got the worst grade in class, so that probably means he's expendable, right?" Kagis asked.

Fucking Kagis.

"Here's the razor." Coach handed me a brand-new flat razor, wrapped in a tiny strip of cardboard. I slipped the razor out of its sheath. Shiny and sharp.

No prob. It dawned on me how easy this was. Just poke a tiny hole in your index finger. Anyone could do it. It wouldn't hurt or anything. Everyone was staring at my finger. I hammed it up, holding the blade in the light above me, inspecting the edge, turning it over in my hand. A couple of students laughed. I brought the razor down.

And down.

It came to rest a millimeter from the soft pink bubble of skin on the tip of my index finger. In my brain I wanted to do it—I *was* doing it—but the hand holding the razor wasn't responding. I couldn't look at Jaimy. This was too humiliating.

"Okay, Nick, looks like you bit off more than you can chew. Anyone else think they can do it? And this time all you wimps out there can keep your hands down."

Kagis raised his hand, the teacher handed him a fresh blade, and I could tell from the look on Kagis's face that he had total confidence in himself and would succeed. I think right then I noticed something weird about Kagis. He was my friend, yet he always had to make me look like an ass. Everyone redirected their eyes toward him, not me, and even Jaimy's mouth was slightly askew, almost wincing at the sight of Kagis gripping the blade.

I shouted, "Wait, I'll do it," and gritted my teeth while plunging the razor down a little too fast on my innocent index finger.

Minutes later Coach was explaining to the school nurse that I had employed a slashing motion with the razor. Apparently this must have cut an artery, because there was more than enough blood for the demonstration. I felt dizzy, Jaimy gaped at me as if I was demented, and I kept asking her, "Did I beat him? Did Kagis do it before me? Where the hell am I?"

For the rest of the week Jaimy addressed me in the halls with phrases like, "Hey, psycho," and sometimes she made a stabbing motion reminiscent of Anthony Perkins in a wig. I'd laugh, do the motion back to her, and she'd give me a tense smile.

❧ ❧ ❧

One day toward the end of fall semester I walked with confidence into the cafeteria during study hall and sat down right next to Jaimy. She was sitting with Maggie Shaughnessy and Missy Means. Jaimy nodded and smiled at me before continuing her conversation. I looked around to see if anyone had noticed me sitting with them.

"Question, Wang Chung Park," a voice roared. It was

Giles, standing in the double door frame of the cafeteria, wearing a Whalers practice jersey and stonewashed jeans with matching premeditated rips at the knees. Technically, it wasn't my name, so I ignored him. "Is it time for everybody to have fun tonight? Seriously, bud, is it time for everybody to Nick Park tonight?"

He cackled and walked off, singing his version of the chorus. Conversations started up again, and I silently prayed Jaimy had somehow not heard him. The best way to get someone to forget that they've heard you get slurred is to look like you've forgotten about it yourself, so I immediately started sketching an impressive-looking mansion. I had drawn this very same one so many times I could do it with my eyes closed.

"How's science?" Missy asked Jaimy.

My ears perked up.

"It's okay. Kind of boring. Well, except for Crazy Guy over here," she said.

"Nick's nuts," Maggie added, flicking a used straw at me.

"What's that about my nuts?" I asked. "You didn't finish your sentence."

She stared at me with her mouth open.

"How's your finger, anyway?" Missy asked. How had she known about it? Then I realized: Jaimy must have told her. She'd talked about me!

"Oh, it's fine, and yours?"

They stared politely at me for a few seconds, then Missy turned back to Jaimy and they promptly forgot I was sitting there. I mentally cursed myself. Missy started complaining about how scratchy her shoulder pads were, and I went back to work on my mansion with a goofy smile on my face.

"Tomorrow's my last day with Randy in seventh period," Missy said.

"I wish I was in that," Jaimy said. "There aren't any hotties in science. Well, I guess there's Keith, but he doesn't count—he's like my brother."

"I've always thought he was . . . ," Missy babbled on, but there was a roaring in my ears and I couldn't hear her anymore, so eventually I stopped listening.

I sat there for a few minutes and realized they weren't going to talk to me again. Jaimy didn't even notice that I had mentally switched my brain from stun to kill and was giving her a death-ray stare. I excused myself to get a drink. I hunched over the water fountain, slurping away even though I wasn't thirsty. The bell rang, and I kept drinking so I wouldn't have to see them again. I swallowed three more gulps of water. Surely enough time had passed that I could return to the table and grab my notebook. I shut my eyes for ten seconds to make extra sure that no way was she still there waiting for me or something, and when I turned around the cafeteria was empty.

twelve

Since being a frosh guy was the lowest notch on the social totem pole, I didn't go to a single party all fall. I took solace in the fact that this was old hat for me, whereas the rest of the soccer guys were shocked to suddenly be considered dirt while the girls in our grade went to upperclass parties. Kagis and Company were finally getting their first taste of what I'd been dealing with for three years already. By the time the open-to-all bonfire party was announced, we were all rabid to go.

That year the bonfire party was being held at a rich senior guy's house on the Friday after Christmas. The story was that he normally spent every winter break skiing in Vail, but he'd broken his leg playing football and was being allowed to stay in Renfield by himself over the holidays. The house had been built before the Revolutionary War and sat at the edge of miles and miles of cornfields, with a barn and everything. It was going to be huge. Apparently kids from neighboring towns even knew about it.

My first report card arrived in the mail the day of the party, and luckily I intercepted it before my parents could see it. I locked the door to my bedroom and sat at my desk for ten minutes staring at the unopened envelope. There was a small chance I'd done better than I thought. I made a silent prayer and then opened it.

Renfield High	Academic Performance Report	Fall Sem 19__
Student: Nick Park	Year: 9	
Course	**Level**	**Grade**
Intro to Psychology	(Honors Level)	C-
Latin I	(Honors Level)	D
European History	(Honors Level)	C+

American Literature	(Honors Level)	D
Algebra 2	(Honors Level)	D-
Earth Science	(Honors Level)	D+
Physical Education	(N/A)	A+

| Sem GPA: 1.77 | Cum GPA: 1.77 |

I groaned. My grades had actually *dipped* after receiving those progress reports. Fortunately, I have a knack for finding the positive in any situation. Technically, I reasoned, if these were remedial classes I would be getting mostly A's. The phone rang.

"Yo, it's Mitchy Mitch. I talked to Kagis and he said it's cool if you and Will want to tag along with us. We're meeting up at my place tonight."

The bonfire party. There was no way I'd be able to go if my parents saw the report card. I knew what I had to do. It was already official. My parents were eventually going to kill me. The only question was when. I'd waited too damn long for this only to let myself get grounded because of something as silly as four D's and two C's. It wasn't even a decision. Since it was just a single piece of paper, I opted to slip it in my ceiling hiding spot. I had tacked a Gabriella Sabatini tennis poster to the ceiling above my bed, and it served as a good hiding spot for empty boxes of cigarettes. I got on the chair and slipped the report card inside the poster.

I put on my Spyder jacket, since it was an outdoor party (otherwise I never wore the thing), and went downstairs. My parents were sitting in the living room watching a rented Korean soap opera. My mom was flipping through a *People* magazine, and my dad was standing next to the sliding glass door to the porch, gripping his new putter. They rarely seem to watch the shows; I think they just like hearing people other than themselves talk in Korean inside the house.

"I swear one of the characters on this new show looks just like you. Very handsome," my mom said, pointing at a wimpy-looking Asian guy with pointy, elfin sideburns as he lilted like a falling maple leaf across the screen.

"I don't look anything like that," I said. "He doesn't even look human."

"Come sit and watch with us," she said.

A car horn honked outside. It was Will and his pops.

"Maybe another time. That's my ride."

Mitch, Paul, and Kagis were waiting for us outside the garage by the time Will's dad dropped us off. Since none of us was old enough to drive, we had to walk through the woods behind Mitch's house for about forty minutes to get to the party. I started doubting Mitch knew where we were going, but eventually the woods gave way to cornfields and a view of Talcott Mountain. We caught sight of the barn ten minutes later. Lights and sounds rolled out to greet us. Will looked frightened. I was nervous about being there, too, but kept a poker face. As we neared the barn the voices grew louder. The roof of the barn shimmered in the moonlight. We stopped at the clearing, where four tiki torches were propped up, one in each corner. We were waiting for Kagis to take the lead.

"Holy crap," said Mitch. "There must be three hundred people here."

We saw some Renfield varsity booster jackets and immediately made our way over. I was shocked when I realized who they were, but it was too late to turn around: Giles, his buddy Hursley, and half the wrestling team. Everyone on the squad had shaved their heads with number two razors; they looked like a pack of feral Hare Krishnas. I stiffened, took a deep breath, and stepped into the light.

"Long time no see, Giles," I said, visibly frightened. "Hurse."

They all looked over at us with vicious smiles.

"Hey, it's the frosh soccer douche bags!" Giles announced. Kagis cringed.

Giles was wearing a Choate sweatshirt with the neck cut off—it made him look like a squat chunk of gray muscle. Hursley was wearing a Van Halen *Monsters of Rock* concert T-shirt with mildew stains around the shoulders that looked like gray freckles.

"How's the rager?" I asked Hursley. I sounded like an impersonator.

He glared at me through bloodshot eyes. Steam was rolling off his shoulders because of the cold.

"Even Pauly could get laid in a place like this," said Giles. I breathed a sigh of relief—Giles must have decided to pick on Paul instead of me. "Hey, Nick, why's your goddamned face so red? I didn't know VC explode when they drink liquor."

Hursley laughed.

"Must be all that napalm you inhaled growing up. Gooks are fucking flammable!"

None of my friends said anything, and I didn't expect them to. I tried to smile at Giles as if I thought he was hilarious, but turned so my friends wouldn't see me appeasing his ass. We followed them into the barn, and over to the far side, where eight kegs were lined up against the prop doors. Bales of hay were stacked on top of each other against the far wall, forming a pyramid. An Asian girl wearing a drenched red tie-dye gave us all cups, including Will, who slipped his inside his pocket. It was a rarity for me to see other Asians my age, and I reacted as if I'd happened upon a yeti. Kagis noticed my expression and started laughing. I reddened, worried he was going to publicly acknowledge that there were two Asians in the barn, but he seemed interested in her and struck up a conversation. I realized it was actually Peggy Su, the reverend's daughter. She ignored me.

Giles took each of our cups and filled them with foam. He looked at Will, who was again eyeing his shoes, waiting for the laces to somehow come undone.

"Hey, One-Eyed Willy, you don't drink?"

"I had a lot to drink earlier," Will lied.

On the walk over we had all ripped on him for not drinking—it was kinda pathetic, how scared he was, but in this case we kept our traps shut.

"I had a lot to drink before I got here," Hursley mimicked in a high-pitched voice. He sized Will up, shaking his head. "You'll need to get loaded to talk to these chiquitas, Freckles. Do you even know where to stick it in?" he asked, slapping his hand down on the small shoulder of a girl who had just walked up to the keg. Her initial reaction was similar to that of a squirrel caught in the headlights of a passing car. Then she frowned at Hursley and promptly scurried off.

"I can drink—I'll drink in a little while. I'm just taking a break," Will piped up.

"Will already did some shots with us," I added, hoping I could help out.

Kagis glared at me, and I felt like an idiot for bringing Will along.

"Don't defend him, Slanty," Giles said. He smiled at me with an especially hard expression I hadn't seen since soccer season ended.

♣ ♣ ♣

Will and I ended up sitting next to the bonfire by ourselves for over an hour, feeling more cold than warm next to it, watching others toss empty beer cans into the fire. The cans melted on the burning logs. Giles was sitting on the other side of the fire, making out with a curly-haired girl from another town.

"I hate Giles," I said, punching the dirt.

"You should go over there and waste him," Will suggested.

"If they didn't know everyone here, I'd suggest we all jump him."

"Are you upset he called you Slanty?"

"Shut up."

Kagis was hooking up with Peggy Su off in the cornfields behind the barn. Paul and Mitch had ditched me and Will an hour earlier and were nowhere in sight. Although I was psyched to at least be at the party, it was obvious we didn't belong. Not yet. The girls looked like women, and we were the only freshmen guys there; everyone's eyes felt like spotlights as they looked at us. Still, I liked being there, watching the drunk, hot girls flirting with older guys. I daydreamed about being an upperclassman and owning the crowd at parties like this. I wondered if Giles had been a nobody, too, when he was a freshman. I sat there wondering if this was one of those moments that I'd one day look back and laugh at, and I asked Will about this.

He said no.

❦ ❦ ❦

It was past midnight. The skylight in my parents' master bedroom was dark, which meant that they were probably both asleep, but I wanted to make sure, so I stood in the front yard for an additional twenty minutes, surveying my house for any signs of life. Finally I crept over to the back porch, pulled the glass door open just enough to slip inside, and tiptoed up to the second floor. There was a crack of light under the door to my bedroom. A good sign. I'd left the light on before locking the door so it would give the impression that I was in there. I slid my Renfield Public Library card through the crack in the door, turned the handle slowly, pushed the door open, and gasped.

My parents were sitting on the bed in the far corner of the room. My mom was clutching my junior Louisville Slugger and breathing heavily. Her eyes were closed, and I could see them moving back and forth underneath the eyelids as if she was in deep REM sleep or something. A strange, dry rattling sound was coming from deep inside her chest. On the carpet between us was just about everything I'd ever stashed or hidden in my bedroom. My Sabatini poster had either fallen or been torn down and was ripped to shreds. It was awful.

Lying in little piles on the carpet were the following pieces of evidence:

<u>Item #1:</u> a handful of empty, crumpled cigarette packs

<u>Item #2:</u> a Ziploc bag filled with uncut NutraSweet that I'd collected over a period of months from various Friendly's booths in Unionville (after seeing *Scarface*)

<u>Item #3:</u> my sawed-off Crossman 650 pump air rifle

<u>Item #4:</u> a handful of M-80s

<u>Item #5:</u> my two *Playboy*s from third grade

<u>Item #6:</u> Eric Louie's Game Boy (I'd been meaning to return it)

For a moment I scanned the piles fondly. It was like opening a time capsule of my life. I'd actually lost the M-80s and wanted to ask where they found them. The Louisville Slugger tapped lightly on the bed. "First of all, most of this stuff is Will's," I said, feverishly trying to come up with explanations for all the items, but then she produced the final piece of evidence:

Item #7: my report card

I could feel the blood leave my face.

"You've been lying to us, Nicholas," my mom said in a disturbingly throaty voice, squeezing the junior-sized bat so hard her fingers turned bright white.

"Are you in a gang?" my dad asked me.

"I didn't lie to you about anything," I whimpered.

"You said you were in the running for some academic award," she said softly.

"I'll probably win another academic fitness award," I said.

"Were you planning on killing someone?" my dad asked, picking up an M-80.

"Are you serious?" I asked him.

"Why is your face so red?" she asked. I glanced in the closet mirror. *Uh-oh.* My face was still beet red from drinking beers, and my eyes were bloodshot. I had assumed it would have gone away by now.

"That's from being out in the cold," I said feebly.

"Come here." She pointed to the ground beneath her feet with the bat.

I shook my head.

"Get over here this second," he barked.

I trudged over.

"Down on your knees!"

I got on my knees, and my parents leaned in and started sniffing me.

"You've been drinking and smoking!" they both shouted.

"No, people were doing that bad stuff around me, that's why you smell it."

"Breathe out of your mouth."

"I prefer the nose. I don't want to catch a cold. It's not healthy to switch temperatures so quickly like this."

"Just do it!"

I breathed out the mouth.

"*Guhjeemal, yaminishekya!*" she screamed. The rough translation from Korean is "You worthless liar, son of a bitch."

She let go of the bat and pulled my plaid button-down off me. The buttons popped, and she ripped the left sleeve completely off. My dad grabbed my T-shirt around the collar and pulled as hard as he could. Soon I was sitting there naked from the waist up. I started crying and screaming, "Sorry," over and over. In the closet mirror I saw that my entire chest was red and bumpy from alcohol. I looked like I had chicken pox. I didn't even know my skin did that. My mom raised the bat over her head and slammed it down on my alarm clock. It disintegrated immediately. She then proceeded to poke me repeatedly in the chest as she interrogated me.

"Who gave you alcohol? Huh? Do you just want to kill yourself? Huh? You want to just throw your life away? Huh? Answer me!"

"Why do you have a firearm in your closet?" my father asked, picking up the sawed-off.

"It's not real! It's just a pellet gun, a toy—I got it at Service Merchandise. It can't even break the skin of squirrels—it's totally harmless. Jesus, don't point that thing at me!" I shielded my face and cowered.

"*Aigoo, jugeta.*" He sighed, letting the BB gun fall to the ground.

In Korean, *aigoo* means "Oh, God," and *jugeta* means "You're killing me."

"Who gave you the cocaine?" she asked, picking up the Ziploc bag. She looked at my dad. "I told you he shouldn't have quit jazz band. He's now a drug dealer."

"It's NutraSweet. I got it at Friendly's," I said. "I was only pretending it was coke. Taste with your pinkie and you'll be able to tell it's artificial sweetener."

They stared at me.

"It was for a play," I lied softly.

She dropped the bag back on the floor. They both stared out the window at the full moon and repeatedly howled "*Aigoo*" and "*Aigoo, jugeta*" like a pair of coyotes for a minute, shaking their fists at the stucco ceiling.

"You're flunking out of school," my mom said between *aigoo*s.

"Einstein flunked out of school in the fifth grade," I retorted.

"You're no Einstein."

"That's what his mother said, too."

She suddenly went berserk again and slammed the bed with the bat as hard as she could a dozen times. Feathers from my pillow puffed out into the air above the bed and started floating around us. It looked like nuclear winter.

"Honey, calm down," my dad said, reaching for the bat. It caught him on the wrist, and he yelped. "*Aigoo! Yoboh*, you're out of control!"

Yoboh means "honey," although with my parents it usually means "stop."

"You should have made him go to church, not these silly tennis tournaments."

"I want to go to church," I lied, knowing their weakness, but they ignored me.

They argued about my fate in Korean for a minute. Every now and then my dad would plead in English, "No, he's just a stupid boy," and she'd talk louder. They finally stopped arguing. Now that her rage had dissipated, my mom suddenly looked exhausted. The lights flickered as she stood up. She was still gripping the bat and was now smiling oddly at me. Tiny feathers were settling in her curly hair.

"Go on up to your room, Nicholas," she said in a daze.

"But I'm already in my room, Mama."

"Then just go to sleep, honey," she said gently.

My dad looked apologetic. I suddenly realized she was about to club me as if I was a baby seal. I took a deep breath, and with my eyes solemnly acknowledged that I understood what was about to happen. I prayed for a clean death, a soldier's death. I lay down where I was on the floor, shut my eyes, and waited for the beating to begin. Tears dripped sideways down my face. A minute later, they left the room. I opened my eyes and looked at my reflection in the closet mirror.

Fuck me.

thirteen

I can't remember exactly why, but one Friday afternoon in tenth grade soccer practice was canceled at the last minute. Even though I was now a sophomore I still didn't drive, and only frosh geeks took the bus, so instead of taking it I decided to hang out for a while before hitching a ride home from my mom. I loitered in the "Sports Hall of Fame"—the hallway between the caf and administration wing where framed photos of the sports teams lined the walls. Generations of Renfield High athletes posing in outdated uniforms. Soccer teams from the early eighties wearing short shorts. Tennis players cradling wooden rackets and wearing aviator sunglasses. I noticed that girls' boobs in the seventies were a lot pointier. Legend had it that in one of the hundreds of framed photos there was a subtly exposed dick. Once a month I'd examine a row of pictures, casually searching for it.

The door to the auxiliary gym opened down the hall, and I heard the familiar squeak of the janitor's sneakers as he mopped the wooden floor of the basketball court. I scanned the hundreds of team pictures and wondered if I'd have been as much of a nobody in previous decades. I looked at the faces and realized I really was the first Asian student in the history of Renfield. There weren't any minorities ever at Renfield High. The only other black guy besides Monty Banks had been his dad, over twenty years ago. There was a little plaque next to the team photo that explained that Mr. Banks won the state open for the javelin toss back in the mid-sixties. Scratched into a cartoon bubble in the lacquered photo was MONTY'S DAD: SPEARCHUCKER. I traced it like Braille and pictured a future bubble above my face in a tennis photo, pointing out that I was the same color as a goddamned tennis ball or something.

"Hi, Nick."

I turned around and mentally gasped.

"I might try out for the tennis team this spring," Sam Foley said, shifting from one foot to the other. "The varsity team lost a lot of seniors."

"That's great," I replied. Even though we'd gone to school together for years, we'd never actually spoken. I felt confused and wondered if I should introduce myself.

"Do you want to give me a lesson sometime?"

"Really?"

"I called Farmington Farms during lunch. There's a court available tonight at eight," she said.

I felt dizzy. I slumped against the wall.

"What about the football party? Aren't you going?" I said this casually, hoping to convey that I was invited, too, and maybe we could carpool to it after the lesson, but my voice sounded too desperate. Luckily, she didn't notice.

"They're boring," she sighed. "Besides, there are parties every weekend. So do you want to play or what? My dad can give us a ride both ways, because he's playing in the night league. So, it's a date, right?" Immediately she blushed.

"I didn't know you belonged to the club," I said quickly.

"I've seen you practice on Saturdays. You're, like, totally going to be the next Michael Chang, I bet!"

"Not really—he's wicked short. I'm more like Thomas Muster."

"I don't know who that is. Okay, so I'll call you tonight?"

I nodded. I wanted to stand up straight and shake her hand to seal the deal, but I realized I had a serious woody and so I scrunched down, faking a stomachache.

"Are you okay?" she asked.

"I'm fine, it's just a stomach cramp," I said, waving her off. I blatantly stared at her butt as she walked away; it had a little shimmy to it I hadn't noticed before. Sam Foley. Best friends with Amber Milwood, known for having the best legs in our grade. I had a date with Sam Foley. I repeated the sentence in my head a couple of times. Frankly, it sounded like bullshit. When the exit door closed I let out a primitive holler and banged my elbows against the lockers in celebration. After my elbows stopped hurting, I grabbed my backpack and walked to the convalescent home to beg my mom to immediately take a break and drive me home because I had less than four hours to get ready for my first date.

❧ ❧ ❧

It was appalling to discover that I had no clothes worthy of Sam Foley's presence that night. My usual tennis outfit consisted of a pair of ratty gray sweatpants that accentuated my gonads and a corny Ziggy T-shirt. I frantically searched through my parents' walk-in closet, and picked out my dad's best collared tennis shirt and a pair of shiny Ellesse warm-up pants. I then spent a full hour working on my hair. By the end my bangs were sore from manipulation and I somehow looked worse. Then I had to take a dump, which warranted taking another shower—I'd die before going on a date with Sam Foley smelling like poop, and this of course forced me to redo my hair, which wasted another half hour. Before I knew it it was seven-thirty. Sam called to say she was en route and then hung up. My mom had listened to the entire phone call with a hand covering the receiver.

"Quit spying on me," I yelled downstairs.

"I was only on for a second."

I was about to criticize her for being such a lousy liar, but then a car horn honked in the driveway. I barreled down the stairs, nearly tripping on the last step and ramming my head through the front door. I slung my green Prince tennis bag over my shoulder, jammed my feet into my Asahi Bones without untying the laces, and went out through the garage.

"Go back inside," I screamed at my parents, who had followed me out. Thankfully, they just waved at the headlights and scurried back inside. I hopped into the backseat, expecting to find Sam sitting there. I was about to smell her! But she was sitting up front. Mr. Foley shook my hand before backing out of the driveway. It was an old brown Mercedes with cracked leather seats. My back sank into the seat a few inches.

"So, can you transform my Sammy into a star player?" Mr. Foley asked as he backed out of the driveway. She punched him in the shoulder.

"I'll do my best, sir," I replied. I hadn't planned on using words like *sir*—it hadn't occured to me to plan ahead how to address the guy—but it sounded appropriate.

"Nice manners, this kid," Mr. Foley said, jabbing Sam in the arm.

"Ow," she said, rubbing the spot.

No one talked for the rest of the drive, but occasionally Sam glanced over her shoulder and smiled at me. I didn't know how to react, so I just nodded politely, but she couldn't really see me anyhow. She looked miniature in the front seat. I quietly mimicked the cute way she'd said "ow," and it made me smile in the dark.

The parking lot was full. Mr. Foley ran ahead without saying goodbye, five minutes late for his doubles match. Sam took the keys out of the ignition, reached over and locked his side, then stepped out of the car. She swung an old Head racket without the cover back and forth. My Prince bag felt heavy. Earlier I had stuffed it with two dozen old issues of *Tennis* magazine, my roses to her. The bag repeatedly banged against my thigh as I struggled to keep pace.

We started out slow, hitting balls at opposite service lines. She could consistently make contact with the ball, but that's about it. She accompanied every forehand with a 180-degree twirl, so she ended up facing the wall. No discernible backhand. I hit painfully slow shots; she'd try to run around them, and ended up catching the ball with her free hand as if she was some sort of a sped or something. Basically, she royally sucked. After ten minutes of this she came over to my side. It felt like she was about to kiss me, and I nervously glanced around.

"Okay, we're warmed up," she said. "Now teach me something."

"Well, you have a natural forehand, which is great," I gushed. She rolled her eyes. "Maybe I'll teach you a backhand."

"Yeah—I want to be able to nail a backhand down the line."

"Obee-kaybee."

I showed her my backhand grip, then kept modifying it in order to make it more teachable. Her racket looked too big in her tiny hands. We were nearly touching, and I could see the goose bumps on her thighs. Finally she announced she was ready to hit some balls. She whiffed on the first two, this time doing a 360 clockwise.

"Why do you keep spinning around like that?"

"I can't help it. How do I stop?"

"Just don't do it."

"Oh, you're a great teacher," she said, and I winced.

We hit some more, and eventually she developed a basic, awful backhand.

"Here, let's play a game," I suggested. I was actually a little bored. I wanted to make out. I caught myself daydreaming about the party at Missy's. I pictured entering the party with Sam at my side. I tried to think of a casual way of asking her to go. I let her win a couple games of mini-tennis. It made her happy, and soon I wanted to feel the happiness of winning, too, and started hitting the ball harder. Without thinking I beaned her in the head with a forehand. She fell over. I hopped the net, but she waved me off.

"Are you okay?"

"I'm fine. Get back on your side," she snapped. I let her win the next game easily.

The hour ended, and we retreated back to the lobby. She treated me to a can of Tab, and we split a Twix bar. She didn't catch me feverishly licking both sticks of Twix before handing it back to her. I stared in fascination as she proceeded to swallow my saliva; according to the transitive property, we were technically making out. We swiveled in plastic chairs while her dad played doubles for another half hour. I showed her the magazines, and she was touched but took just one. At first I was dejected.

"You can give me a new one every Monday at school," she added.

I briefly made eye contact when our legs swiveled into each other, but I couldn't maintain it. I glanced at her again a few seconds later, and she was still looking at me. I panicked at the near certainty that there was a booger hanging from my nose, so I turned away and discreetly wiped at it. When I turned back she was waving at her dad.

"How'd the lesson go?" he asked.

"I'm a certified pro," she said, hugging him. I flared with jealousy.

"I'm going to hop in the shower. Want anything to eat, Nick?"

"No, thank you, sir," I replied.

He dug a hand into my shoulder and squeezed till I yelped. Jesus.

"Loosen up, Nick. You're on a date."

She screamed.

It was a perfect night, and when Mr. Foley drove me home Sam sat in the back with me and we held hands (hers was sweaty). "Every Rose Has Its Thorn" by Poison played softly through the back speakers. She hugged me in the dark backseat when he pulled into the driveway and even kissed me on the shoulder, on the shirt, and I vowed to never wash the shirt again. It felt like a relationship, I could smell her on my clothes, and I went to sleep feeling the happiest I'd ever felt in my life up till then.

❧ ❧ ❧

The following Monday everyone at the table was gossiping about the party at some junior's house. Mitch looked over at me.

"You didn't miss anything, Nick. The party was nothing special," he said. His face held an expression of boredom that looked practiced.

I smiled at him.

"Yeah, I know those parties are lame. Sam told me. That's why she doesn't go anymore," I answered confidently.

"When did she tell you that?" Mitch asked.

"We went out on a date Friday," I answered.

"Bullshit alert," Kagis said in a robot voice.

I glanced over at Sam's table, across the cafeteria. She was sitting with her friends and looked tired. Maybe I'd walk over and say hello. Mitch tapped me on the shoulder.

"What do you mean exactly, that you were out on a *date* with her?"

"Just what I said. We went to the club to play tennis."

"Really?" Tinman was interested now. He stared at me through bloodshot eyes.

"It started out as a lesson, but it got more interesting, if ya know what I mean," I said, thinking about the hand holding, the kiss on the shoulder. Could it really be possible that she'd kissed my shoulder, or was I making it up?

"You're so full of it," Kagis said, and everyone laughed at me.

"If you're going to lie, at least make it slightly believable, like have it be some sort of animal you were hooking up with," Rollo added thoughtfully.

"What happened and where, and seriously, Nick, are you lying to us?" Mitch asked as if he was a game show host; he held a fist in front of my face like a microphone. I'd have preferred to change the subject, but it was too late now.

"No, I'm not making this up. I'm dead serious. Really, on the drive back we held hands, then we kissed. Her dad was focusing on driving, so we sank down onto the floor of the car," I said. They were all staring at me. I couldn't think of anything else to say, but I had their rapt attention, and didn't want to lose it. "We necked for a while, and then, you know, I got to go to third base for a couple of minutes," I said.

"What?" Tinman shouted, squeezing his Capri Sun so hard the juice squirted out in a thin line and hit him in the chin. The entire cafeteria hushed.

Suddenly I felt afraid. Very afraid.

"Trap it, Tinman. This is all confidential, right?" I whispered.

They all nodded their heads. I wanted to freeze the moment. The à la carte line behind us resumed like a machine.

I took this as a good moment to stop talking. It kinda felt like I'd had an out-of-body experience and was just now returning. Rollo and Mitch practically carried me out of the cafeteria. I felt happy, but then I noticed Tinman. He had walked off, in a daze from the story, then veered like a diving kamikaze pilot toward Sam's table. I didn't have to wait to see what would happen next. I calmly exited the cafeteria, desperately soaking up my hero status among my friends before it came to a crashing end.

🐦 🐦 🐦

"Nicky," Mitch said. It was now sixth period, and I was hiding out in the library. "I'm on bathroom break. What are you doing? Don't you have a class right now?"

"I'm skipping," I said. My plan was to sit in the carrels all afternoon because the rest of my classes were with Sam.

"You're ballsy." Mitch laughed. "Glenda's having a party Friday. You in?"

"Whatever," I said.

And that was the first time any of the soccer guys ever invited me to go with them to a *real* party. It was a major moment, and I was thrilled, but at the same time it was a colorless happiness because of my lies. I tried to play *Where in the World Is Carmen Sandiego?* on one of the old

Commodore 64s to get my mind off it, but I was too frazzled
to look things up in the almanac. I spent the afternoon devising an alibi for Sam. My first inclination was to deny the
whole thing. I'd lie if questioned and claim that I'd mentioned holding hands, apologize for saying even that, then
express shock and dismay at Tinman's outrageous lie. Then I
came up with the idea to just play dumb. *Huh? He said what?*
Come again? Bad ear, bad ear. Satisfied with my options, I let
myself enjoy the good news. I was finally invited to a party!

fourteen

At last I was the few, the proud, the officially invited. At
around 10 that Friday Mitch called and told me to hurry up
and get over to his house. I prayed my thanks to God for
granting me this chance for a reprieve. As far as I could tell,
none of my friends knew the truth. My plan was to feel things
out with Sam and if everything went well to have the guys see
me talking privately with her, which would seal their belief in
the lie. Then I'd tell them we broke up, and then after that I'd
never lie again for the rest of my life. It felt weird—I'd been
wanting to go with the soccer guys to a party for years (the
bonfire party didn't count, since everyone was technically invited to that) and now that I finally was going all I could
think about was straightening things out with Sam.

At the party I stared unsubtly at the adult outfits the
girls wore. No longer wearing wool sweaters, the Bolis twins

were now in matching frilly halter tops that showed considerable cleavage. They looked like a pair of pirate's whores. Missy Means was the sole proprietor of the zipper skirt that had been circulating among the girls in my grade, a velvety miniskirt with the zipper undone at the bottom, barely suppressing tightly woven fishnet stockings. Maggie Shaughnessy was sitting on a couch next to one of the cocaptains of the varsity basketball team. He was flexing, and she was squeezing his biceps with a sarcastic look on her face, but the fact that ten seconds had passed and she was still trying to fit both hands around his biceps made her sarcasm look like a disguise.

The girls didn't notice me, and I got the vague impression that the soccer guys were mildly annoyed by my presence, because they crowded around me as if I was something to hide. Just like the bonfire party, I was surprised to find that despite all the buildup in my head, I was kinda bored. I mentally shrugged; I assumed parties were like yogurt and eventually I'd grow to like them. Still, it was a bit of a letdown, but then I saw Sam standing by the doorway.

"Hey, Sam," I said casually, then flinched, expecting a cross-handed slap.

She pretended not to notice me.

Shit. She knew.

"Can we talk?"

She turned and walked down the hall. I sighed, but then she turned and motioned for me to follow. Instinctively I looked for Mitch and made eye contact. Despite a lingering guilt at having lied about her, I couldn't help but goad the deception further. I winked at him before running after her. She was sitting at the bottom of the staircase. Midnight Oil's "Beds Are Burning" clanged out of ceiling speakers.

She glared at me.

"You're an asshole. I can't believe how slimy you are. Why would you make up those things about me? I hate your guts," she yelled without taking a breath.

"But you kissed me on the shoulder," I blurted.

"No, I didn't."

She looked serious, and I silently cursed my imagination. But then—

"What about holding my hand in the car?"

"It didn't mean anything," she said. "If I knew you were going to think I liked you, I never would have held your hand in the first place."

My windpipe tightened. I stared at her. Mitch, Kagis, and Rollo approached us. Could they tell that Sam hated me? I felt panicked.

"We're outta here, Nick. You staying?"

"No, wait," I replied. I turned to Sam. "I have to go. Just call me later tonight and we can continue the conversation. But seriously, make sure it's midnight on the nose this time, or else my parents will pick up before me again. M-I-D-N-I-G-H-T."

"Are you joking?" She pushed me away. "God, get away from me, you loser!"

Mitch snickered. When I snuck one more glance back at her she was hunched over hugging her bare shins.

"Don't stare at her. We're in a major fight about me

telling the whole world about our hookup," I whispered. They clammed up immediately and nodded seriously at me. "It was a rookie move, man. I'm an idiot."

I walked off, stifling the urge to cry. At the same time I felt victorious because I'd stocked up authenticity points with the guys. I figured they had to be good friends, otherwise how would their belief in me feel so good?

Later that night in bed I racked my brain, trying to figure out if Sam had really kissed my shoulder. I replayed the conversation at the party to gauge if she had given any signs that she was denying the truth about our kiss. Or was I really that blind? Maybe she was just embarrassed about her feelings for me and didn't know how to respond. Then again, at the party she'd really sounded like she hated me. Back and forth. The sun was rising, and I was still awake.

I felt electric.

SUNDAY
1:33 PM

Blue and gold balloons (the school colors) have escaped their knots on mailboxes and are floating overhead. I can hear the neighbors watching the Red Sox game through sliding screen doors, and the repeated clang of what has to be rocks being chucked against the backboard of a basketball rim in someone's driveway; a distant lawn mower. Through a gap in the trees I catch a flash of a chocolate Lab chasing a wet tennis ball on a dark patch of chemical grass. Through another gap I can see three little kids in bathing suits form a line in the Shumperts' backyard, shivering as they wait for the banana slide. As I resume taking laps around the edge of the water tower I recall the perpetual ache I had in my belly after lying about my date with Sam, worried that my lie would get exposed to the general public, but then I abruptly stop, because I recognize the boulder below and it reminds me of something.

I wonder pretty much every day what people think about me, and yet I'm only just beginning to see what Kagis has made obvious for years. I never really considered the fact that he might just be an asshole.

fifteen

I spent most of junior year worried Sam would go public with my lie, but she never did. Socially that was pretty much my year.

At the end of junior year Mitch and Paul went to Nantucket for the Memorial Day weekend, and since I wasn't signed up for a tennis tournament, I had absolutely nothing to do that weekend. The phone rang and, despite the fact that I'd already seen the infomercial for *Creedence Clearwater Revival's Greatest Hits* a zillion times, I found it difficult to part with the TV. I felt lethargic as I reached for the receiver.

"What up, hos. It's Kague. What are you doing right now?"

"Talking to you."

"Come over and we'll hit the club. The pool's supposed to open today," he said.

I slung my Prince tennis bag over my shoulder. The garage door opener hummed to life, and I raced my tenspeed under the closing door like Indiana Jones, but the door hit my back and I got off the bike and jumped in pain around the driveway for a few minutes. Boris stared at me from the window above the garage. I couldn't maintain eye contact. I'd recently made a pledge to spend more time with my cat because he always looked so dejected, but whenever I remembered the promise, I'd have something else to do. It confused me, and I nearly crashed my bike into the neighbor's mailbox thinking about it.

♣ ♣ ♣

It took twenty minutes to reach Kagis's house. He was already outside by the time I arrived.

"Carry my racket?" he asked.

I nodded. We rode our bikes to the club. After we'd been hitting at the tennis courts for twenty minutes the sprinklers came on. The courts were red clay, and Rick, the club pro, shouted for us to get away from the sprinklers. Kagis was using his racket to redirect the water so that it sprayed me in the ass. Our shirts were stuck to our red clay torsos by the time Rick chased us off the court. We headed up to the pool.

My stomach fell a little. All the pretty girls in our grade were there, lounging on beach chairs and nodding along with Ziggy Marley's "Tomorrow People" playing on a yellow waterproof Sony boom box. I'd been dying to see what they looked like in their bikinis, but the truth was I'd have felt relieved if Kagis had suddenly suggested we go back to his house to play pool. We sat in a corner and watched Tinman and Rollo repeatedly toss the Bolis twins into the pool. The school year had ended weirdly. I was finally hanging out with the soccer guys on the weekends, but only Tinman and Rollo went to upperclass parties, while Kagis, Mitch, Paul, and I played pool by ourselves in Kagis's basement. Apparently I had officially joined the group during a transitional period or something.

I couldn't believe how adult-looking the girls' bodies were. Everyone had a deep tan except Missy Means, who made up for it with her marble-sized nippons. Their legs were long and thin. Rollo shouted our names and waved before pounding his chest like a caveman and executing a perfect swan dive off the board. Kagis shook his head.

"I wonder if he's scored with Missy yet," he mused out loud.

Missy was hiding her face but sticking her boobs out as she writhed away from his cupfuls of pool water.

"I doubt it."

"You're clueless, Nick," he muttered. He actually looked angry. It was understandable. It was a mystery to me why the girls hooked up with Rollo and Tinman but not Kagis. I didn't feel like I had any reason to be pissed, but Kagis was a good-looking guy. He was built, too. I was praying I was just still in my awkward stage. My hair was a horror show no matter how much hair spray I used, and my chest still looked sunken even though I could do fifty push-ups in one set. The year before, I could only manage twenty.

I decided it was an apt time to do some push-ups, so I rushed off to the locker room to do a set. For a moment I wondered if I was doing push-ups for my sake or for Kagis's. I was about thirty into my set when Rollo and Tinman showed up. I stopped. I was lying on the cold and wet tile floor when they saw me, and I tried to look casual.

"What are you doing, Park, humping the tiles?" Tinman shouted.

Even though Tinman had invited me to two out of three

birthday parties in middle school I'd never really gotten along with him.

"Ouchy Nicky," Rollo cackled out of tune, messing up the lyrics to the Prince song. He already had the physique of a bodybuilder and played stopper for the varsity soccer team.

They ran out of the locker room. I peed quickly and peeled off my shirt before heading out. My chest didn't look bigger, but it was definitely red; at least it was a reaction. Everyone in the beach chairs started applauding when I stepped out. Kagis stared at the pool. I walked briskly back to my seat, and a couple of seconds later everyone forgot about me and resumed flirting with each other.

Kagis poked me in the shoulder.

"They told everyone you were spanking it on the floor."

"Those dick-noses—I was just doing some push-ups," I muttered, and stood up to publicly explain things. Kagis grabbed me by the wrist. I sat down.

"Your pants are all wet," he said evenly. Of course they were wet—I'd been doing push-ups on the wet tiles. And then I realized that they probably didn't believe Tinman and Rollo, therefore it would be stupid to explain that I was doing push-ups in the locker room, so I pressed my back deeper into the seat.

We biked back toward my house. When we got to Summit Drive we had to walk our bikes—it took fifteen minutes just to get up the hill. Thick beads of sweat dropped from my neck. I glanced at the trail of sweat behind us. It looked like blood.

"Remember that time I got a bloody nose in the second half against Somers, and it was all down my jersey?" I asked.

"Yeah. So?"

"It looked like I got shot," I said. He looked at me. "Sorry about the club."

"Nick, all I'm saying is that it's hard enough without you doing something lame like that. It embarrasses both of us, you know?"

"It won't happen again," I promised.

♣ ♣ ♣

A stroke of luck. Well, sort of. A stroke of luck would have been Maggie Shaughnessy or Jaimy Ginsberg suddenly falling in love with me. A stroke of luck would have been the Bolis twins appearing out of the woods buck naked and jumping us and bragging about it to everyone at the next party. A stroke of luck would have been Missy Means giving us a striptease on my back porch with Rollo and Tinman forced to DJ. In reality, my strokes of luck were pipe dreams that ultimately made me more depressed than excited. Instead, there was a rustling in the woods, and Kagis put a finger to his lips and motioned for me to follow him through my backyard, along a branchy path that led to the Shumperts' backyard.

There were two girls sitting on boulders below the water

tower. We stepped off the path, so that we were hidden behind trees, and looked at each other.

"It's just Paulette and that freaky-looking chick she hangs out with," Kagis said. "Should we check it out?"

I nodded. Staring at the pretty girls in their bikinis all morning had given me a mental woody. I hopped up and down, waiting for Kagis to take the lead. He frowned at me for a second, then stepped back out onto the path. They noticed us immediately.

"Who's there?" Paulette slurred.

"It's me and Nick," Kagis said.

Little giggles.

"Hey, guys," I said, and my voice sounded too high. I offered them a cigarette.

"We got our own. Wanna join us?" Keely took a small sip from a bottle of Captain Morgan. Paulette grabbed at it and accidentally spilled some on her white T-shirt.

It happened quickly. Kagis took Paulette—a chunky, chesty brunette in our grade—and I ended up with Freaky Keely. She had dyed black hair that looked blue, and her skin was freckly. We'd been neighbors for six years and had never spoken. I was amazed at how Kagis didn't even say a word—he and Paulette just started making out in front of us. He looked pissed off, actually. Keely smiled at me with big horse teeth. I walked over and held her hand for a couple of minutes, then leaned in and kissed her. I tasted peanut butter. This was my first real kiss. I'd been imagining it for years, and it had been nothing like this. Or this was nothing like that. Keely took off her tank top. She wasn't wearing a bra. Her breasts were perky but she had no nipples, just inefficient little circles in the centers that were the faded pink of weak lemonade.

"Let's separate," Kagis said, staring at us. We sat for a moment before I realized he meant for us to leave. Keely and I walked around to the other side of the water tower and started making out on the ground. Dried leaves and twigs scratched my legs, but I didn't want to move and disturb her. She started making sounds, and for some reason it embarrassed me.

"Shhh," I whispered. She opened her eyes.

"You're scratching me," she whispered back. She closed her eyes again and made no sound.

A minute later Kagis tapped me on the shoulder. He stared at Keely, and she leaned onto her side.

"Do you have protection?"

I didn't. He looked at the trees for a minute, thinking real hard.

"Forget it," he said.

In a minute I could hear them doing it on the other side of the tower. I pulled my shorts down to my ankles. Surprisingly, it wasn't as embarrassing or exciting to do that in front of a girl as I'd anticipated. I pretended she was a goose-down pillow, and it made me blush. Beads of sweat on my brow threatened to fall, and I couldn't think of what to do next. She informed me that she was on the pill. What the hell? Even the losers in my grade were having sex. Then I realized she could compare me to someone. Giles appeared in my brain, chanting, *Rice dick, rice dick*. I suddenly remembered the soccer guys at lunch explaining the definition of Kent Cole's nickname: Tripod. I recalled the time I'd watched a horse take a four-minute pee in the petting farm at the Big E. I reached down to pull my shorts up, but right then she pulled her own shorts off completely, and I immediately forgot my worries. A minute later I was focusing on the fact that the sensation was real and a million times better than *The Stranger*—where you sit on your hand until it falls asleep before jerking off—but at the same time a part of me felt like I was one of those toothless Appalachian guys in the movie *Deliverance*.

With eyes closed I couldn't help but picture the Bolis twins naked with fake wings strapped to their backs, floating toward me in a mist. And then I collapsed on top of her with my eyes still closed, and I felt like I was falling asleep. Even though only a minute had passed since we finished having sex, I already couldn't remember what it felt like.

"Was that your first time?" she asked softly.

I didn't say anything.

"It's okay. I won't tell anyone," she said.

"Sort of," I said. "Who have you slept with?"

"I was dating a guy from Canton for a while," she said. "We broke up last year."

It felt like we were two random adults bumping into each other at the grocery store, reaching for the last can of Sheba cat food and ending up talking casually about our sex lives because we'd been having sex for decades. I was amazed. Keely Glick. She never said a word in school. It wasn't fair that she'd already done it before, because if we were both suddenly struck by lightning, she'd die having had more sex than me.

"What are you thinking?" she asked.

"Nothing." I was suddenly cold and wanted to immediately take a shower, so I slid my shorts back on. She did the same. We sat next to each other in the dirt and listened to Kagis and Paulette on the other side of the water tower for a while. Then she stood up.

"I should go," she said. We awkwardly hugged, and then she walked away. The reality of the situation dawned on me. I closed my eyes and pretended I was an owl in a tree watching the two of us going at it. I remembered that I'd been resigned to thinking that I was never going to have sex in high school. I said it out loud a couple of times. "You just had sex. I have now had sex." My brain was flooded with love for girls again. Around that time my thoughts about them were usually laced with a tinge of resentment, but at the moment I was reaffirmed in my dedication. Girls were what I lived for; they were all I'd ever wanted. Only girls could make me feel truly happy—I wanted girls for breakfast every day. I climbed onto the huge boulder next to the water tower and waited for Paulette and Kagis to finish.

❧ ❧ ❧

Paulette wasn't leaving. We both wanted her to hit the road, but she stubbornly clung to us. She tried to hold Kagis's hand, but he was having none of it.

"We should go," he said, staring at his shoes. It was his first time having sex, too.

"Do you think Keely is home?" she asked me.

"How the hell should I know? Does it look like I have infrared vision or something?" I half wondered why I was suddenly so pissed at Paulette. Actually, I knew. It was because she was a woofer, simpering pitifully over Kagis, and I could tell he was feeling just as embarrassed that we were standing around with this cow.

"Bye-bye, Paulette," I said, and walked toward my back porch. Kagis followed without saying goodbye. We were a couple of cool assholes.

"Nick," he whispered urgently when she was out of earshot. "Don't tell anyone."

"Why would I tell anyone? They're heinous," I said.

He nodded. I thought about what it had felt like to lie next to Keely. For a minute Kagis and I both stared up at the sky and watched the clouds stream by. It didn't seem real, how fast the clouds were passing overhead. Kagis looked at me. We both acted repulsed for a few seconds, but secretly I no longer felt gross and in need of a shower and instead felt incredibly satisfied with the situation. I could tell he was thinking the same thing because he had a distant look in his eyes. Then they turned coal again.

"Okay, I'm outy," he said, and got on his ten-speed.

"Latersky," I said.

I went inside my house and immediately called Mitch in Nantucket and related the afternoon's events. I couldn't help but grin as I bragged about our conquests.

♣ ♣ ♣

The next afternoon when Kagis came over, I told him about my call to Mitch, and then he put me in a half nelson and somehow proceeded to repeatedly slap me in the back of the head. Then he put me in a full headlock and started ramming my tailbone into the garage door.

"You stupid ass," he huffed, pushing my face against the driveway. I growled, but that was about all the resistance I could muster, and it failed to frighten him. "I told you not to tell anyone, especially Mitch. Now everyone's going to find out."

"Big deal, and no, they won't. I made Mitch promise to keep his trap shut. It's . . . cool . . . Kagis," I squeezed out the words between breaths.

"Another rookie move." He let go of me. "You're amazing."

"I'm sorry. But no one's going to find out," I reasoned. "Dude, it's summer."

He shook his head. Then he nodded. Then he shook his head again.

"Whatever," he said.

We sat there for a minute, catching our breath.

"And by the way, you mess with me again and I'll kill you," I said.

"You want more, bitch?"

I held up my right hand.

"It's over. It's over," I said.

Then we went inside and called them up. Kagis made me do all the talking. His face was pressed against my cheek, trying to listen in on the conversation.

"What are you two doing?" Paulette asked.

"Not much. Kagis's taking a dump—whatever you do, don't picture it," I hollered, and he punched me in the shoulder. The punch stung so I bad I nearly dropped the phone. Kagis glared at me. "So do you want to get together?" I asked. He rolled his eyes.

"Get together?" Kagis whispered. "Give me the phone."

"Come over to Keely's," Paulette said, and before she could hang up I heard them giggling like two elves. I stared at the receiver.

"Well?" Kagis asked.

"Let's go get laid," I said.

We exchanged high fives all the way up the driveway.

Keely and Paulette were sitting in her backyard when we got there. Keely actually looked pretty in the sunlight—her hair looked purply and her eyes were big. Paulette still looked like a porpoise. I could tell Kagis recognized this, too, because he stopped dead in his tracks. They waved at us. He looked at me. We shuffled forward.

"Here, catch," Paulette said, tossing me a yellow sponge ball.

I caught it and giggled out loud. It sounded girly, and my ears singed. The four of us sat in a little circle, tossing the sponge ball around. At first Kagis rolled his eyes and stuck out his tongue, pretending he was a special kid with an elevator pass, and I felt unchallenged as well, but then Keely and Paulette started pretending the ball was a hot potato, and I got Kagis to pretend also, and soon we were all laughing and enjoying our stupid little game. I thought to myself that this was a really nice moment. Who would have guessed, the two of us hanging out with Butterball Ruben and Freaky Keely on a humid, summer day?

I smiled at Keely. Before we'd had sex I had identified her as an unpopular weirdo who willingly dyed her hair black (why would anyone do that? I wondered), but when I looked into her eyes I could tell that she was a genuinely happy person and really liked me. She had a nice smile. It was poor luck she wasn't one of the popular girls. I liked Keely's personality, but I wasn't totally attracted to her, whereas I hated the pretty girls' personalities, yet I was involuntarily obsessed with them. What was wrong with me?

"You guys are the best athletes in school," Paulette said.

"Got that right," Kagis said.

"Don't you play in tennis tournaments?" Keely asked me.

"I'm ranked ninth in New England," I said. Actually I was fourteenth.

"Let's play tennis," Paulette said suddenly.

"Let's not," Kagis replied, and jokingly bear-hugged Paulette. She shook him off.

"Is that all you want?" Paulette said, batting her eyelashes. Kagis didn't say anything. "You can't kiss me until you teach me how to serve."

"But I don't want to kiss," he said.

Paulette giggled. I looked at Keely. She looked down at her gray sneakers.

"Come on, Kagis, let's just hit for a bit," I said.

"Where?"

"I don't know . . . Renfield Middle?"

"Nope."

"The club?"

"Wrong again, chief," he said. I knew immediately what he was subtly refusing to do: risk being seen in public with these losers. I didn't want to take the chance, either, but I liked teaching tennis. If my grades stayed as low as they were, I figured I might want to become a teaching pro someday.

"The Oaks has a court, right?" Keely asked innocently. She was right. The Oaks was a nearby apartment complex. No one hung out there. It would be a miracle if anyone showed up. Kagis knew this, too. He looked at Paulette one last time with an attempt at a sexy grin, only he looked livid.

She didn't bite.

"Let's go," she said, getting to her feet.

Once they retreated into the garage to dig around for old tennis rackets, Kagis muzzled me with his big fat hand.

"We could bang them now. Say you have a dentist appointment or something. We'll keep tossing the sponge ball around until they give in."

"It's too late," I said. My voice sounded nasal because his catcher's mitt of a palm was crushing my nose. The girls emerged from the garage wielding four wooden rackets. Kagis muttered something.

"No one's going to see us," I whispered in his ear.

Kagis refused to walk on the road with us, opting instead to follow in the woods as we half jogged to the Oaks. He had trouble keeping up, hopping over fallen logs and pushing through pricker bushes. Idiot. I knew how he felt, though— I felt the same way to a degree, but it wasn't worth getting all scratched up about. Paulette was panting, hunched over, trying to keep up. Any second I was expecting a burst of steam to shoot up out of the back of her shirt.

"How long can you stay out of the water for?" I asked, thinking no one would understand, but Keely punched me in the back. Paulette stopped jogging and stared at me so hard I had to look away for a moment.

"You little prick," she whispered. I flinched, expecting her to let loose with a slur or two. I deserved it. "Don't talk to me," she said, and walked past us.

Keely stared at me as if I was a stranger.

As if God was warning me (or mercifully hydrating Pauline), a thirty-second downpour suddenly fell. It was a warm rain, the kind where steam rises off the tops of people's heads. The sky was gray and I could hear rumbling in the distance, but I couldn't make out much above.

I immediately felt horrible and turned to Keely. "I'm sorry," I told her, and I must have looked adequately remorseful because a few seconds later she placed her head on my shoulder, then took it off.

A sign of forgiveness.

As expected, the Oaks was deserted. The sun broke through full force again, and my head felt greasy from the humidity. A thick raindrop from an overhead branch plinked the top of my scalp and spread slowly over my head like a raw egg. Kagis ran onto the court.

"Come on, let's get this over with," he shouted.

Paulette walked onto his side of the court but didn't say anything. I had really screwed things up. But she must have really dug Kagis, because suddenly he was flirting with her, hugging her, and she was giggling again. I fixed Keely's grip and taught her a rudimentary forehand. She was a natural. Her first three tries went over the net. Kagis slammed inside-out forehands at us but missed. I instructed Keely to follow through with her racket, and she held her finishing pose and flitted her eyelashes at me. We laughed, and at that moment the last thing on my mind was sex or any of the popular girls. I was focused on just me and Keely, playing tennis.

A car pulled into the parking lot. I was showing Keely my serve, with my back to the lot, but could see Kagis's jaw drop. I froze, too. I was having a great time, but I still froze.

"Hey, Kagis! Teaching tennis?" an obnoxious girl's voice shouted, followed by laughter and a car horn. I turned around. A silver Volvo wagon had pulled into the parking lot. Missy Means was at the wheel, with the Bolis twins riding shotgun. Tinman and Terry Robley gaped at us from the backseat. I felt awful for Keely. I didn't care about Paulette's feelings, but it was obvious they were laughing at both of them. I wanted to nail a flat serve as hard as I could at the windshield.

"Bye, boys, enjoy your hot date!" they shouted, and backed out of the parking lot. Keely looked frightened. I dropped the racket and pulled her close. It was in this brief moment I felt like I'd finally grown up and could feel good about my actions.

"I told you we'd get busted with these losers," Kagis shouted. He hopped the net and barreled straight at us. I shoved Keely out of the way. He tackled me—well, he sort of missed, but I still went reeling. I grabbed the fence to keep from falling down.

He chased me around the tennis court. Keely shouted for him to stop, but he was blind with rage—he probably didn't even realize he was mechanically shouting, "Mother-fucker!" over and over. Paulette looked dumbfounded, or maybe that was her normal expression, and I sprinted two more laps around the court with Kagis in pursuit before snatching up one of the wooden rackets. I pivoted and swung twice to force him back. Keely started crying.

"You jackass," he screamed.

"Relax—we can say we just ran into them," I shouted, then flinched and prayed Keely hadn't heard it.

I swung my racket again and almost hit him. His eyes were liquid and he grew more aggressive, coming in a little closer after every swing, so I had to keep backing up a step.

"Keely, this is not a proper follow-through," I said, continuing the tennis lesson, almost tripping. "Dammit, Kagis, chill out."

I glanced over at Keely, who was being escorted off the tennis court by her best friend. Paulette looked like a nun, the way she was comforting her. Right then, Kagis found an opening and lunged. I desperately swung blindly and caught him square above the right eyebrow. He dropped to his knees. I threw the racket away, crept over to Kagis, and placed a hand on his shoulder.

"Bro, I'm sorry," I said.

He leaped at me like a trap-door spider and punched me in the stomach. As I staggered backward I managed to grab the racket and swung just in time to stop him from leaping onto me.

"Stop it this instant!" a voice shouted. Tenants from the apartments had formed a crowd behind us. "We'll call the police," the voice threatened.

"Screw you," Kagis roared.

I held up the racket again. I was thinking about Keely and how she was crying because of what I said, and I was also thinking about how damaging socially it was that Missy, the Bolis twins, Terry Robley, and Tinman had caught us with these losers, and on top of that I could hear the adults behind me yelling and threatening to call the police, and I couldn't help but start bawling. My body heaved and I dropped to all fours, not caring if anyone saw me. Through teary eyes I could see Kagis's expression change. He rushed over. I coughed. Out of the corner of my eye I saw a shadow of my body on the court, heaving and shaking.

"It's okay, I'm sorry," Kagis soothed, rubbing my back furiously. "Hey, man, it's no big deal. I'm sorry," he repeated, adding a fake laugh to make me feel better.

I couldn't form words because I was shaking so much, but Kagis somehow read my thoughts because he suddenly shouted at the people watching. I couldn't bear to turn around and see their expressions.

"Get out of here," he screamed. He had a pretty thick scream.

Footsteps disappeared behind us.

"Hey, man," he whispered, rubbing my back some more. "It's okay, Nick."

I was watching my shadow—it buckled less and less. My nose was wet, and there were drops collecting on the green concrete. I could sense a few people still watching, probably from behind their windows. Kagis patted me on the back a few times and asked if I was okay, but I focused on my shadow.

sixteen

After getting deflowered at the end of junior year by Freaky Keely Glick, I figured the ladies would detect a subtle new musk seeping from my skin when I arrived at school as a senior, but it turned out that I was still scentless. I wrongly assumed that socially things had finally come full circle. In theory, I was finally a senior at the top (and therefore start) of the dating cycle, about to hook up with hot freshmen, and on the first day of classes I graced the halls like a debutante, letting the frosh girls check me out. I got the distinct feeling that some of them felt a momentarily confusing horny sensation as I walked by. They looked at me and saw a guy with a driver's license, wearing the prestigious Varsity Renfield Express soccer pullover. Freshman guys, by comparison, looked like ten-year-olds. I had even grown a goatee in preparation—albeit a pathetic excuse for one—which the senior girls ended up making fun of during homeroom. I still believe that the freshman girls were impressed I could grow any facial hair at all. At last count I had twenty-four eyelash-curly hairs protruding bravely from my chin.

There was a huge rager the first Friday night of the school year that all the frosh girls would be at, and I couldn't wait to go. The only problem was that my friends weren't interested. Weeks earlier we had planned a pool tournament in Kagis's basement, and I couldn't believe it wasn't being postponed in light of this golden opportunity and in light of the fact that all we ever did was shoot stick in his basement. They were more interested in trying to hang out with the senior girls, who were suddenly paying attention to us again because last year's seniors were gone. For three years the girls in our grade had ignored us—except for Rollo and Tinman—and dated older guys and prep school guys, and now they were acknowledging our existence again? My friends were blind.

On Friday night we met up at Kagis's house as planned. Paul brought a dry-erase board and made up a draw and rankings for the nine-ball tourney. Everyone just sat there silently watching Tinman repeatedly attempt a stupid pool trick, but he kept shooting the balls off the table. Whenever a song ended I looked at my watch.

"You're going to chip the cue ball," Mitch said.

"Dude, I can make it," Tinman replied.

I sighed.

"It's not too late guys—we can cut our losses. Let's hit that party," I pleaded.

"Nobody's stopping you," Kagis said.

"I'm not going by myself. I can't believe this," I said. "You'd prefer to have a sausage fest instead of go to a party full of totally available frosh chicks?"

"Missy said she might come over," Mitch said. "She'll probably bring Alicia and some friends. You love the twins, Nicky."

"We're not hanging out with those bitches, are we?" I asked. Mitch stared at me. "We're seniors now. We're supposed to be dating frosh girls, just like the seniors before us, and the seniors before them. This is how it's always been. You don't mess with tradition."

"We hated those senior guys when we were freshmen, remember?" Kagis asked.

"All the more reason to claim what is rightfully ours now that the time has come. We paid our dues. Dammit, we've suffered long enough."

"Okay, Moses, if you really want to bag a frosh chick so bad, go ahead."

"The senior girls are using us."

They didn't listen. I felt hunger pains. At a quarter till midnight I took off from Mitch's, and on my way home I drove past the house that was holding the party. All the lights were off. Maybe it had gotten canceled? I felt relieved. I felt encouraged that I hadn't missed anything major.

But my worst nightmare came true. At school on Monday I discovered that there *had* been an epic rager, and by the end of it all the hottest freshman girls were snagged. The football guys were passing around a purple hairbrush, combing out their hickies. My friends didn't even care, because some of the popular senior girls now sat with us during lunch. Whoop-de-fuckin'-do. I sat with my arms crossed, visibly pouting, watching the frosh girls giggle with their new senior boyfriends. I groaned. For years I'd wanted to become a full-time friend with the soccer guys and hit all the cool parties. I'd gotten my wish, but now that there were once again parties to go to, they decided they preferred hanging out by themselves in Kagis's basement. And all the frosh girls were now taken.

Cue Beethoven's Piano Sonata No. 14 in C Sharp.

❧ ❧ ❧

Every weekend the frosh girls hung out with the senior guys at the McDonald's in Avon. On the third weekend spent putrefying in Kagis's basement (Friday had become poker night), I finally got fed up and struck out on my own. I drove to Mickey D's. The place was packed. Even Andy Cordello the Trumpet Guy was there, sitting on the hood of his old Audi with two hot frosh girls he'd met in concert band. Immediately I knew this was where I belonged. To actually have a chance at getting a girlfriend. One of these frosh girls was my destiny—I could feel it.

It was easier to talk to the hot frosh girls compared to the hotties in my grade. Frosh girls were like Mogwai—utterly harmless at the moment, but destined to turn into evil, flesh-eating Gremlins like Missy and Terry Robley. It was stupid that these hot frosh girls saw something in me that the girls in my grade missed. It crossed my mind that if I were three years older I'd have probably had one of the hot girls in my grade interested in me, but rather than be appalled by all the politics, I struck up a conversation with a quiet and surprisingly hot blond frosh named Lauren in the McDonald's parking lot. We shared a cigarette. By the following Wednesday I was platonically giving her rides home before speeding back to school in time to make the soccer practice bus.

One night I made a spontaneous trip to the Farmington Valley Mall, where I purchased a plastic ring off the quarter machine at the arcade. Then I bought a bunch of plastic spiders, stickers in plastic eggs, a fluorescent orange bouncy ball, and some trinkets next door at Themes. Later I poured the contents on Lauren's bed. "I wanted to get you this ring, but I kept getting spiders and tattoos," I said with a defeated tone. Her eyes sparkled. Even though she was kinda boring and never talked, it felt good to pretend she was my girlfriend and to do things like this for her, and for her to appreciate them the way I always dreamed a girl would.

Soccer season ended in early November. For the first time in seven years the Renfield Express didn't win the state championship. It was a big deal, but I was surprised how little I cared. At lunch the Monday after we lost in the quarters, the soccer guys sat around assessing the team's chances next year, and it dawned on me that I was utterly disinterested in their debate. Lauren was sitting with her friends in the opposite corner of the caf, and I focused on just staring at her from a distance.

"You know Tinman and Robley disappeared at your party, Kagis," Paul said.

I turned around.

"You had a party this weekend?" I asked Kagis.

"Not really. We were just hanging out, and people started showing up."

"Oh. So what's on tap for this weekend?" I asked half-heartedly.

"It's only Monday," Kagis said.

"True, but I haven't been around much."

"You haven't been around at all," Kagis replied.

Mitch quietly read the nutrition facts on his carton of milk.

"What's that supposed to mean?" I asked.

I had been hanging out with Lauren for only a few weeks, but apparently it had been a few weeks too long.

Kagis looked out the window.

"What—are you jealous that I've been hanging out with someone?"

"Yeah, that's it, Nick, exactly," Kagis said.

He got up and walked away. Paul followed him.

"What's his problem?" I asked Mitch.

"He's just pissy you ditched us for that frosh chick," he said.

"I didn't ditch anyone. He's jealous."

"That's not true."

"So? What, do I have to apologize to him?"

"It's nothing, forget about it," he said. "Come on, let's bolt."

❧ ❧ ❧

Kagis and I didn't talk the rest of the week. During final period on Friday I heard random underclassmen talking about a party at his house. It was weird that I hadn't heard about it already. Nobody had mentioned it at lunch. I drove Lauren home but didn't feel like hanging out. We shared a quick cigarette, and she mentioned that she was going to the movies with a friend. I said goodbye and drove over to Mitch's house. While I didn't think spending time with Lauren made me a bad friend, I also realized it didn't exactly make me the most loyal one, either. Kagis and Mitch were sitting on the back porch.

"How's it hanging, Nicky?" Mitch shouted.

"Oh, a little to the left. Listen, Kagis," I said. He looked shocked that I was talking to him. I held out my hand, and he awkwardly shook it. He had a crooked smile on his face. "You were right, man. I've been away. Thanks for making me realize."

"No problemo," Kagis said. He looked at Mitch. "I gotta hit the road."

"Peace out," Mitch said.

We watched him walk off without saying anything.

"He's still mad at me, huh?" I asked.

"Don't worry, it'll blow over."

"I've been thinking lately," I started. Mitch looked at

me, exhaling smoke through his nose like a cartoon bull. "I realized you guys are the best thing I have going."

"Are you dying?"

"Lauren's cool, but you guys are definitely more important. I kinda spaced and forgot that for a while. I'm definitely hitting the party tonight."

"It's good news to hear you want to hang. We missed you."

That night I actually felt nervous about going over to Kagis's house. Things were definitely strained between us. *Make the peace tonight*, I thought. I was quiet throughout dinner, just nibbling on leftovers. My mom read the Korean Bible in her nurse's uniform, and my dad circled items in the Holabird ad at the back of *World Tennis* magazine using a yellow Sharpie highlighter—our official marker. He put it down and took off his glasses.

"What's wrong?" he asked. I fumbled with a pair of chopsticks I'd found in the silverware drawer. I tried to pick up an egg roll with the chopsticks but failed, so I started playing air drums. "You look like you're talking to someone, but no words come out."

"I'm just figuring out my friends. It's nothing."

"Forget your friends, focus on school," my mom said.

"They're my best friends. You have no idea what you're talking about."

"Why did you ask me, then?"

"I didn't ask you anything."

"Nick, your mother is just saying you should study more."

"Thank you for the brilliant advice," I said, and scraped the contents of my plate into the trash even though I was suddenly kinda hungry again.

By the time I arrived at Kagis's house there were already at least twenty cars parked outside. Missy Means was sitting on the curb between two prep school guys. *I knew it. She's just using Kagis for his house*. My theory about the senior girls was right after all.

"Hello, Missy," I said, shaking my head.

"Nick Park," she slurred.

"How's it inside?" I asked, not meaning to be friendly, but sometimes I felt intimidated by her. She ignored me and resumed flirting with one of the guys. The other kid glared at me. I kept walking. The living room was packed with freshmen guys and girls. I felt like saying hi to some of the frosh girls I now knew (friends of Lauren's), but my first priority was to find Kagis and clear the air. I tapped the shoulder of a freshman. He turned around with a big quid of tobacco tucked behind his lower lip—some of it had slid down his chin, and his face was pale and quivering like Vesuvius. He was obviously about to puke any second and I kinda wanted to see it, but I was on a strict mission.

"Frosh, where's Kagis?"

"Who's that?"

"The guy who lives here, pud," I said, pushing past him, giving him a little extra shove. I could hear him stumble behind me. Stupid freshman.

I made my way down the creaky wooden steps to the basement. It was much quieter down there. Guys were standing around shooting stick; the pool table had a big beer stain in the middle. I was shocked when I realized who was down there: The Bolis twins were standing in a corner with Tinman; Paul, Mitch, and Rollo were talking to prep school kids and all the popular senior girls. It was weird the way Paul was talking to some of the prep school kids—it looked like they were all old friends. How long had I been gone? For a moment it seemed like everyone was looking at me, but I assumed I was merely deluded because of my resurfaced shyness.

"Nick," Kagis said from behind me. I turned around.

"There's a lot of people here," I said, jabbing Kagis in the shoulder.

I followed him into the dart room.

"Listen, I wanted to apologize, man," I said in a rush. I felt noble, making the peace like this. "I honestly didn't even realize I was ditching everyone. What you said at lunch the other day was a wake-up call for me, man. Thanks." I felt like hugging the guy.

"You ditched us to become a chauffeur for those frosh chicks."

I winced. It was like he had socked me in the stomach. I stared at him. His eyes were bloodshot and his pursed lips rippled a little as he stifled a burp. He finished his beer, let it drop to the floor.

"It's not like that," I said. "We hang out alone. Lauren likes me."

"She's using you, man. You're just a means of transportation."

"That's not true. Dude, I'm trying to be a good guy here."

"You're pitiful, Nick. It's pathetic how hard you're trying to score with that frosh chick. Here's some advice: don't bother. It ain't worth it."

"Why's that?"

"They're not gonna go for you, man. Are you blind?"

"You're just jealous I met a frosh chick while you were still whacking off in this basement every night."

"Everyone's here," he said. "Why would I ever be jealous of you? That little freshman betty doesn't like you. I just talked to her—she called you her smoking buddy."

I moved within inches of his face. We could feel each other's breath.

"Bullshit. Is Lauren really here?"

"I tried to put in a good word for you, but she whispered in my ear that she wanted me. Actually, you probably *could* hook up with her right now. She's sloshed."

I suddenly shoved him against the wall. He looked stunned for a moment, then peeled himself off; some tools fell from hooks.

"Why are you giving me shit, Kagis?"

"Because you're a joke. You don't even realize that I'm trying to help you. Tell me something, Park—how come you never go for Asian chicks?"

"What? You know I hate Asian chicks," I said, confused

by the question. "First of all, there aren't any around. Second, I'm not attracted to them."

His eyes lit up.

"You should be going for Asian girls, Park. Quit wasting your time trying to score with Renfield chicks. You're deluded because you happened to score with a skank like Keely. Asian chicks are hot. Remember Peggy, that girl at the bonfire I hooked up with? I bet you could get her."

I turned and walked out of the room. The people in the basement must have heard the commotion because they were all staring at me. I smiled and tried to act normal, but my hands were shaking. I stuck them in my pockets, and my pants started vibrating.

"Let's shoot some stick," I said to Mitch, and my voice cracked.

I wanted to just soak up time with Mitch until I felt right again. I felt as if I was underwater; my head was buzzing. I turned around. Kagis was standing right behind me.

The basement was bone quiet.

"Nick, leave right now," he said loudly. "Come on, get lost, you fucking *loser*."

In slow motion I turned to Mitch for support.

"Mitchy, let's get out of here," I whispered. But Mitch just looked down and contemplated his beer. Rollo had an evil grin on his face. Paul focused on the pool balls. The Bolis twins and all the senior girls looked shocked. The prep school guys were itching to jump me. I managed to turn around. I couldn't tell what was making me more embarrassed, that my close friends were witnessing this or that the popular girls were. It seemed to take forever to get up the stairs. Kagis occasionally pushed me in the back to keep me going. I wanted to wheel around and belt him in the face. The shakes spread from my hands throughout my body, but luckily the kitchen was packed and no one noticed.

I navigated my way out to the car and started it up. I backed up so I wouldn't have to drive by the house. Kagis was standing in the doorway talking to a frosh girl. He had a stern look on his face. A group of freshmen losers clustered next to the front stoop, waiting to get inside. He waved them all through. My throat had a lump in it as I drove off. I almost forgot to turn on the headlights. I just drove. By the time I pulled into my driveway I was calm. My jaw ached because I had been clenching it the whole drive back. I pictured Mitch and everyone else down in the basement, but it was too embarrassing even in the privacy of my head to think about it, so I blocked the image out. I couldn't think. Not yet. There would be time enough for that. But this much was certain: Kagis had made a formal, public break from me, and everyone else had just watched, without saying anything in my defense.

And just like that, I no longer had friends.

seventeen

I can remember that it rained the day after Kagis kicked me out of his party. I huddled in my dad's La-Z-Boy in the afternoon, watching a PBS documentary on hyenas. I found my soul brother in a little hyena whose mother had been killed. He was tiny, with pointy ears and fewer black spots on his back than the rest of the clan. With no adult protector around, the clan rejected him, and eventually he found himself sitting in the middle of a skanky pond to avoid their snapping teeth. I got all choked up as the little hyena, all alone in the middle of the pond, shrank lower and lower while the others barked and growled at him. He made dismal little yelping sounds as he tried to creep back to the pack, but then he got chased away.

The deep-voiced narrator explained that from here on out, the hyena would never be part of the clan and would have to get by on its own. I cheered for him. I cheered for myself. "We'll make it," I said out loud. It sounded feeble, but at the same time it made me feel strong. "We don't need friends." I felt relaxed for the first time all day, secure. Then the music turned ominous, and the camera zoomed in on a gold tail flickering in the underbrush. Suddenly a lion hiding in the brush bounded across the pond and crunched its incisors into the little hyena's throat, audibly snapping its neck in two.

Every time I thought about those faces from the party

the night before, I'd shudder. I dreaded hearing classmates whispering about me behind my back the following Monday. I had no desire to ever see Paul, Rollo, or even Mitch again. They'd had the choice to back me up, and they'd chosen to stay with Kagis. Mitch at least should have left with me. I wanted to kill Kagis. I was shell-shocked. After being humiliated in public like that, I immediately knew there was no chance (unless they really went out of their way) that I would ever be friends with any of them again.

Things began to click in my brain as I thought about what Kagis had said. It was fine for him to hook up with whomever he wanted—a Korean chick, even Paulette—just as long as I didn't do better than him. In his mind, some Asian girl was the best I could possibly get. The notion of me and not him dating a hot Renfield chick was almost a crime, in his opinion.

🍃 🍃 🍃

I was obviously uncomfortable at school. It took a few days to adjust to no longer being friends with the soccer guys. Mitch's face looked apologetic every time I saw him, but he never stopped in the hallways to talk. For his sake I stopped walking past his locker when he was there. Soon enough Mitch and Rollo and Paul switched over to lockers next to the alpha male, Kagis—an act of unification. It accentuated the off-kilter feeling I already had. To make matters worse, it soon became clear that Kagis was having huge parties every weekend that all the popular girls went to.

The soccer guys (minus me) were now officially the kings of the school.

I started eating lunch with Will and his friends, while Kagis and Company now regularly sat with the popular senior girls. I was so out of it that one time Will pretended to nurse me at lunch by spooning some applesauce into my mouth, which made everyone at the table laugh. I slowly chewed on the applesauce without using my teeth, swallowed, then opened my mouth again without blinking once. It freaked everyone out.

About a month later I noticed that Mitch no longer looked sympathetic about my plight, and everyone else, including even Lauren, no longer seemed to acknowledge my existence. At this point I made a pledge to myself that I'd stop daydreaming about better days. I was like the parent who finally decides to clean out his dead son's old bedroom and turn it into a rec room. I made the decision to disappear.

🦋 🦋 🦋

There was a minor snowstorm in early December, and though it didn't snow again until after Christmas, it stayed cold from then on. Winter in Renfield is a major drag if you don't ski. If you do, there are weekends at time-share condominiums up at Okemo and Killington; there is a ski club at Sundown on Wednesdays after school. The elimination of outdoor activities motivates you to go bowling or shoot stick at the pool hall in Plainville. If you're dating a girl, winter isn't nearly as bad. But even for those who do ski and have girlfriends, the winter is still ridiculously cold. The main weekend activity when there isn't a party is still to hang out in the parking lot of McDonald's at night. Once the fuzz kick you out there are any number of cul-de-sacs to loiter at, and it's boring as hell, standing around in the dark, chugging beers and slap-boxing. Will invited me a few times to go driving, but I firmly said no. I was dedicated to my plan.

I was happy for winter. Well, *happy* might be an overstatement, but by January I was definitely used to my new life as a hermit and felt solid antisocially. Then one Thursday night I realized I could actually understand a little of my parents' conversation. I couldn't spend another night at home. I needed to see people. I needed a distraction.

Girls.

I needed to at least see one in person to help me feel alive. I needed to actively look at one; maybe she'd work as a tonic. So I called Will. I didn't expect him to be home; usually he hung out at a random cul-de-sac drinking out of flasks with his boring friends, then killed a couple of hours driving hundreds of miles within a five-mile radius searching for a party that they all knew didn't exist but wouldn't admit to each other. It was 9 p.m., but he picked up right away.

"Long time no hear," he said.

"Been busy. What are you up to?"

"I don't know."

"Let's do something," I said. My suggestion was met with an uncomfortable silence—Will's way of showing his frustration that only now was I finally wanting to do something with him. I was in no mood to deal with his selfishness. "Come on, I'll pick you up in ten minutes."

I picked Will up and we drove over to the pool hall in Plainville. The name of the town epitomized the type of low-life kids that hung out there. The male contingent at the pool hall that night was primarily high school burnouts. One of them was Asian. He was shorter than me, had a crewcut with two lines shaved into the sides of his head (probably not sports-related), and he was wearing a tight Kool cigarettes T-shirt that showed off his veiny biceps. It was shocking to see another Asian guy who might actually be more bananarific than me. At first I felt a tinge of brotherly love for him, despite his cheesy greaser look, but whenever we made eye contact he tried to engage me in a staring contest. I got the distinct feeling he was planning on mugging me in front of his friends as the final act of his initiation into the group or something, so I stopped matching his gaze. Will and I shot eight-ball for a while. "Alone at Midnight" by the Smithereens was playing on the sound system. I ran two straight racks before two girls slid over from the next table to bum cigarettes off us. I couldn't believe our luck. We let them shoot with us once we deemed them single.

It felt surreal the way things happened. We met two girls at a pool hall. We shared a couple of butts. They agreed to come with us to a second-class rager Will had heard about.

The pool hall girls wore revealing tight shirts and tight jeans, and my first impression was that they were big-boned girls. One of them was pretty, with plump lips, high cheekbones, and big hazel eyes. But she wore more makeup than the other girl, which was too much to begin with. Bright blue eyeliner to match their acid-washed Jordache jeans and mashed-on red lipstick. They looked like a couple of dirty American flags.

♣ ♣ ♣

I did some doughnuts in reverse in the icy cul-de-sac before parking on Holworthy Terrace. We walked up to the front entrance of the modern mansion. The thump of bass rattled the shutterless rectangular windows as speakers inside blared Public Enemy's "Cold Lampin' with Flavor." We looked at each other for a few seconds before Will took the lead and opened the door. The entrance was crowded with high schoolers, the majority of them underclassmen, with a handful of particularly loserish bearded seniors standing around like corrupt prison guards.

Everyone stared at Kara's Plainville High football jacket. I patted Will on the back and led Penny, the other Plainville chick, upstairs to the first room with lights off. I pressed the door shut behind me and blushed as I locked it, but she didn't seem to notice. I wondered about Will and tried to listen for his voice out in the hallway. Feet shuffled past the room; a foot kicked the door. Penny guzzled from a silver flask that had her initials engraved on it.

It was quiet and dark in the guest bedroom, and Penny was boring. The clock on the windowsill read 11:30. She casually pulled her shirt off and sat next to me on the bed. Almost a romantic moment, ruined only by the fact that she had programmed the song "One" by U2 to play over and over on the stereo. She also reached over and placed a couple of CDs inside her parka pocket when she thought I wasn't looking.

In addition to having nice big blue eyes, Penny's other distinguishing feature were her round, cream-puff melons. I accidentally touched them, and they didn't make sense—so huge and firm, yet soft, as if filled with helium. Her bra was industrial-strength, with four clasps in the back. It would have probably worked as a pretty good slingshot for large pieces of rotting fruit. On the ride home from an away soccer game toward the end of the season Mitch had held court in the back of the bus describing a way of rating girls he'd heard about from a cousin, comparing them to metals. "Coppers" were beer goggles, or just plain ugly girls; "silvers" were one-night stands, as if any of us regularly had them; "golds" were decent hookups, worth seeing again; "platinums" were girlfriend types; and occasionally you'd come across the perfect girl, whom Mitch referred to as an "unobtanium."

Despite her name, Penny was a silver.

I leaned in and kissed her once, lightly. I leaned back.

"Sorry, I just like you so much," I said, and cringed at how phony it sounded.

"Oh, Mick," she said, and kissed me back. "Did you ever think this would happen?"

I didn't know how to take this, given the fact that we'd known each other for just over two hours, so I tilted my head to the side to simulate deep thought.

"No, but that didn't stop me from praying." I flinched as I said it. She giggled.

A door shut down the hall, and for a moment we both looked over at the doorway. Penny had an overall bluish hue to her face, and I couldn't decide if she looked better with the lights on or off.

"You're really good at pool," she said, then started to kiss me.

In the background, Bono was singing, "Did I disappoint you, or leave a bad taste in your mouth?" and this made me uncomfortable, fearful Penny might actually listen to the lyrics and somehow Bono might ruin my present situation, so I started doing army push-ups on top of her just to drown the music out.

She touched my chin with her left hand. "You know . . . don't take this the wrong way, but . . . I've never hooked up with an Asian."

I stopped.

"What?"

"I've never been with one before. We don't have any in Plainville. That's why I had a crush on you. I think you're the most beautiful Asian guy I've ever met in my whole life," she said in a slightly singsongy voice, and her eyes were actually wet.

She leaned up to kiss me, and I let her. I didn't say anything.

"You don't get it. I've *never* been attracted to Asian guys before. That's how hot you are," she gushed. She looked down at her belly.

My night had unraveled. Maybe I should have taken it as a compliment, even though she basically said I was the best of the worst. She could tell I was thinking this, or at least something, and she whispered, "Are you okay?"

"I'm just worrying about Will and Kara," I said.

"They're fine," she said.

She went on about how Will and I should hang out in Plainville sometime, and the more she talked, the more I wished I could get out of there. The word *Asian* was stuck in her throat—I could almost see it. It was shocking to think that she considered me the same way I saw her—as a hookup, or maybe in her case something to talk about with her friends. I didn't want to be an experiment, or a guinea pig, or an exhibit at a fair. I was dumbstruck by how in a matter of seconds a girl could go from being the one thing I most wanted (at least temporarily) to the one thing I hated most in this world.

I wanted to leave but couldn't, so I just lay there. I suddenly remembered what I hated most about being different: the fact that everybody knew it.

♣ ♣ ♣

The sound of shouting. I could make out a ringing sound, but I knew it was only tinnitus. I recognized Will's voice, rolled off Penny, quickly dressed, and ran out into the hallway, where I found Will surrounded by three underclass football guys. They were all wearing hemp ponchos they'd bought at the Trading Post in Canton. It was the only store around where preppy Renfield jocks could buy hippie clothes to wear while they listened to the Dead and smoked pot out of a Coke can in their newly leased Jettas on Friday nights. I was immediately livid.

"Nick, we should go," Will said. "Kara was stealing stuff."

Kara was crying in the bathroom. One of the football players shouted at her, told her to shut up, get out of his house. Just the fact that he was younger than us and had a baby face made me feel fuzzy, or maybe he just reminded me of Kagis. I felt a surge of adrenaline when he tried to push past Will, and before I knew it I was on top of him, choking him. I had his left cheek pressed against the floor like a vise, and he couldn't move. Will got between me and the kid's friends, then pulled me off him. He didn't seem hurt, but his face was bloody and my knuckles were all bloody, too, from scraping against the wood floor. I'd never understood how high school fights worked. I'd witnessed a few, and the fighters always looked gawky, swinging weak roundhouses a mile a minute like spastics, out of control, barely connecting with anything, but by the next day both miraculously had black eyes and cut knuckles. Will squeezed my shoulder.

"Let's go, slugger," he said.

Penny exited the guest room and her drunkenness immediately evaporated when she saw Kara crying, the kid pressing his nose in the middle of the hallway, and me with my bloody knuckles. She rushed over and hugged me. A crowd formed at the bottom of the steps—kids wanting to know what was going on. We pushed through. We made it out the front door, and suddenly we were all booking it for my car. I half expected to hear shouting behind us as a lynch mob with torches flared out of the entrance in wild pursuit.

I fumbled with the keys, caught up in the fantasy, but no one came out. I looked at the mansion. It was dark and quiet—hard to believe there was a party going on inside. I flipped the latch so Will and Kara could get in. I was surprised to find Penny sitting in the passenger seat. My hands were numb from the cold and from punching a face. Kara shoved her head forward from the backseat.

"You're a bad-ass, huh?" she asked. I looked at Will.

"Can we please get out of here?" he asked.

I started up the car and peeled out, then stopped, because we were now facing the house, so I did an Atari logo turn and drove off again, slower.

We went to Buckley Park, a popular makeout spot in Renfield, and at this point I felt nasty. Nasty that we were with these girls, postfight nasty, remembering that all the beautiful people were hanging out at Kagis's house and that it didn't cross anyone's mind for even a second that I'd once existed nasty. The fact that Penny would even hook up with me made the rift between me and the hot girls in Renfield seem even greater. Penny was in my league, and she sucked. To top it off, Will motioned for me to get out of my own car and take Penny for a walk so he could be alone with Kara.

Penny and I walked up to the bridge that overlooked a frozen waterfall. She was cold. She wrapped both arms around my right arm.

"You're my hero," she said. "You kicked ass. Do you know karate?"

I didn't say anything.

"Bet you do. You can beat the living shit out of people twice your size, right?"

I kicked at the wood base of the bridge.

"I'm right, aren't I? You're a kung fu master," she said, making the martial arts whine with her mouth all twisted and making chopping motions with her bony hands.

"Shut up," I said halfheartedly. "I'm only a third-degree black belt. I should be a fourth, but I quit training in order to focus on tennis. I can barely throw chopsticks through two-by-fours—it's actually kinda embarrassing."

"Seriously, you know how to take care of yourself. I like that in my men."

"You have really high standards."

"Come on, block my kick," she said, and kicked me square in the shin.

"Ow!" I winced, staggering as I clutched my leg. "Watch it, you stupid slut."

She punched me in the nose. Her swing was alarmingly masculine. I barely dodged a second left hook, and her momentum or drunkenness caused her to fall.

"You ugly, squinty-eyed chink!" she screamed, slapping her palms against the floorboards like a little kid. I stared at her. She had an evil look on her face all of a sudden. I felt a burn inside and couldn't believe she had said that. It felt worse when a girl said it. I didn't want her to say more but couldn't resist lashing back at her.

"I fucking dare you to call me that again," I said.

I was frightened by the sudden urge coursing through my veins to kick her in the face—to pull a Mike Tyson and aim to bulldoze the bridge of her nose back into her brain. Was I really about to do this . . . to a girl? In my head I reasoned that she was an ugly, stupid whore that no one would miss. I pictured Kagis. Bubbles of saliva formed on the outside of my front teeth, and I could hear myself almost snarl at her. I *was* snarling at her.

"Don't . . . Jesus, I'm sorry," she pleaded. "Calm down, Mickey."

I stopped snarling. I felt heavy. She just sat there, her hands up in a defensive position. She looked like she was staring at a killer. It felt awful and great.

"Run away," I growled, picturing Michael Jackson in the video for *Thriller,* and I looked up at the cloudy sky and imagined a fake-looking full moon emerging. "Get away from here. Don't look back. You'll die if you stay where you are. Run for the woods."

She stared at me, her lips trembling.

"There's a path, a 7-Eleven at the end—you can make it. For God's sake, get the hell out of here," I hissed. I stared at my hands as if they were changing; they bristled in the cold. Incredibly, she got up and ran away, across the bridge and into the woods. Did I really look different? It felt like a dream. Then I remembered my words. *Stay on the path.* There was no path. *You'll find a 7-Eleven at the end.* There wasn't a 7-Eleven in Renfield anymore. From where we were, the nearest pay phone was miles away. Her parka was lying on the ground, by my feet. I glanced over at the car to make sure no one was watching, then kicked the jacket over the edge of the bridge. It landed on the snowy frozen lake with a silent puff. The snow was bright blue. I could hear the sound of breaking branches. Penny was moving around in the woods.

I headed back to the car.

I opened the driver's-side door, and the overhead light clicked on. Kara was sitting on Will's lap. Her eyes were bloodshot. Will's face looked a little green.

"Penny needs to talk to you," I said, holding the door open.

"Tell her I'm busy," Kara said.

"It's important. She's over by the bridge," I said. "Come on, it's *my* car."

I handed Kara her coat like a true gentleman when she stepped out. I pointed at the bridge and hopped in the driver's seat. I almost started the engine before realizing Kara hadn't left yet; she was still standing by the windshield looking in at me. I nodded at the bridge. Eventually she stumbled against the front hood and walked toward it, calling out Penny's name. Will stared at me in the rearview mirror. Once Kara was out of sight I quickly turned the ignition and backed out of the spot. The tires spun in the snow as I drove out of the parking lot with the lights off. I glanced at the bridge and saw Kara jumping up and down, waving at us.

"What are you doing?" Will asked.

I drove a couple hundred yards before pulling over. I banged my fist against the door, chipping a piece of plastic above the lock. I turned the car around and pulled back into the parking lot.

"Hey, guys," I said cheerfully, but my voice cracked. "I was just fooling. Get in."

Penny looked scared and pissed at the same time. She

refused to sit up front with the werewolf and instead forced
Will and Kara to make room in the backseat. Will tried to
kiss Kara, but the magic was gone. He glared at me in the
rearview mirror. We dropped the girls off at the pool hall
and Kara sat down on the curb, leaned over, and threw up.
"Yuck," Will said.

It took twenty minutes to drive him back to his house. I
used the emergency brake to turn into his driveway, nearly
clobbering the mailbox. Out of belated fear I cut the ignition. He got out without saying goodbye. Even with the car
stopped, it felt like it was running.

eighteen

Now that my weekends were open, I started watching
movies at night with my mom. She slept most nights on the
sofa in the living room because she got home so late from
work. She explained that she was so wired after running
around the convalescent home all evening that she couldn't
just go to sleep. So we'd sit together in the living room,
watching old movies on cable past midnight. I found out that
my mom was obsessed with movies and would talk constantly
during her favorites: *Sunset Boulevard*, *Wuthering Heights*, *The
Best Years of Our Lives*. All war movies made her cry. One
night we were watching *The Goodbye Girl*, and she was being
unusually quiet, and just when I thought I'd actually be able

to get through a whole movie uninterrupted, she let out a wail.

"Ooh, this is my favorite scene. Watch. Richard Dreyfuss's play bombed, and just look at his expression! I sobbed the first time I saw this," she said.

"Maybe you'd cry again if you didn't yap so much," I said.

She ignored me.

"Your father and I were both learning English, and we saw all these movies in Charlottesville," she said, staring at the ceiling. "He was getting his Ph.D. in engineering, and I was already a registered nurse. We went to the Tuesday matinee every week because no one was there, so we could explain things to each other in Korean. Some parts I understood better, some he understood better."

I thought about my parents. Aside from the occasional church gathering, no family friends ever called to invite them to dinner. My dad didn't have coworker buddies outside of the lunch hour, maybe because he didn't drink. Once a year my mom got a phone call from her former nursing school roommate, who now lived in Guam, and that pretty much covered her social life. It suddenly occurred to me that they were lonely people. I prayed my loserdom wasn't hereditary.

"Nick, why don't you go out with your friends anymore?"

I didn't say anything at first. Boris was curled in a corner, eating spiders. I reached over and picked him up. A second later he hopped off my lap and returned to his corner. He started licking his left front paw, eyeing me suspiciously.

"They're boring."

"Did something happen with them?" she asked.

"No," I said. "I just got tired of going out. I guess I'm growing up, focusing on the important things in life."

"But you aren't doing anything with your life."

"You can't rush progress."

"Do you want me to invite your friends over sometime? I could bake apple crisp."

"Huh? Jesus, no. I'm just taking a break from them, that's all."

She wasn't buying it, so I improvised.

"I've actually been thinking of getting a job," I said.

"Really?"

Her eyes lit up.

"Yeah, I mean, I want to earn some money for college."

"I think that's a wonderful idea. This is so great. Seung!" she shouted. I flinched.

He came running downstairs, and I told him the news. It felt good even though I knew I was talking out of my ass and had no intention of working for the man if I could help it. My dad vigorously shook my hand. "I knew it! I knew it! We just needed for you to find out on your own, realize that life is more than just going to parties." I nodded.

And that's how I ended up getting a job at the tennis club in Wheatogue.

❧ ❧ ❧

Almost immediately I was working thirty hours a week, sitting behind the front desk. I'd close up the club at night on weekends, then drive straight home, past the teasing golden arches where everyone from Renfield was hanging out. In my bedroom with the lights off I'd smoke two cigarettes with my torso hanging out the bedroom window, feel nauseous and almost throw up, chew a stick of Fruit Stripe and spray the living hell out of my bare chest and hands with Right Guard, then lie in bed feeling nauseated for ten minutes before finally going to sleep. Sometimes Boris would scratch at the door. I'd let him in and spend an hour or so trying to trap him in an overturned laundry basket. He's pretty slippery, but once you get him in there it's a riot to watch him move around the room, dragging or pushing the overturned laundry basket all over the place.

For some reason I could never manage to do more than one thing right at a time. I had a job now, and this gave me even less time to study. Unbeknownst to me, my parents were somehow alerted to this minor problem. One night in early February I was home alone, and instead of studying for a test I was sitting in my bedroom rearranging my trophies. I kept reentering the room, pretending I was a stranger noticing the trophy collection for the first time. I couldn't tell if I was impressed. Headlights flashed across the walls. It was eight o'clock. My dad walked into the house and marched straight to my room with my mom trailing behind him. She wore her white nurse's uniform, right down to her tiny white nurse shoes. I braced myself—I knew that if my mom came home early from work, something major was up. They stood together in the doorway for a couple of seconds, observing me as if they were at the zoo, so I scratched my head and hopped up and down on the bed a few times, shrieking, thinking this would alleviate the tension. Instead, they frowned.

"Listen, Mr. Monkey Man," my dad started, sitting down on the bed. "We just went to your school for a conference. According to your guidance counselor, you're doing so poorly that even if you do manage to get accepted to a college, they might possibly rescind their offer. The last semester of high school *counts*, Nick."

"I don't know what you're talking about," I said, pulling Boris onto my lap and tickling him under his chin.

"You need to shape up!" he barked in a militaristic voice, guttural, rising in a sharp crescendo. It jolted me. Boris swiped my knee and hopped off the bed.

"*Nappunum*," my mom added. They had once told me it means "disobedient boy," although I think it means something worse because one time I said it to her Korean friends during dinner at a restaurant and their faces turned white. "We spoiled you. When Reverend Su's daughter disobeys, he whips her with a sapling. We rarely even ground you."

"In this country it's illegal to strike your child," I noted.

"No, it isn't," she said. "Mr. Chan makes his son stand outside with his arms raised above his head for hours. Hours! We never made you do that."

"It's not fair," I agreed. I crossed my arms and frowned, but they didn't laugh.

"Don't joke. He gets straight A's, regularly attends church, and can do push-ups for two straight hours! He'd end up at Harvard if his heart wasn't set on Annapolis."

"I truly have no aspirations whatsoever to attend an Ivy

League school," I said in a British accent. I kinda sounded like C-3PO. My dad giggled. I had him. "Pardon me, sir, but do you have any Grey Poupon? But of course."

My dad lost it and started nodding and repeatedly slapping his hand on the desk, unable to breathe. He loved that commercial. I patted him on the back.

"Okay, breathe," I said between giggles. "It was nice talking to you guys."

I started leading him toward the door. His laughter was turning into tears. My mom stopped us. His face became serious again. He turned to me.

"You're coming to church with us this Sunday. But this time you're going to keep going, every Sunday, no excuses. No more tennis tournaments. You go to church."

"This fall I'll be in college, so you won't have to worry about me anymore."

"Nicholas, that's what this is about—you're not guaranteed to get into any college at all," he said. "This is serious, son. We don't understand. What's happened to you?"

"Look, I get what you're saying, I'll be good and study hard and stuff so I don't sabotage myself, but as for going to church tomorrow—"

"You are coming with us to church *from now on*," he said. "Case closed."

They started walking out of the room.

"What? And I don't have a say in this?"

My father turned around.

"The problem is we didn't force Korean ways on you. We should have made you go to church and become a good

Christian, but we wanted you to make your own choices. We never forced you to do anything because we wanted you to try to fit in, but you only picked up bad traits from your white friends."

I was stunned. My parents had never referred to my friends as "white."

"Don't say that about them," I said, even though technically we were both referring to nobody. Well, besides Will.

"These kids at church—they do so well in school, they never get in trouble."

"Losers, Dad. The lot of them. Trust me, they don't have friends at their schools."

"They have friends, but they study, too, and respect their elders, speak Korean. They're good kids. It's not too late. You will go to church and learn to be a man."

I stared at them, confused. I was overtly Korean to people like Kagis and not Korean enough for the church kids and my parents.

"You go to church this Sunday," my dad repeated, trying to talk in that deeper, tougher voice again, but this time his voice cracked. They left the room.

A minute later I heard a strange sound. Water was spraying against the window by the bed. I opened it.

"Nicholas!" my mom screamed. She was glaring up at me, squeezing the hose with her yellow-gloved paws. My dad shook his head, rubbing his temples beside her. "Are you smoking cigarettes out the window?"

Directly below me, forming a bed on top of the bushes,

were a couple hundred cigarette filters. They seemed to glow in the moonlight. I'd never noticed them before. In fact, I'd never really wondered what happened to the filters once I let go. I'd just assumed they dissolved after a few days. I made my face look as innocent as possible.

"You could have set fire to the house," my dad wailed. "Who are you?"

I shook my head vehemently.

"Those aren't mine," I replied, and it sounded nakedly feeble.

My mom cursed in Korean, and my dad tried to calm her down. I just closed the window. Eventually she stopped spraying water and went back to work.

🕊 🕊 🕊

My parents continued with the reeducation of their son the next night by making me watch a movie they rented, *The Killing Fields*, after dinner. It turned out to be a great flick about a Cambodian translator and the last days before the country gets taken over by the Khmer Rouge. He never makes it to an evacuation chopper. For years he has to survive one of the worst genocides in history before escaping. At the end of the movie a tearful Sam Waterston greets the dirty though smiling translator as John Lennon's "Imagine" gently floats around their long and tearful embrace.

My parents started bawling.

"Can I go now?" I asked. I wanted to send a message

to my parents that I refused to be broken by their cult methods.

"Son, don't you see?" my dad asked. "This man endured so much pain, but in the end did he feel pity for himself? No. He was just grateful to have survived. And he continues to work hard, no matter what."

I couldn't look at him. On the rare occasions he cried, it made me feel horrible. My mom pressed pause on the VCR, so the Cambodian translator was frozen with a smile.

"Look at that man—he's a hero," she said.

"I know what you mean," I said. "For the past two hours he's suffered unspeakable pain, torture, and frustration, and yet at the end, covered with dirt and with insects visibly burrowing into his forehead, he's so happy and eager to do something good with his life, right? I get it."

"He's an example you ought to aspire to," my dad said. "This man was no bum."

They were right, of course. It made immediate sense. None of my troubles compared to his. That, and I was a total lazy ass. I was well aware that I'd probably never experience a tenth of that guy's misery, and if he was going to be happy and decent and work hard, I had no right to ever slack off or feel pity for myself. Only guilt.

"You be grateful for what you have. How would you feel if you had his life?"

"That would honestly suck."

"So remember this man, this movie, next time you feel sorry for yourself, or when you're listening to music instead of studying. He had nothing and was happy."

"Say it," she instructed. "Say the movie title as . . . as a . . ."

"Mantra?"

"Right, mantra. *Killing Fields, Killing Fields*."

"Can I please go now?"

"Do what your mother says," my dad warned.

His expression softened, and they both stared at me with wide eyes.

"*Killing Fields, Killing Fields*," I mumbled. "Yup, you're right, it gives me a fresh perspective on things. A new lease on life, if you will. Can I please go now?"

"I knew it." My dad smiled, pumping his fist in the air as if we were watching sports. "You're on your way already, Nicholas."

As I left the room they repeated the phrase in unison, "*Killing Fields, Killing Fields*," in different keys, like a Gregorian chant in a horror movie, and it scared the living bejesus out of me.

But as my brain relaxed I started actually feeling positive about my future. I had the opportunity to transform myself into something better—like those kids I saw in infomercials late at night. They're born missing a limb or two and attending a summer camp for kids with physical deformities, but were still so happy with life despite their misfortune. They truly understood the point of living and didn't take it for granted. I'd lost some friends who were assholes anyway. Boo, hiss. That was nothing compared to being born with one leg, or three.

I paced back and forth in my room. I shadow-boxed. This

was a golden opportunity, the more I thought about it. A chance to find out what I was really made of. This was perfect timing. It was the winter of my senior year of high school—there was still a chance to concentrate on school and to graduate with a more promising future. I felt like I was going off to prison, and for the first time I saw how prison can actually be a good thing. Prison is a test for convicts. They can either sit and stew and get tats and shiv people and network with top-notch getaway drivers they wouldn't otherwise connect with and then five years later come out the same exact person, or they can use the time to their benefit and upon parole reenter society armed not with a gun, but instead with the rare ability to cook for hundreds, a self-taught law degree, and an improved physique. I was going to be a good prisoner for the rest of my sentence in Renfield and come out of this stronger than ever.

I was going to make something of myself.

What actually happened: I continued to ignore everyone at school except for Will. I picked up more hours at the tennis club, and soon I was essentially working full time. On Sundays I regularly attended church with my parents. I sat through the services without looking at anyone and avoided interacting with the Korean teenagers.

And then one day toward the end of February it suddenly dawned on me that I was completely over losing my friends and that I no longer cared about not having a social life. I'd thought the moment would never come, and now I was suddenly a changed man. There wasn't a discernible click, a specific moment where I actually transformed—

when the realization came, it felt like I had been this way for a while, and I exhaled. But it wasn't really closure; I only felt partially cleansed, like when you take a shower on a humid summer day and immediately start sweating again.

nineteen

This March it was unseasonably warm and rained practically every other day. On the second Sunday of the month the rain temporarily let up and the sun came out with a rainbow and everything. I sat out on the back porch for hours watching the drowsy bees stumbling around, flying slowly and bouncing off the railing. They were carpenter bees, and I made note of every cavity in the porch they climbed into. I grabbed a roll of duct tape and sealed up every hole. Some were already filled with bee cement. I pictured hundreds of baby bees suffocating to death. When my parents returned from church I was still admiring my handiwork. This was my first time missing church since they'd made it the law—I'd overslept, and they hadn't made a stink of it. I think they were kinda sick of me at this point. My dad came around back and looked at the dozens of crisscrossed patches of duct tape. My mom slammed the garage door, and the entire house shook.

"What did you do that for?" my dad asked.

"Trapping bees. You'll thank me later."

"The porch looks broken," he said, scratching his chin.

My mom slid the glass door open and stepped onto the deck.

"You've been invited to Grace Kim's party," she announced.

"She invited you especially," my dad added.

"You're joking."

He shook his head.

"You know the deal," I said. "I hate going to church, but I don't fight it. Your end of the deal is that you don't bug me about not going down to the basement after the sermon to hang out with those nerds, and we all go home happy. Remember?"

"But you might like it," my dad said. "Korean girls are quite attractive."

I nearly threw up on the spot.

"No offense to your race, but they're kinda nasty-looking," I pointed out.

My parents laughed.

"And what race would that make you?" My dad laughed. "Besides, they're not unattractive. Grace might be a little fat, but what about Reverend Su's daughter?"

My mom pinched his shoulder, and he recoiled.

"Don't call Grace fat," she said, smiling. "She'll grow."

"That's the whole problem," he replied.

"Peggy Su is very beautiful," she said to both of us.

For a second I pictured Peggy. She wasn't ugly, I had to admit, but then I remembered that Kagis had hooked up with Peggy at that bonfire party freshman year, and I immediately felt appalled again.

"The party is next Friday," my dad said.

They smiled at me, thinking I was daydreaming about Peggy, which I was, but in my head she was making out with Kagis in the middle of a cornfield.

"I command you to go to the party next week," my mom said, waving an imaginary wand at me. I went up to my room, sat at my desk, and thought about the basement Koreans. I'd always felt it was an easy, cowardly life they led, not being friends with white kids, only being friends with themselves, even though they lived in a state where they were surrounded by 99.9 percent non-Asians. They conveniently eliminated the need for acceptance. But now I kinda felt sorry for them. They'd been railroaded into an adolescence of academics and orchestra rehearsals by their parents and would never know what it was really like to actually make choices. Whereas I was my own man and had focused all my energies on my social life and the pursuit of girls, and as a result I was now a senior with no friends, no girlfriend, a shitty transcript, and a cat. . . . Maybe my theories needed a tune-up.

I realized I no longer hated the basement Koreans, but I still couldn't justify being friends with them, let alone going to one of their parties. If you're Korean (at least in Connecticut), either you hang out with the majority and develop a deep-seated ambivalence or you're part of the roving minority, the small gang of Asian geeks at the mall looking like exchange students on a field trip. It's one or the other. Regardless of the fact that my Renfield friends had dumped me, I figured it would be hypocritical of me to join the

Korean group. The last sign of defeat—hanging out with Asian kids with my tail tucked between my legs. Besides, the Korean church kids hated my guts.

I paced back and forth in my bedroom, my hands curled like angry crabs, but I felt nothing besides confusion. *Fuck me. Do I go to the party or not? They're putzes, Nick.* But something indiscernible (was it blood?) was compelling me to go. Maybe loneliness.

Eventually I decided that I was definitely *not* going to the party on Friday.

❧ ❧ ❧

It was already dark on Friday night when I changed my mind and decided to attend the Korean party after all. My parents watched me get into my car. It pissed me off that they were still worried about my driving, and I was edgy about going to the party to begin with, so I floored it in reverse. I accidentally ran over the entire bed of flowers next to the driveway, flattening everything. My mom pressed her hands against her cheeks. I rolled down the window to apologize. "Now you know not to watch me drive," I yelled instead, and peeled away before they could respond. I looked at my face in the rearview mirror and winced.

I almost turned back. Through some trees I could see a silhouetted cross on the roof of the Kims' house. The Kims were apparently religious freaks; maybe Grace had telepathic powers like Carrie. The house was otherwise modern-looking, with skylights. I cut the ignition and debated leaving before anyone ID'd me. I considered my alternatives. It was too depressing to go back home—I didn't want to watch Korean soaps with my parents. I could have gone for a solo drive, but that would've made me even more of a loser. I felt like these Asian nerds were the only potential friends I had at the moment. At school I saw that Will was starting to hang out with Kagis and Company. I felt betrayed, in need of comfort. It was ridiculous that I turned to the basement Koreans for answers, but I stepped out.

As expected, Grace and Peggy and a bunch of Sunnys and Graces were standing around in fluorescent pink and green cocktail dresses next to a coffee table littered with open bags of chips. When they saw me they froze. Their eyes turned mischievous, and I immediately regretted showing up.

A Franky advanced on me.

"Hey, dude," he said.

"Hi, Nick," Peggy chirped quickly, as if she'd been waiting for someone else to break the ice. I realized that part of the reason I thought Korean girls were so ugly was only because I feared being seen with them. Since there weren't any white kids around, she almost looked pretty. The house was filled with Koreans as far as the eye could see.

"Howdy, Peg," I replied.

"Isn't there a party in Renfield tonight?" Grace asked. "I have a friend at AOF, and he said there's a huge kegger tonight."

I pictured Kagis's basement. I frowned at the table in front of me, covered with a half dozen bowls of different-flavored chips and fruit punch. I prayed we wouldn't play Pin the Goddamned Tail on the Donkey later.

"You've been MIA from church for a long time now," Franky said. "I didn't think you were going to show up here tonight."

I'd been going to church all winter. Did *anyone* notice me anymore?

"Well, I was in the neighborhood," I joked.

"The neighbors warned us about you," Peggy said.

"Right." I laughed. She was definitely flirting with me. I could tell because I had a boner, my first Asian-girl-induced-boner ever. Everyone stood around in a circle eating chips. The stereo in the corner played "The Logical Song" by Supertramp. A pimply Korean kid eventually showed up with a sixer of Heineken. He placed the bottles on the table, cracked one open, and actually started pouring beer into tiny plastic Dixie cups.

"Heineken? That is *so* Vietnamese," Grace said.

"Lighten up, Grace," he replied.

I chugged my cup. I mingled. It was boring as balls, but as the minutes passed I realized that I felt comfortable in public, something I hadn't felt in a while. I glanced at my watch. I'd been there for all of twenty minutes and wanted to leave, despite the fact that they were all nicer to me than I deserved. As hypocritical as it was to have these thoughts anymore, I still felt they were all beneath me, regardless of my current social standing in Renfield. I wanted another ounce of beer, but the cups were running low.

Peggy started talking to a girl by the snack table and I

noticed that she didn't have the slightest Korean accent. Maybe it was just my ears, but everyone else sounded slightly foreign. She alternated between speaking in fluent Korean and English. Then I noticed that everyone else was starting to sound less foreign also. My throat tightened, because I suddenly saw them as potentially normal people. I walked outside and lit a cigarette. *Maybe I could be more like Peggy when I get to college*, I thought. I saw a chalkboard wiped clean. Was it really a possibility to no longer feel secretive about my skin? The boundaries widened, and I felt like I could breathe again. *Who knows*, I thought, *maybe next fall in college I'll feel comfortable enough to even make fun of my race while hanging out with white guys and actually willingly draw attention to my ethnicity.*

Peggy walked outside. I could tell she wasn't wearing a bra. The clink of bottles and the sound of laughter drifted through the open window.

"So are these your best friends?" I asked.

"Are you kidding? I've known Grace forever, but we aren't that close."

"I figured you guys all hung out with each other. Life's a perpetual study group."

"Hardly. Tonight's a rarity," she said, staring at the crowd. "Is that what you think, that we're all best friends?"

"How would I know?"

"If you don't know, how can you be embarrassed by us?"

"I'm not."

We stood still for a few seconds, feeling uncomfortable.

"I see how you glare at us at church," Peggy said softly.

"You act cool—you always have a grimace on your face the entire time, as if you hate being around us. You never come down into the basement after the service."

I was surprised she noticed.

"I'm not a morning person."

"You seem different now, though."

"I don't hang out often with Koreans. Okay, so you're not best friends with these people, but you see them regularly. I don't. There aren't any other Asians in Renfield."

"Do you want to?"

Her voice sounded foreign all of a sudden. Was it my imagination?

"I don't know—I guess, maybe," I said. "I'm just explaining how I feel uncomfortable. You can speak Korean and stuff."

"No, I can't. I can say hello, answer the phone, say thank you. That's it."

"But you spoke so fluently inside."

She stared at me for a second and then laughed.

"God, you have a pretty distorted view of me."

We stood together, not saying anything for a minute. I shut my eyes and then opened them; I tried to mentally pry my brain wider. Peggy was a normal person, likable. No, she wasn't. She still had a trace of an accent, but maybe it was my imagination. She was too academicky. Her shoulder glanced my shoulder.

"Do you smoke?" I asked.

"You could teach me," she said brightly.

I lit one and watched her take rookie puffs. Her eyes got

all squinty, practically shut. She leaned over a bit, and I could actually see her boobs. She giggled. I inhaled up the nose and blew out my mouth.

"I feel dizzy," she said.

"That means it's working," I said. We were about to make out. She wavered, her hand on my shoulder, and smiled softly at me. But I didn't kiss her.

"What's wrong?" she asked.

I felt paralyzed.

"I forgot, I have to leave," I said.

"Why?"

Seeing Peggy as an attractive person went against everything I believed in about Korean girls. For that matter, slurs didn't feel so hurtful now that I knew she was normal like me. I almost felt stupid for having been bothered by the racism I'd experienced before. Being nicknamed Charlie by Mr. Weller in fourth grade. The martial arts whine from Penny on the bridge. Giles the soccer bully. Simsbury townies at the Farmington Valley Mall following me through D&L, laughing and pulling at their eyes to make them look like mine, which I never thought looked like mine, but that's how ambivalent I was. Slurs felt less biting now that I hated Korean people less.

Embarrassingly, a gong suddenly went off in my head.

Grace stepped outside and started talking to Peggy. I laughed out loud. The girls looked at me, but I ignored them and focused on this serious epiphany. Racism was no longer an issue with me anymore! No more flinching at origami, gagging on orange juice when someone used the phrase "chink in the armor," blushing when someone pointed out that my face was red from drinking beers. No more blushing anytime I saw other Asian people in public, for that matter. And how could any of this upset me, anyhow? People assumed I was a freaking genius just like every other Asian in the history of mankind. Cool. Feeling attracted to Peggy was proof I could change. I chose to build this shell. What I thought was racism was in some instances subtle expressions, flickering eyes, smiles behind my back that might have been my imagination. Although I'd been called slurs thousands of times, I'd always felt a little guilty that the racism I experienced growing up in Connecticut was nothing compared to the old blue television footage of blacks getting sprayed by fire hoses as police dogs lunged at them.

Grace looked over at me.

"All Korean guys smoke," she said. "Why is that, Nick?"

I felt a confusing combination of self-disgust and ethnic pride as I pondered my cigarette. Someone called Grace's name, and she went back inside. Peggy resumed gazing at me with those squinty, come-hither eyes. She started talking, and I broke into a sprint away from her. I laughed, but it wasn't typical laughter, more like a confused chuckle; I was running away from Peggy. The facts: she liked me, I found her attractive, I'd just had this big epiphany about race, and I was ditching her. The conclusion: I didn't know why.

I got in my car and drove away.

"Ghost in You" by the Psychedelic Furs played softly on the radio as I cruised home slowly, taking the back roads. I could have kissed Peggy. Her braless Korean skeeters were staring at me in my head. Forget her. I couldn't suppress the fact that deep down I still wanted a girl like Missy Means or Maggie Shaughnessy—a popular Renfield girl from the popular crowd—even though I really hated them.

When I got home my parents were waiting for me in the living room. They attempted to look casual, but my mom's magazine was upside down and my dad was turning the VCR on and off with the remote. Even Boris had been waiting eagerly to hear how the party went; he was gazing at me with one front paw motionless in the air as if he had been shot with a freeze ray, his tail all fluffy. We all stared at each other for a few seconds. Then my mom tossed the magazine in the air, my dad dropped the remote control, and they both broke out in wide smiles.

"Thank you for going!" my mom shouted. "I'm proud that you went."

"How was it?" my dad asked.

"I've never felt so Korean," I said.

Boris meowed.

"Don't you feel Korean every day?" my mom asked.

I didn't say anything.

"So you had fun tonight?"

"It was great," I said.

My dad walked over to me and clapped me on the shoulder.

"A year ago, would you even recognize the person you are right now?" he asked.

"No, I wouldn't," I replied.

SUNDAY
2:00 PM

Graduation is in two hours. There's a locked gate at the far edge of the dirt path that leads away from the water tower, and past it I can see Summit Road. An invisible haze spreads over the curved pavement, the kind that makes the air look blurred like shower glass. As a car passes, I catch a wisp of the bass line to "Voices Inside My Head" by the Police out the open windows. I stand to stretch and immediately recoil in pain. I reach down and rub my right shin and it makes me wince. It hurts to touch it directly. I forgot about the bruise.

twenty

Three months ago it happened.

I was sitting on the brick wall outside the administrative offices during my second-period study hall. A plane etched a trail across the bare blue sky. I was now barely even a student anymore, more like a grim exchange student from Korea circling the halls in a holding pattern until graduation.

"Hi," a voice said.

Maggie Shaughnessy sat down next to me. She was an anomaly, a hot senior who happened to also be a brainiac. One time in middle school I'd tried to realistically draw her face on my pillow with a permanent marker to make our makeout sessions more realistic, and therefore I should have welcomed the prospect of talking to her, but she was still one of the popular girls, which meant she was friends with Kagis, so I steeled myself.

"I know you hate my guts, but it looked nice out," she said.

I frowned.

"I don't hate your guts."

"You ignore me anytime we pass each other in the halls."

"I'm not friends with your friends. I had a falling-out with Kagis which I'm sure you know already."

"I don't know what you're talking about. I hardly hang out with Keith."

I didn't say anything. I suddenly felt foolish, worried she was going to say I was being an idiot and that I invited my own isolation. I had a sudden flash. Was it only Kagis and those few guys he hung out with that were jerks? Were girls like Maggie really not like him?

"Do you want to hang out tonight?" she asked.

She blushed.

"Okay," I answered slowly, a break between syllables, ready to laugh knowingly if this turned out to be some sort of sick joke.

"I'll call you then," she said with a perfectly straight face, and left.

I was too stunned to speak. My rib cage felt tight. "What the hell just happened?" I asked out loud. The bell rang for third period, but I stayed out on the wall for a few minutes, waiting for my hands to stop shaking. It made no sense. I prayed this wasn't like that ABC After-school Special where the cheerleaders conduct an experiment to see how a fat girl would respond to suddenly becoming popular, followed by another experiment—seeing how a fat girl would respond to suddenly becoming a loser again. Who else was on the inside? I went to English class and kept my ears peeled around Maggie's friends—Missy Means and Alicia Bolis—listening and watching to see if their expressions gave anything away when they looked at me. Nothing seemed out of the ordinary. They still routinely paid no attention to me.

Why the hell would Maggie ask me out? This was the first time we'd had an official conversation since she tried to get me to ask out Paige Cooper for Class Nite. Maggie was best friends with Missy Means, and despite the fact that she seemed cooler and less materialistic and shallow than the rest of her clique of snotty popular friends, she was still one of them. She'd gone to the senior prom as a freshman *and* sophomore. Her ex-boyfriends were frat guys in college. I pinched myself on the forearm.

I felt real.

By the time dinner was over I was convinced it was a prank. I ordered my parents not to use the phone. I ran upstairs and locked the door to my bedroom and sat crosslegged, staring at the phone. Eventually it rang. I waited a couple of rings, then picked up the receiver, breathed twice, and said, "Hello," in the most casual and cool voice I could muster. I sounded like a drag queen.

"Mr. Suck Park, please," a woman's voice said.

"It's Seung—that's my dad. He isn't home."

"It's okay, I'm calling from New England Bell, all I need is to confirm your address before we change you over to our new long distance plan and—"

"Are you kidding me? Stupid telemarketing bastard!" I slammed the phone down and resumed testing out different voices.

Ten seconds later the phone rang again.

"Okay, Nick. You can do this. Relax," I said out loud before picking up.

"Go back to China, you chinkoid," the same female telemarketer barked into the line before hanging up. The receiver felt like a cube of ice in my palm.

I set the phone down in its cradle and went over to the window. I watched a squirrel hop from one branch to the next. It stopped and wrapped its tail around the limb like the stripe on a barbershop pole. I sat at the desk and flipped open my European history textbook. I started reading the assigned pages but couldn't get past the first sentence.

The phone rang again.

"It's probably just a lawn company," I warned myself.

I could hear my dad talking downstairs.

"Nicholas, you have a phone call," he hollered. I could picture him not covering the receiver, his mouth inches from it, making the person on the line temporarily deaf.

Maggie was laughing.

"Please. Hang. Up. Dad," I said, squeezing the doorknob until it made a cracking sound. "It's for me."

He hung up.

"Your dad seems like a nice guy," Maggie said.

I couldn't think of a clever response. I realized I was breathing heavily into the phone, so I immediately cupped a hand over the receiver.

"So Nick, about tonight. This is the fishy part," she said slowly. I tensed. "My dad needs the car, so can you drive?"

"Oh," I said, and my stomach gnarled as I realized why she'd asked me out—she needed me solely as a chauffeur, a conduit between her and her friends. "Who are we meeting for coffee? I'm not positive I can make it, actually."

"We're meeting no one. Why wouldn't you be able to go?"

I exhaled.

"Where do you live?" I asked.

This sounds a little creepy, but I knew exactly where she lived. After I got my license I'd sometimes go on midnight drives past her house and Terry Robley's house and the Bolis twins' house, but mostly I'd just drive past Maggie's house. I mean, I never stopped and climbed a tree with night-vision goggles or anything, but just driving by the dark structure that I knew she was asleep in every night had been enough to excite me. I still felt deceitful lying to her on the phone, however, while taking down directions.

We agreed that I'd drop by in half an hour. I stared longingly at the phone; I already missed talking to her. I picked out potential outfits. I settled on a pair of jeans and a T-shirt

I'd received for playing in a tennis tournament. "It's casual, yet shows my interests," I said to my reflection in the window. I spent ten minutes French-rolling the cuffs of the jeans as tightly as possible. It looked stupid and I felt stupid doing it, but I couldn't help it, just like I couldn't help wearing only one shoulder strap of my L.L. Bean backpack in the hallways during school. As the blood shunted away from my ankles and my bare feet began taking on a mottled complexion I went over to the mirror in the bathroom and started fucking around with my hair.

It had been a very bad hair day. I hated when my hair looked poofy, so I dabbed my hands with water and matted it down best as I could. I tried some hair gel. I combed the front. I mussed it up again and added more gel. Then I sprayed the clumps of gel in my hair with Aqua Net. After fifteen minutes, I donned my trusty Stanford baseball cap. It was more brown than white from dirt, and the top half of the maroon S hung over as if it was bowing in apology. How fitting.

Maggie lived in a green Colonial with black shutters on the corner of Iris and East Aurora, not far from where I lived. It was a quiet neighborhood. The other houses on the street varied little—some had gardens in the corner of the front yard with spiraling wire fences surrounded by moats of worn wood chips spilling onto the grass. Other yards were untended, weeds left unpulled in bunches all over the yard. It was a solid middle-class neighborhood, and I wondered if our similar economic positioning was responsible for her sudden attraction to me.

I considered her dating history, and what a dense history it was. I suddenly remembered my first party sophomore year and recalled the image of her trying to fit her hands around that jock's swollen biceps. I flexed my left biceps; despite thousands of push-ups over the winter, it was still more garter snake than python.

I hoped her tastes had changed.

❧ ❧ ❧

I popped in a mix tape and blasted Ice-T's "I'm Your Pusher" out the back speakers as I drove to Maggie's house. When within Renfield lines I never bothered turning the volume down or rolling up my window—aside from Monty Banks, I was technically the closest thing to a black guy in this town. Once I reached her neighborhood, I pulled over and stared at my face in the rearview mirror. I made different faces, trying to find the one that had attracted her. A red Fiero drove by slowly, so for a few seconds I focused on the nearest mailbox as if I was lost before resuming staring at myself. Finally I drove to her house and parked on the street. I killed the ignition and stepped out. I silently prayed she wasn't watching as I lurched over to the front steps because I'd suddenly lost the ability to walk normally. A battered brown Honda Civic parked in the driveway. There was no doorbell next to the front door, just a rusted brass latch. I rapped it a couple of times. Maggie opened the door. She was wearing a white tank top and had wrapped a denim button-down around her waist. She looked ethereal, the light in the kitchen outlining her body with a furry, yellow glow.

"Can I use your bathroom?" I asked.

She looked puzzled. Though I was scared to meet her parents, I couldn't resist the opportunity to see the inside of her house. I saw the stairs she had raced up as a kid, the carpet she'd spilled food on, the silver urn resting on the hallway table. I squinted at some framed photos on the far wall, but she led me in the opposite direction. I went to the bathroom, smelled the towels before washing my hands, and frowned at my reflection in the mirror. A red toothbrush rested on the counter. I picked it up, considered it, then stuck it in my mouth. I brushed my molars a bit because I'd forgotten to do so at home. I licked the bristles and feverishly smelled the bristles and prayed that someday I wouldn't have to do this sort of psychotic shit in substitution for actually kissing a pretty girl.

"Sweet bathroom," I said, closing the door behind me.

"It's just me and my dad. He sleeps down here, so it's like I have my own apartment upstairs. I pretty much only come down here for meals."

"Do you use this bathroom?"

"Never," she said.

It took considerable effort on my part to conceal that I was gagging on the inside, realizing I had in effect just tongued her dad.

"Okay, I'm leaving," she hollered at a dark room.

"Take the key," a deep voice rolled out from the blackness.

I stared at the door as it closed slowly before following her outside.

"The car overheated this evening so my dad couldn't use it anyway," she said, pointing at the Civic.

"I can tell," I said.

She smiled, but I kept a straight face. I opened the passenger door for her, and she seemed pleasantly surprised. I got in, turned the ignition, and realized I couldn't feel my fingers. We got large coffees at Dunkin' Donuts, then drove to Fisher Meadows in Avon. Renfield didn't have a home soccer field, so the soccer team had to practice in the neighboring town. I showed off my ability to skirt death by weaving fast around the ribbon-thin roads past Avon Old Farms, the prep school—past the painted bear in the tree—before the last turn opened up to the soccer fields. We parked and sat on the warm hood of my car for a while and sipped our coffees. I took out a pack of smokes, and she asked for one.

"I didn't think you smoked," I said.

"I just like the smell. Is that weird, that I actually like the smell?"

"Not really. I love the smell of gasoline."

"Me too!"

"Hey, we're like soul mates," I said.

"Or nose mates," she joked. God, she was funny. I couldn't believe my luck.

"We were in frosh science together," I said.

"I know, psycho," she said. "You almost cut your finger off trying to impress Jaimy. I remember thinking you were funny."

"Do you remember when you got me to ask Paige to Class Nite?"

"But you didn't ask her," she said. "She was mad at me because I told her you were going to."

"Right, but she and I danced at the end."

"You were weird back in middle school."

"Maybe we should stop reminiscing," I said.

She placed her hand on my right forearm. A car sped by.

"I really have to pee," she said, staring at her empty cup.

"That's bizarre—so do I. You first."

"Where's the Porta Potti?"

We looked around. The far parking lot across two soccer fields had one, but it looked painfully far away, even by car. Her face echoed my doubts.

"I don't think I'll make it," she said. "Turn around, I'm going."

She reached in through the open window and grabbed Dunkin' Donuts napkins. I turned around, and she ran over and peed in the grass next to a tree. I peed behind the car. It was all very romantic. We sat back down on the front hood.

"I should probably go home," she said.

I didn't say anything. She looked at me for a few seconds, trying to interpret my expression. I wanted to ask her out again but didn't have the courage. I suddenly felt weepy, thinking this was my first and last date with her.

"We can hang out tomorrow," she said. "I have a track meet, but I'll call you when I get home."

"Sounds like a date," I said, and immediately clenched my teeth.

"Let's get out of here," she said, and hopped off the hood.

The entire drive back to her place I debated whether or not I should kiss her goodnight. She hadn't corrected me when I used the word *date*, which implied that she considered it one. A second date meant she considered the first date a success. The fact that she'd scheduled the second date for the following night made it clear she had enjoyed the date and wanted to experience the pleasure of my company again as soon as possible. There could be no doubt about it: Maggie Shaughnessy dug my shit. I pretended to adjust the side mirror and giggled silently at my reflection before pulling into her driveway. We were about to kiss—I knew it. As expected, she didn't hop out of the car when I stopped. She just stared unblinking at me, like in the movies.

"Okay, have a nice night," I said quickly, involuntarily reaching over and unlocking her door, pushing it open with an extra shove.

"Um, okay, thanks for the ride," she said, and stepped out of the car.

I immediately turned my head so I could back out of the driveway, while she took forever to close the passenger-side door. Eventually it shut. The tires screeched because I stepped on the gas too hard. I didn't look in her direction once, just drove off.

Soon I was back in my own driveway with the engine idling.

"Fuck me," I sighed.

✦ ✦ ✦

And for the rest of March we were together almost every night during the week. Mostly we just hung out or watched rented flicks. The only movie she seemed to have ever seen was *Ghostbusters*, so I introduced her to *Repo Man*, *Electric Dreams*, *Sharkey's Machine*, and, when I felt she was ready, *The Warriors*. We usually had her house to ourselves because her father was a pilot for Pan Am. Her parents had gotten divorced when she was two. Her mom lived in Long Island with a new boyfriend that Maggie didn't approve of. When she told me this I murmured appropriate sounds of sympathy.

"I'm an only child, too," I said. "And my parents have opposite work schedules, so it feels like divorce. I rarely see them together."

Even though we were alone, no funny business went on. I couldn't tell if she was interested in me. Maggie was now five-six, and she still had those green eyes that seemed to change color in the light—just like my cat. I spent countless hours debating in my head whether I could have kissed her, and whether I'd missed my only chance. I was on the verge of willing myself to death, like the Aborigine in the movie *Walkabout*, but then a little over a month ago it happened for real.

I finally kissed her.

By then it had become our daily routine to get coffees and hang out at Fisher Meadows after school. I was paranoid that she was going to stop hanging out with me if we didn't kiss, but that didn't override my hunch that she'd react in horror if I tried. My stomach perpetually rumbled as we drove to the soccer fields, wondering what to make of things. I felt happier than I had ever been in my life. I reminded myself to just be grateful for this nice moment—I could wake up any second and be stuck right back in the furthest depths of hell.

Despite the warm weather, the soccer fields were still snowy thanks to a freak storm at the end of April, with large patches of dark green grass exposed by the sun. We walked over to a park bench. I wiped the snow off the top, and we sat down. My butt immediately began to freeze, but the sun touching my face felt warm.

She sipped her coffee. The fact that we were mere inches from each other was heightened by the flat lands around us. Acres and acres of snow. The sun. A clear blue sky. No passing cars. We finished our coffees.

"I'm glad we came out here," she said.

"This is nothing, come on," I said.

Her green eyes glowed from the glare of sun on the snow. She pulled on my shirtsleeve and kept asking me what the surprise was, but I refused to tell her. We tramped through the slushy snow, not caring that the cuffs of our pants got so wet they clung to our shins. Finally we reached the lake. It was a quarter mile across the middle. During Hell Week all soccer recruits had to run around it at the end of practice. The thawing top of the lake was a layer of steaming blue ice. Near us, at the edge, were some holes, some cracks under the surface, and the ice looked like X-rays of molars.

"I've never been here before," she said. "It's beautiful."

"Wait," I said. "Shhh."

A few seconds later we heard the sound, and she grabbed my forearm. Her grip loosened, but she didn't let go.

"Oh my God," she said. "It's amazing."

Deep bellows like a whale, belches that sounded like the ice was about to implode, followed by the sound of ice cracking. It was the sound the lake makes when the top is frozen.

"It's so loud," she said.

"I didn't think of it until we got here. I heard it once, a long time ago."

She stared out across the lake and I watched her. I took little breaths. She finally turned to me.

"Do you ever feel like kissing me?" she asked.

I didn't know what I felt. She looked at the frozen lake again.

"Yes," I said futilely.

"Well, you must really want to now, because you're not even looking at me."

She was staring at me, and I forced my eyes to match her gaze full on, in this light. I was still too shy, and couldn't move closer to her. After a few seconds she rolled her eyes and laughed, then leaned in and kissed me on the lips. It made me dizzy. This was by far the happiest moment of my life. We hugged. We walked around the parking lot a dozen times, not talking, just holding hands and feeling content with each other.

Finally I drove her back to her house.

We started kissing again in the car, parked in her

driveway. She had to meet some friends at the library for a study session.

"I have to go," she said.

"Will I see you tomorrow?"

She smiled.

"No, this is a dream, now wake up," she said, and we kissed again. She pulled back. "So are you going to be my prom date?"

My heart stopped. Even though I had no friends, if I went to the prom with Maggie, everything would be okay. I would be with the most beautiful, funny, smart girl in the entire high school, and I would win. Kagis would lose. I did win, I realized.

"Okay," I said.

All morning at school the next day she was standoffish with me. After the one class we shared I tried to talk to her, but she was in a rush, and I watched her Frogger the hallway and disappear inside a classroom. My stomach bubbled. It had only been fourteen hours since our first kiss, but it was more than enough time for doubt to set in. She felt regret, I knew it. Prom was a month away, more than enough time for Maggie to lose interest in me. What she needed, what we both needed, was for me to kiss her again, so she could remember how she truly felt about me.

I had another reason to kiss her—the night before I'd barely slept, eager to have people see me with her. I had finally returned from the darkness, ready to premiere the Nick I always knew existed: cool, appreciated, the cause of envy. It was a little frustrating not to have any friends to brag to that I'd kissed her—it was like being in the middle of a state forest when you see a UFO float overhead, but before you can tell someone about it you get lost and a few days later you die. That afternoon I collared Will at his locker before lunch and whispered the whole story.

"Prom with Maggie Shaughnessy?" he asked. "You're shitting me."

"I'm dead serious."

"Congratulations, Nick," he said, clearly impressed.

I nodded, gravely.

At lunch, Will tried to prod me into visiting her, but I was too high-strung. Maggie was sitting with Beth, Missy, Sam, and the twins at the table adjoined with Kagis and Company. Will started doubting my claims, but then she walked over and sat between us.

"Hi, Will," she said. She gave me a covert smile, and I slyly smiled back.

"So Nick tells me you two necked last night," Will said in a fatherly voice.

I spit out my milk and kicked Will in the shins under the table.

"Ouch," she cried.

We all laughed. I glanced over at the soccer table and caught Kagis staring at me. Mitch mouthed a question at me, but I couldn't read it. I shrugged and tried to glare back at Kagis, but he had already turned away. He looked pissed off, actually, and I couldn't remember the last time I felt so good being in school.

❧ ❧ ❧

And that's how I got to prom last night with Maggie. There was only one hitch—which at the time I was too excited to digest. Our companions at the last dance of high school would be Maggie's friends, which meant, of course, that we'd be sitting with Kagis and Company.

twenty-one

The prom was held last night at the Jade Gardens Events Center. The Jade featured one of the largest Japanese gardens in New England. If I hadn't gone to that church party back in March this would have probably been my worst nightmare, but thanks to my night with Peggy Su I'd evolved and could now at least *stomach* all things Asian. We checked out the garden before heading into the ballroom. The entrance was a large wooden gate opening into a fenced-in area that felt like a movie set. There were a bunch of stone lanterns that had lightbulbs inside them. Water trickled from a bamboo pipe that extended over a water basin in the corner as wooden flutes played over the sound system. The surrounding fence blocked the garden from the highway sounds on the other side.

Smooth granite stones formed a path next to a fake stream, and we hopped from stone to stone alongside the man-made stream. Kent Cole was standing in the opposite corner of the garden shielding his dog, Nugget (decked out in a doggy tuxedo), as it peed against the fence. The stream curved around the centerpiece, an ornate pagoda that had rounded benches on the inside. On the other side of the pagoda was the ballroom where our prom was being held. The French doors to the ballroom were open but were obstructed by a series of slightly bent rice paper walls.

Will saw me just as he was going inside the ballroom, and waved. Student Council brown-nosers sat at a table by the entrance, passing out our senior yearbooks. Maggie returned with two. We spent a couple of minutes flipping through them in silence. I'd submitted a single photo of me as a little kid wearing a raincoat for the senior section, and someone on the yearbook staff had added a caption underneath it: *Data!* I realized that the reason girls never forget their first time having sex is because they all write the date down in their senior write-ups. Two limos with purple neon along the bottom panels pulled into the parking lot. We watched as the soccer guys and Maggie's girlfriends filed out. Maggie slinged the camera strap over her shoulders and stared at the limos as we headed inside.

The ceiling of the ballroom was filled with balloons. Everyone was already sitting at the round tables. It looked just like lunch at school, only people were all decked out and the round tables had white tablecloths. "Hey guys, over here," Missy said, and gave us each a hug. The Bolis twins approached us, too. They exchanged pleasantries with me as if they didn't ignore me in school. Rollo's bow tie was undone, just draped over the collar, as was Tinman's, and I wondered if I should undo my tie, too. Maggie grabbed my hand, and we followed the twins to the tables. At each seat there was a

voting card and mini pencil for picking out the prom king and
queen:

RENFIELD HIGH SCHOOL PROM
JUNE 17, 19__

More than Words

Nominees for King and Queen

(Circle 1 per category)

Male	Female
Kent Cole	Terry Robley
Mark Steeley	Alicia Bolis
Rollo Tivares	Glenda Berrenger
Mitch Wertz	Jaimy Ginsberg
Keith Kagis	Maggie Shaughnessy

"Hi, Keith," Maggie said as Kagis put his hands on the
back of her chair.

"What's up, cutie?" he asked, giving her a big hug from
behind, looking past me. "It's crazy, everyone's voting for
you and me. Missy's depressed she got negged."

"How you doing, Keith?" I sounded obnoxious. He
shook my hand without looking at me, and then Rollo
hollered for him and he disappeared around the corner.

"God, I hope we don't win," Maggie said to me.

"Who's we?" I asked.

"Any plans after the dance?" Paul asked us from across
the table. "We have the limos until two. We're gonna go
into Hartford and cruise around—you should join us. We're
getting dropped off at my place. Tomorrow we'll all go to rehearsal together."

"We'll think about it," I said diplomatically.

A little while later everyone sat down at the tables, and I found myself sitting at the popular-people table. I didn't have an appetite. I felt so uncomfortable I actually volunteered to take pictures so I'd have an excuse to get up. Within seconds I had three cameras draped around my neck, banging into each other, and a couple more in my hands and pockets. I have to admit, it felt inherently natural to be taking so many pictures like this. For years I'd felt humiliated by those loud Japanese tourists who don't seem to notice everyone staring at them, and now I could suddenly see myself in ten years wearing an ill-fitting plastic green visor, using twenty rolls of film just to document standing in line outside the enormous golf ball at Epcot Center, gutturally instructing Maggie and my now hunchbacked mother to repeatedly shoot me the thumbs-up sign.

"Let's have someone else take a picture," Maggie suddenly announced, waving me toward her. "Nick's doing all the taking. I want some group shots with him in them."

I cringed on the inside. Terry Robley took back her camera from me, and as I stood behind Maggie everyone groaned. "Can we please take a break?" Mitch asked.

"Just a few more," Maggie insisted.

Even I rolled my eyes as the flash went off. Everyone grunted and departed, streaming away from the tables toward the dance floor.

"Can you get one more shot of just the two of us?" Maggie asked Terry.

She quickly took a picture and handed Maggie the

camera, then immediately rushed back into Tinman's arms and dramatically sighed. They gazed at me.

"Do you want to dance?" Maggie asked, waving at Missy.

"Actually, I see Will out back. I'm going to say hi."

I didn't see Will, but I pretended I was communicating with him with my hands as I walked away from the table. I went outside to the garden and sat down on a stone bench. There was a foot-wide crack between two of the rice paper walls that stood in front of the open French doors, and I freely stared at Maggie and her friends. I hated how bored all the popular people looked. Mitch was making fun of the plastic champagne glass with the theme, "More than Words," stenciled in white calligraphy on the sides. He looked around a couple of times and then chucked it onto the dance floor. It shattered silently. Missy looking around in obvious disgust at the loser couples, probably rating their gaudy prom dresses. I felt relieved graduation was the next day. "So long, suckers," I said.

I scanned the other tables. All the nonpopular girls' dates were guys from other towns—men in their twenties with mustaches and receding hairlines, taking secret swigs from concealed, silver flasks, and it suddenly dawned on me that all the mutants in my grade didn't give a shit what the popular people thought of them. Eric Louie, still the obligatory fat guy in our grade, was wearing tails and had a shiny black cane and a fake monocle—he resembled the guy on the Monopoly box. He looked like he was enjoying himself. Freaky Keely was standing at the edge of the dance floor leaning against her date, who looked like a foreman at a mine or something.

Kagis sat down next to Maggie. Terry was smiling, taking pictures of them and seemingly enjoying it. The flash kept going off. Maggie had her arm around Kagis. I leaned forward and my eyes focused in on her hand even though I was fifty yards out, it was resting on his back just off his shoulder, and a second later I saw it.

I blinked twice.

I squinted. I leaned forward and forced myself not to blink. There it was again! Maggie's thumb. Seemingly immobile from a distance, in actuality it was very slightly, almost imperceptibly, *moving back and forth*. Maggie was gently, affectionately rubbing her thumb on Kagis's back. Was I seeing things? I looked at my watch. I waited ten seconds before focusing in on her thumb again. It was still suggestively massaging his back! There was no denying what this meant. I charged straight at her.

"Can I speak with you, please?" I asked politely, grabbing her by the wrist. Maggie stood up, and I basically pulled her across the dance floor, bumping into strangers, out the open French doors, sideways through the foot-wide crack in the rice paper walls and out to the stone bench.

"What's going on, Nick?" she asked. "What's wrong?"

"I saw it, Maggie."

I'll give her this much: she had a good poker face.

"You saw what, exactly?"

"Your thumb."

She stared at me.

"Don't play it off like you don't know. You're busted. Time to come clean."

"What the heck are you talking about? What about my thumb?"

"You were rubbing Kagis's back with it."

"What?"

"Don't lie to me," I said slowly, wiggling my index finger in her face.

"Okay, stop right there, Nick. First of all, I don't know what you're talking about. I don't think my thumb was rubbing his back, but even if it was, what's the big deal?"

"Maggie, you can't look me in the face and say that doesn't mean anything." I imitated the thumb rub on her back. She twisted her back, so I did it softer. "You're telling me that's totally benign? Can you look me in the face and tell me that that type of rub doesn't mean anything?"

"I don't like your tone. And I didn't do that."

For a flicker, I questioned my vision. I immediately remembered the car ride home from my tennis date with Sam Foley in tenth grade, that debatable kiss in the backseat of her dad's Mercedes. No, I knew what I'd seen. I sighed. I took off my jacket and my bow tie and methodically hung them on the bamboo wall, feeling like a detective. I sat back down on the bench, then reached over and tilted a floor lamp so it shined directly into her face. She covered her eyes, then turned away.

"You know how I feel about Kagis!"

She started crying.

"Scratch that, my bad, I'm sorry, new subject," I said quickly.

"You're overreacting, Nick! I thought this could work

even if you didn't like my friends, but I can't take this any-more!"

Kagis and Missy came outside.

"What's going on? Are you okay, Mags?"

"Hit the road, Kagis," I said. "We're talking here."

"Why are you so concerned?" Maggie asked, wiping her eyes with the back of her wrist. "Why don't you trust me?"

"Why do you have to hang out with him and his friends when you know that they're complete dicks to me?" I shouted.

"Maggie, are you okay?" Kagis asked.

I stood up.

"Go back inside, Kagis."

"I think *you* should leave, Nick," Missy said. "You've obviously upset her."

"This is none of your business. Don't try to talk to me like I'm a little kid!"

"Stop it, Nick!" Maggie cried.

"You're defending them," I said. "Why are you defending him?"

"She's crying," Kagis said. "Don't you care at all that she's upset?"

I shoved him backward a few steps. He shoved me back. Missy had a horrified look on her face and tried to pull Maggie away, but I grabbed Maggie's free hand.

"Let go of her," I shouted in a surprisingly deep and menacing voice, something I must have picked up from my mom.

"I can't take this anymore," Maggie screamed.

I let go. She ran inside. Missy glared at me before chasing after her. Kagis started to leave, too, but I reached over and pulled him back, crushing his boutonniere.

"Okay," he said, turning around. "You really want to go, bitch?"

Our eyes narrowed. Mine more than his. I couldn't decide if my fingertips felt like they were on fire or frozen—I just knew I couldn't make a fist at that moment. We started circling each other. Kettledrums started playing through the outdoor sound system.

"Quit dancing around me, bitch," I said.

"Anytime you're ready, go ahead and let's see if you can bring that shit, bitch."

"Bitch, don't call me a bitch," I replied.

"Bitch, I'm about to make you my bitch, bitch," he said.

Before I could come up with a good response he took a wild swing at me, and we were both immediately out of control—a pair of spastics blindly swinging wild hooks and haymakers with our elbows locked. If our aim wasn't so terrible, we'd have cracked our arms in half. Kagis grabbed me around the shoulders, I countered by putting my arms around his waist, and we proceeded to knock over three stone lanterns in a brutal waltz. An usher on a cigarette break saw us and gasped. We trampled a row of bonsai trees and kicked up fresh mulch and then I lost my footing, but Kagis refused to let go, and our combined momentum sent us flying headfirst into the rice paper walls. There was a loud ripping sound as we crashed through them, tumbling onto the dance floor. Everyone gaped at us.

It was silent for ten seconds.

"Yeah, a fight!" someone finally shouted. "Kill each other!"

"Fight, fight, fight . . . ," the chant started.

Kagis had landed on top of me, and my hands were crossed as if in a straitjacket. I was helpless. He shoved me into the floor and simultaneously launched himself up. People cheered and laughed as he bowed dramatically and then began fixing his bow tie. As everyone laughed at me I could feel a gentle heat coming from the overhead colored lights, and something from my long-ago past suddenly returned, as if it had never left. The warm watts from the yellow spotlights enveloped my very being. The sound of the crowd dissolved, and I could now hear the trickle of water outside falling from the bamboo pipe into the water basin. I closed my eyes. My right leg flew out from under me as I simultaneously put my weight on my left hand and effortlessly twisted like Ozone in *Breakin' 2: Electric Boogaloo* onto my side and brought Kagis down with a perfectly executed scissors kick. I took a little force off it so I wouldn't maim him. There was a stunned gasp.

"Sand Snake Scissors Kick," Will, Mitch, and Paul audibly muttered from three corners of the ballroom, recognizing my patented third-grade kung fu move. Kagis looked befuddled. He got up, unclipped his cummerbund, and threw it to the ground. I rose and did the same. Things were moving real slowly. I looked over at Will.

"Triceratops," Will mouthed silently. I nodded. Kagis came in with a southpaw boxer's stance, and I pretended to get into a stance, too, then surprised him by suddenly kicking him squarely in the crotch. The entire crowd gasped for him. After the perfectly placed mini kicks to deflate his balls, I confidently turned sideways and executed a right-handed Hummingbird chop at his left forearm. Bad move—it felt like I'd broken every bone in my hand. I leaned over, squeezing my right hand, and grimaced so hard a little bubble formed and popped in my left nostril. I was totally vulnerable this close to him, and I realized I'd lost. I nobly looked up at him, ready to take a fist on the chin.

And that's when Kagis went down.

"Get up," I immediately shouted. It was obvious he was down for the count, but I felt like juicing up the machismo in front of everyone. Victory. I'd won. Where was Maggie? I forced myself to stop squeezing the pain out of my right hand. I caught Kent Cole shaking his head in disbelief. It dawned on me that I had grown up into a total bruiser.

"Why don't you throw a punch, you sissy pansies?" a voice hollered.

"Huh?" I turned around and saw the football table laughing at us, and at that moment Kagis took the opportunity to toe-job me in the right shin. I looked down and saw him curiously smiling up at me through teary eyes. A couple of seconds later the pain hit me like an aftershock. I gasped, "Oh, God," and crumpled to the floor. Everyone watched with fascination as Kagis and I lay there in the middle of the dance floor, writhing around and bumping into each other with our eyes closed like a pair of tuxedoed maggots. A minute later the waitstaff and the manager of the Jade Gardens descended on the dance floor, pulling us off in opposite directions. A pair of waiters dragged Kagis toward the bathrooms, while the manager personally picked me up in an upside-down bear hug with my legs flailing over his head and stalked out the French doors, past the shredded rice paper walls, and into the garden.

I could hear laughter.

"Stay here," the manager said. "I'm going to get your ushers, and then I'm calling the police. You're in a lot of trouble, son. Don't you dare move from this spot."

"Can't move . . . leg . . . need ice pack and splint," I said softly. I groaned.

The manager rushed back inside. The second he was out of sight I immediately got up and limped out through the gates and into the parking lot. My shin throbbed. It felt like it was bleeding. I realized I'd left my cummerbund on the dance floor. I got to my car, unlocked the door, and climbed in. I stuck the key in the ignition but didn't turn it. I looked back at the garden. It was empty. I sighed. I couldn't make myself leave. Ten minutes passed before Maggie appeared at the passenger-side window. She got in.

"They're looking for you," she said. "Drive me home."

"You don't have to go with me if—"

"Don't talk. Please." She looked out the window. "Just take me home."

We drove all the way back to her house in silence. I parked in her driveway and we sat there for five minutes, staring out the windshield at the garage. I almost fell asleep.

"I hate you," she finally whispered, tears suddenly trickling out of her eyes.

She got out of the car and stomped away, toward the

back of the house. I got out and followed silently at a distance of around ten feet. I felt like I was part of a funeral procession. She took off her heels, and her feet made a soft padding sound as she crossed the yard. She started climbing the steps to the treehouse in the backyard. Her dad had made it when she was little. Strips of two-by-fours nailed into the side of a big tree that served as a makeshift ladder led up to a treehouse. The roof had shingles and everything.

"What are you doing?" I asked. "That thing's old, it's not safe. Come down."

She ignored me, and scraped her knee against the tree, which only made her climb faster, recklessly. She hoisted herself up over the floor and into the treehouse. I could see the back of her head through the miniature window.

"Come down," I repeated. She didn't reply.

I stood under her for a few minutes. I contemplated throwing a couple of acorns at her, but there weren't any in sight.

"I'm going to sit in my car," I announced. She didn't respond.

I did what I'd said. I pictured her up in the treehouse, night all around her. I tried to imagine what her face looked like, but nothing came into focus. Eventually she climbed down and walked over to the car and got inside. She looked bruised and beautiful.

"I won't ask about Kagis anymore," I said softly. "That was dumb of me."

"It doesn't matter. Our relationship's over. I don't want to see you anymore."

"But I'm really sorry. I don't care about Kagis anymore. Hang out with your friends all you like. What I'm saying is that I understand."

"But this isn't *working*," she said.

"Yes, it is. What do you mean?"

"I'm not going to drop my friends for you."

I caught my breath.

"Can we just start over?"

"I feel suffocated. When we're around my friends even for a minute in the hallways at school I can feel how much you hate them."

"They feel exactly the same way about me, Maggie. Trust me."

"Now they do. You just exploded at everyone," she said. I flinched. "But I'm not having a debate about this. I'm talking about you. I'm talking about you ruining our night because you're jealous for no reason."

"It's helpful to know this. I'll just change," I said.

"Being with my friends is important, but you don't see it that way."

"Your friends suck."

"It's useless trying to talk to you. You are the one who created this whole situation for yourself," Maggie said. "I'm going inside."

"Wait," I said, blocking the door handle. She leaned back impatiently. "You're right. I have issues with my former friends—your friends."

She stared at me.

"We went too fast with things," she said. "We can just be good friends."

My mouth fell, and it took considerable effort to shut it. I replied, "No problem," but it sounded more like broken plates coming through clenched teeth. She didn't notice.

"The more I think about it, the more it makes sense. We're graduating from freaking high school tomorrow. This is going to be our last summer before college starts. Senior year's been so stressful, this should be a time to relax. We both don't need this pressure."

"Pressure . . ."

"Do you agree?"

A switch turned in my brain.

"Nick, are you okay?"

We can just be good friends. Her words felt like salt in a bleeding wound, and I wasn't going to let her sting me like this.

"I see how it's better for you to be with your pals," I said softly. "You're right."

She touched my wrist. I didn't brush her away.

"No. I don't want you to say that."

"Really, Maggie, it makes perfect sense to me now. If my friends hadn't ditched me, I'd probably still be immature enough to want the false security of their friendships."

She took her hand back.

"Sometimes, I even miss it. If I put myself in your shoes, I can see how talking about guys and wondering what clothes to trade for school on Monday is an integral part of your well-being. God, Mags, I feel like an outcast thinking that being with cool kids and gossiping about the weekend is no longer important to me anymore, and I miss hanging out with the guy who humiliated me in front of everyone, and I miss talking about the girls in our grade and what their shrubbery looks like and—"

"Please stop."

"Let me finish!" I shouted. "I mean, seriously, Maggie, I thought you were different from everyone else. Even though you were friends with them you were too smart to want the same stupid things they wanted. I figured you were different than everyone else, so forgive me if I'm a little surprised, but really, I had no idea you really are so fucking shallow, you stupid popular bitch!"

I was screaming. Maggie's eyes were buggy, and her mouth was open, and she was breathing strangely, as if her neck was broken. I pulled at my hair, and my cheeks were literally hot to the touch.

"Maggie," I whispered between breaths, and the end part of her name turned into a hiccup.

She punched me in the shoulder.

"Stop crying!" she screamed, and it pierced me for a moment. I forced myself to breathe, and my vision returned. I had hurt her with my words, and now I was scaring her, and the combination was making her crazy. Her eyes were bloodshot, and her cheeks flamed bright with tears.

"I'm sorry," I pleaded, still crying, but lower on the Richter scale, and I said I was sorry over and over.

"Don't say you're sorry," she said.

"Why do you want to break up?" My voice squealed in falsetto.

She patted my back lightly, and I buried my head in her sweater. I felt her body tense. She pushed me off hard and opened the door and jumped out as if she was escaping, barely closing the door behind her as she ran for the front stoop.

I didn't chase after her. Instead, I reached over and pulled the door shut. I sat still and tried to gather my composure by choking the steering wheel. When I felt able enough, I carefully backed the car out of the driveway and left.

twenty-two

I woke up this morning unable to move. My right shin felt soupy. Every part of my body was sore, even parts that had played no part in my epic battle with Kagis last night. My neck was stiff, and even the backs of my calves were discolored. I pressed shuffle on the CD player and the Pixies' "Bone Machine" started playing. I lay in bed until I heard my mom tapping the railing and shouting, "Nicholas, I can hear the stereo. You're going to miss rehearsal. Get your lazy bones out of bed."

I looked over at the alarm clock. It was 9:45. I momentarily pictured everyone at the prom last night laughing at me as I was being carried out upside down. I dressed quickly and went downstairs and directly out the front door without being seen. It was already hazy out. Without thinking I walked around the house and onto the trail in the backyard that led to the water tower. As I climbed up the side my head was swirling. I was graduating in seven hours.

There was a rustle in the trees to my left. For a second, I pretended it was a bear. Getting killed by a bear would solve everything, I thought. My actions at the prom last night would be null and void, and Maggie would be forced to drop her hatred of me and immediately begin mourning me. *That would be awesome*, I thought. But it was only Boris. He gingerly stepped out from under the branches and onto some leaves, not even noticing me up here. I watched as he stood intently over a hole in the dirt for a few minutes, occasionally pawing disappointedly at it. I lay down on my back and stared at the blue sky. A huge cloud above . . . what kind was it? All I remembered from science freshman year was that cumulonimbus clouds were the big fuckers. It was turning into a beautiful morning. *Where did everything go wrong?* I wondered.

❦ ❦ ❦

And now here I am.

It all comes down to this. I couldn't help what I did last night because I'm clueless. I've always wanted a girl, but I've also always wanted to feel better about myself. Ever since I was formally rejected by high school society I've been obsessed with Kagis. I thought that dating Maggie—someone hotter than any girl Kagis has ever gotten—was a way to gain revenge on him for dumping me as a friend and sending me into social purgatory.

The fact is, the last ten years have been a complete

disaster. I've been dying to be in a serious relationship with a beautiful girl since I was nine years old, before I even knew Maggie existed. But I've really just been dying to feel like I'm the same as everyone else. I've been so busy thinking that the people around here have a problem with me being Asian that I didn't realize I have a bigger problem with it than anyone else.

Their problem with me being Asian only surfaces with certain things. In general, everyone can handle the thought of me as a classmate, or teammate, or just Nick—the guy they've known since Crying Stream—but they sure as hell can't swallow the thought of me getting someone like Maggie. There are these expectations, or lack of expectations, about me because of my ethnicity. People expect me to be a brainy pansy, for example. It's not true, but that's irrelevant; the fact is, everyone knows about these stereotypes. It's there when no one says anything. Since it's about me, I feel them, but none of this really matters anymore, because the fact is I *did* get the hot, popular chick—and then I screwed it all up because it turns out I'm just as bad as them. I'm a hypocrite after all.

It was always about me and not about the girls.

SUNDAY
3:27 PM

All that's left to do today is graduate. Commencement begins in less than an hour. The local Y is sponsoring a huge celebration party for the entire graduating class after the ceremony, but of course I have no intention of attending.

So I've realized that I'm an artificial piece of shit. I'd thought I changed over the winter, especially after the church party, but I haven't. I've got issues. I'm a lifelong banana, a card-carrying member. I'm a liar. I'm self-loathing, but deep down I think I deserve better, which means I'm also a whiner. I've always loved girls—just like every straight guy—but it changed at some point to wanting to get the girl so everyone would *know* I had her. So I could get revenge, or so I could win.

I know that now.

And now I'm starving, and sweating, and I feel like I have the formings of a headache, so I hook my legs over the railing and let myself down the side of the water tower. I push branches of pine needles out of the way as I walk back to my house. Even though I've been out here all day, it feels like an abrupt ending.

❧ ❧ ❧

When I enter the house my parents are sitting in the living room in their formal church clothes. They instruct me to sit down. Boris rubs up against my shins. I scratch below his ears as they talk to me.

"Where have you been?" my dad asks. "Today is the big day."

"We're very proud of you," my mom says.

"It must be hard to graduate," he adds. "You already miss high school."

"You father has the camera set up on the tripod. Don't run away."

"Put on your gown so we can take a portrait," he says.

"Can we do this after the ceremony?" I ask.

"It'll just take a second," he says, shooing me upstairs. I pull the graduation gown over my head, and when I go back downstairs again he hands me the mortarboard.

"If you had done better in school, you would have received a special yellow string to wear around your neck," my mom reminds me.

"I wish I had that string." I feign sadness.

"Let's take it out by the flowers," my dad hollers from the garage. "Hurry!"

I sigh and follow my mom out the front door. She points at a spot next to the blooming dogwood. I stand next to it.

"This is kind of fake," I mention. "I haven't even graduated yet."

"You won't be able to tell in the picture," he says.

He snaps a couple of photos. Then my mom runs inside and retrieves my diploma. Actually, it's just a blue booklet made of imitation leather; the real diploma will officially arrive in the mail a month from now. I hold it. "Now me," she says, and stands next to me. Then she switches places with my dad. They finish the entire roll of film. Boris even gets in on the action, squirming in my arms, and when I pull the gown off over my head it's covered with cat hairs. I remember that I won't be able to bring him with me to college, and I reach down and hug him again.

"Good work, son," my dad says, shaking my hand. "You'll do well in college."

"You're just hitting your stride," my mom adds.

I nod. When they stop talking to me I leave.

🌺 🌺 🌺

Since I skipped the graduation rehearsal, I have no clue where to sit when I show up at the Renfield High football field in the afternoon. I can feel everyone staring at me and I hear slivers of whispers, and I almost bolt. One of the underclassmen ushers leads me to my seat in the front row without making eye contact. I sit between Alicia Bolis and Andy Cordello the Trumpet Guy. As we wait for the ceremony to start, I notice my parents' car pulling into the parking lot. There is a tunnel made of wire fifty feet long leading from the parking lot to the football field. Vines and flowers dangle from it, and it's pretty much the stupidest thing I've ever seen in my entire life. The sound of snare drums and trombones erupts as the high school jazz band marches through the tunnel. I can hear some students crying, others laughing.

I look behind me. Kagis and Company are smoking cigars, to the dismay of their parents, who are sitting in the third row. Even their parents hang out together like a clique. Alicia doesn't say a word to me; she stays turned around the whole time, frowning at having to be away from Missy and Maggie. I pretend I'm bored. I even yawn a couple of times, which is easy because the ceremony is boring. The guest speaker is president of some insurance company in Hartford. Ellen Gurvey, aka Princess, the class president, gives a speech about how we're all a bunch of worm-mongering wrens about to spread our wings and fly away from the nest. I snicker, and everyone glares at me as if it's a fresh metaphor. I look to my left through the attentive faces and see Maggie. She's looking ahead but doesn't appear to be listening to the speeches. Then Missy embraces her and they break out in wide smiles. I lean back so she doesn't catch me looking.

The back row stands (not quite in unison, more like a lazy wave at baseball games) to receive their diplomas. A line forms down the middle. Paulette Ruben and Keely Glick are the first students in line. Keely's face looks older, and Paulette hugs her from behind before they return to their seats. Kent Cole jumps onto the podium next to the frightened superintendent and gives the Mötley Crüe sign of the devil with his hands. Nugget bounds up the middle aisle barking its head off. Kent tries to make his dog sit and speak, but instead it stands and craps. The audience groans. Princess kisses her diploma. Someone in the audience throws Sam Foley a teddy bear when she reaches the podium, and it looks premeditated. Monty Banks somehow manages to do the "Running Man" in the thick grass all the way up to the podium and the audience roars. Given that he's the only other minority student besides me, I feel slightly envious about the applause—everyone thinks he's so tough and cool because he's black. But then I think about how he's never hooked up with a girl in Renfield; he always has a girlfriend from Bulkeley High in Hartford or something. Although the football guys imitate his style, they only started hanging out with him like a fad during the last three months of school.

Amber Milwood receives her diploma. She looks anorexic, and I realize I haven't spoken to her once since the fifth grade. Wesley Lipkitz receives a small ovation from his pot clients on the hill. Kagis, Mitch, and Paul approach the podium together in a row. Kagis stands at the side waiting for them to receive their diplomas so they can walk off together. He stands there with the unlit cigar sticking out of his mouth, and he glances over at Alicia, whom he's been dating all spring. We make eye contact, and I flip him the bird. Some prep school kids shout congratulations from the hill at Mitch and Paul. Tinman pretends to moon everyone, and the place goes crazy. Rollo looks pissed off as he stands waiting, but the audience roars when his name is called, and he smiles.

The entire grade sits there watching, clapping

generously for everyone, but louder for some. Paige Cooper, the first girl I danced with, giggles as she receives her diploma. Eric Louie stops for a moment after picking up his diploma, I get the feeling he's about to puke on the principal, but he just bows, and everyone screams as if they all really like him. I make a mental note to find his Game Boy and anonymously mail it back to him this summer. Maybe I'll add a little note of apology with Lipkitz's initials on the bottom. Jaimy Ginsberg looks somber as she rushes forward. I shout and clap when Will gets his diploma. Kagis lofts him a soccer ball, and he juggles it as he heads off the stage. I feel bested. Maggie is in line with Missy, and she's looking at me. I mouth, "Congratulations," and she smiles briefly. The line proceeds. I clap loudly when she gets her diploma. All the popular kids are getting huge ovations from the hill, which is a sea of nylon warm-ups as the prep school kids scream their heads off. Flashbulbs erupt.

Finally my row stands up. Beth Linney is crying as she accepts her diploma. The jazz band drummer repeatedly bangs the crash cymbal when Andy Cordello the Trumpet Guy receives his. Alicia Bolis gets a huge ovation. Maybe the white noise in my ears is distorting things, but I swear the reception dies down to scattered applause when I make the solo walk to the podium. I pick up the pace and snatch at the diploma. The principal frowns at me, obviously because of the prom fight. Will shouts, "Congratulations," but I still feel like a loser. Although I'm aware at this point how stupid it is for me to use the term *loser* or even give it weight, this is still my final moment of high school, and I blush. I stare at the grass as I retake my seat.

"It's over," I say to myself, barely able to hear because of the roaring as the principal announces that we're officially graduated. I remind myself that this is the last step before the slate will officially be wiped clean. This is officially the end of selfish Nick. I feel a glimmer of happiness thinking about college. Then the principal presents our class to the audience, and everyone chucks their mortarboards in the air. For closure, I whip mine in Kagis's direction, on the off chance that it'll poke one of his eyes out, but it veers in the opposite direction and boomerangs back and I end up catching it. I drop it on the seat and walk away, even though my parents are probably hollering for me in the crowd. I keep walking. When the voices grow dim I turn back and stare unnoticed at my graduating class. They're hunched over like a hundred ants, frantically picking up their mortarboards as the crowd rushes forward to congratulate them.

I resume walking to my car. The archway entrance to the tunnel that the Renfield High jazz band emerged from earlier sways haphazardly in the breeze. Purple flowers hang from the top, stretched by the wind, and I start jogging toward the tunnel with the intent of ripping all the purple flowers down.

And I see Maggie. She's clutching her mortarboard against her stomach, standing next to the archway.

My hands are shaking. I take a deep breath.

"Listen, Maggie, we don't have to ever talk again. But I want you to know that I've thought all day about last night and who I am, and you're right, I did awful things, and I've always been a liar, and I'm shallow, and I was a total psycho, and I'm sorry and I don't want you to forgive me for any of it, but you're the only person who's ever made me see myself as myself—not a banana, or a nerd, or a Korean guy, or a loser, or a kung fu master . . ."

I realize my cheeks are wet, and she notices, too. I don't even try to hide it—the tears just start spilling down my face. I'm not even talking, but my throat is making strange, gurgling sounds, which is embarrassing, yet I don't care. We embrace. This is what I've wanted all along. The sun is shining, and people if they looked in our direction would be able to plainly see us together. But for the first time I could care less.

I can hear a jet in the distance, the honk of car horns, the wind. My whole body aches like a fist when you can't squeeze enough energy into it, but I grasp her tighter and pray that nothing interrupts us. I just hold her as hard as I can, because I know everything is going to be different when I let go.

ABOUT THE AUTHOR

NAME: David Yoo
BORN: 1974
EDUCATION: Skidmore College, University of Colorado at Boulder
HOBBIES/PREFERENCES: Boris the Hunter, the Clash, steak burritos, *Repo Man*, standard transmission, Fruit Stripe, The Minutemen, deng jang jigae, ferociously scraping inner ear with bobby pin, straight pool, navy blue, "The Happening," no lefty, food coma naps, BDP, lying, Galaga, *Skylarking*, Prince Original Graphite, lung brush, marinated mushrooms, Let's Active, *The Hustler*, TMJ . . .
RESIDES: Massachusetts